THE NIGHT ISLAND

THE NIGHT ISLAND

JAYNE ANN KRENTZ

THORNDIKE PRESS
A part of Gale, a Cengage Company

LIBRARY OF CONGRESS CIP DATA ON FILE.
CATALOGUING IN PUBLICATION FOR THIS BOOK
IS AVAILABLE FROM THE LIBRARY OF CONGRESS.

ISBN-13: 979-8-88579-028-4 (hardcover alk. paper)

Published in 2024 by arrangement with Berkley, an imprint of Penguin Publishing Group, a division of Penguin Random House LLC.

Printed in the United States of America
1 2 3 4 5 6 7 28 27 26 25 24

As always, for Frank, with love.

And for author and friend Christina Dodd, with thanks. Yes, I know you are not a vegetarian, but your relentless quest for the next great meal inspired Talia's motto: Never waste calories on boring food. *(I'll buy the wine the next time we get together.)*

CHAPTER ONE

There would be nightmares again tonight.

She'd always had a knack for finding misplaced keys, glasses, and pets. She was fine with that. But her new psychic ability for tracking down the bodies of those who had died by violence was not only depressing but frequently led to anxiety attacks and disturbing dreams.

Why couldn't it have been a talent for something more positive — like, say, picking winning lottery numbers? Why did it have to be dead bodies?

Talia March clenched the dead man's gold cuff link in one hand, gathered her nerve, and flattened her other hand against the metal side of the industrial-sized trash bin. She was braced mentally and physically, her core Pilates-tight; nevertheless, the jolt of psychic lightning rattled her nerves and her senses. In the past few months she had learned that the energy laid down by vio-

7

lence always came as a shock.

She had finally figured out that what she detected with her new ability was the psychic stain of the killer's emotions — or lack thereof — and the pain and fear of the victim. It made for a toxic brew that seeped into the crime scene and, to her, was as obvious as a pool of blood.

She was aware of a weak frisson emanating from the cuff link. The owner was dead but the item that he had worn frequently in life was still infused with the hollow echo of his vibe.

She could work with almost any object that had belonged to the missing or the deceased, but over the course of the past several months she had learned that some materials absorbed and reflected paranormal energy more efficiently than others. Gold was a particularly strong conductor, almost as good as crystal.

"Shit," she whispered. She took a quick step back. "He's in there."

Roger Gossard, the head of Gossard Consulting, a crime scene consulting company, studied the trash bin with a pained expression. "Are you sure?"

"You hired me for my best guess," she said. "This is it."

Roger grunted but he did not argue or

demand more details. He knew better than to ask her to explain her conclusion. He looked at the unhappy man wearing a security guard uniform emblazoned with the logo of the company that controlled the loading dock.

"Okay if we take a look?" Roger said. "We need to find out for sure if there's a body inside before we call the police."

The security guard shrugged. "Boss says I'm supposed to cooperate but I'm telling you right now I'm not going into that bin to look for a dead body. You're on your own."

"Right." Roger switched his attention to the two members of his team who were waiting for instructions. "Bailey and Thomas, take a look. We need to make sure."

Grim but resigned, the pair pulled on heavy gloves, climbed into the bin, and went to work sorting through the trash generated by the several hundred office workers employed in the building.

Talia retreated to the front of the loading dock and contemplated the view of the alley. The rain was coming down in the steady way that was typical of Seattle in the late fall. The heavy skies indicated the weather was not going to change anytime soon. The Big Gray was just getting started.

In the past she had been comfortable with the drama of the city's dark season. But the night she had lost to amnesia had changed a lot of things. Now she was aware of a relentless sense of urgency simmering just beneath the surface, a sensation that was intensified by the late dawns and early twilights.

She tuned out the noise of the trash bin excavation process and opened her phone. There was no new text from her mysterious informant. She was starting to lose hope. Maybe she had been conned. It was a discouraging thought because the lead had appeared so promising.

"Looks like we found Clayton, boss," Bailey called. "Wrapped in plastic sheeting. Not a pretty sight."

The security guard backed away from the trash bin as if it was radioactive.

"That's far enough," Roger said. "Don't touch anything else. I'll call Seaton and let him know. He'll be thrilled. It's no longer a missing persons case. He's got a genuine homicide on his hands."

"No question about that," Thomas muttered. "Looks like someone used a hammer on him."

Roger took out his phone and made the call. When he was finished he walked toward

Talia, watching her as if she was a member of the Addams family. This wasn't the first case she had worked on for him and she knew what was coming next. He no longer needed her. She was now a problem. He wanted her gone before the police detective arrived.

Roger was good-looking, smart, well-dressed, and ambitious. Everything about him, from his expensive business suit to his salon-styled hair, projected the image of a man on the fast track to success. He made no secret of his goal. He was headed for the top of the psychological forensics field, building a reputation as a consultant who brought state-of-the-art technology and the latest scientific theories to the business of crime solving. The very last thing he wanted was for his clients to find out that he occasionally employed a psychic.

He stopped in front of her. "You were right," he said quietly. "Ray Clayton did not walk out on his wife and disappear. She murdered him with the help of her lover."

"You'll have to prove that last part."

"It's not my problem. It's up to Seaton to close the case. But now that we found the body for him that shouldn't be too difficult. There will be a lot of evidence."

"There always is on the body."

11

Roger lowered his voice a little more. "You can go now."

She gave him an icy smile. "Don't worry, I'm not going to hang around until the cops get here. We all know Seaton would have a few questions if he saw me. It wouldn't do for Gossard Consulting to admit that they brought in a psychic to find the missing body. Bad for the brand."

Roger winced and glanced uneasily over his shoulder. "Keep your voice down. I told you, Bailey and Thomas think you're a forensic psychologist who figured out the most likely dump site after studying my profile of the wife."

"I won't blow your cover. A job is a job and I need the money." Talia looked at the trash bin and then quickly averted her gaze. "Besides, it's not like I want to be here when they retrieve the body."

Roger frowned. "Are you okay?"

"Absolutely." *Well, except for an incipient anxiety attack and the knowledge that the night ahead will be very long and very dark. What the hell. Not my first dead body. I'm a professional. Don't try this at home.* "I'll ride off into the sunset now."

"Don't forget to send your bill."

"Oh, I won't." She realized she was still holding the gold cuff link. She unclenched her fingers and held out her hand. "You can have this. I won't need it anymore."

"Right." Roger picked up the cuff link and slipped it into a pocket.

She went down the loading dock steps, pulled up the hood of her jacket, and walked toward the far end of the alley. The relentless howl of a siren in the distance announced the approaching police vehicle. The big SUV roared into the alley just as she was crossing the street. She did not look back.

It was a good thing that Roger had not asked for an explanation of how she had located the body of Ray Clayton, because she did not understand it herself. She was not sure she wanted to comprehend it. Her new ability was unwelcome on so many levels. She had not been forced to look at the face of the dead man in the trash bin today, but that would not protect her from the psychic fallout.

Tonight there would be nightmares.

CHAPTER TWO

"Come any closer and I'll kill her," Martin Pilcher yelled.

Luke Rand opened his senses to the nightmarish currents of energy that shivered through Pilcher's threats. It didn't take any psychic talent to figure out that the man was totally unhinged.

Pilcher was in the doorway of the small, shadowed house. He tightened his arm around his wife's throat and put the barrel of the pistol against her head.

"I'm not fucking around here," he screamed.

"He's going to do it," Luke said quietly. "We're talking a couple of minutes at the most before he pulls the trigger."

"Shit." Sam Hobbs's expression was grim but resigned. "I'll signal Wilson to take the shot."

"It won't work," Luke said. "Wilson can't get a clear shot. Best case is the bullet punches through Pilcher and strikes the wife."

"Don't you think I know that?" Hobbs's jaw tightened. "I don't have a choice. We don't have time for any more negotiation."

"Let me try before you give the order to Wilson."

Hobbs hesitated. "Okay, you've got one minute."

"Understood," Luke said.

He and Hobbs were standing behind one of the three police vehicles parked in the front yard of the house. Katy Pilcher had tried to hide in the rural town in Northern California after obtaining a restraining order that was supposed to keep her stalker husband from contacting her. But Pilcher had tracked her down. Katy had managed to dial 911 just as Pilcher broke in through a window.

When the police arrived on the scene it became a hostage situation. Now it was about to mutate into a murder-suicide.

So much for the rural community's promise of safety, Luke thought. Lesson learned. Katy Pilcher wasn't the only one who had chosen the small, remote town as a hideout.

In hindsight, it had been a mistake to accept Hobbs's invitation to play poker on Friday nights, but it had seemed like a small risk. Unfortunately, over cards and whiskey, Luke had mentioned that he had done some hostage negotiation. Now he was paying for that slip of the tongue. Fifteen minutes ago Hobbs had called, asking for assistance at the scene of a crime in progress.

Luke focused on the man in the doorway. "No one here is going to make any moves, Mr. Pilcher. What do you need?"

On the surface, the words sounded calm and reassuring, but they formed an invisible Trojan horse carrying the currents of a psychic trap.

"I need you and everyone else to leave us alone," Pilcher shouted. "This is none of your fucking business. She's my *wife.*"

Luke ignored Katy's panic-stricken face. He had the fix now. He concentrated on the dangerously unstable frequencies of her husband's aura.

"All right, Mr. Pilcher," he said, infusing the words with the counterpoint currents that would send Pilcher's vibe into a wildly oscillating mode. "We understand this is a private matter. Give us a little time to clear out of here."

Hobbs scowled. "What the fuck are you doing?"

"You've got thirty seconds," Pilcher screamed. "If you're not gone, I'll —"

16

He went silent, his mouth open, his eyes wide as he stared at something only he could see.

"Shit," Hobbs whispered. "What's going on?"

Luke did not reply. He had the focus. He continued talking to Pilcher.

"It's over, Pilcher," he said, continuing to lace his words with the frequencies that would suppress the erratic wavelengths of the other man's aura. "You don't want to kill your wife."

"Stop," Pilcher said. But he sounded dazed and disoriented. "What are you doing?"

"The situation has changed," Luke said. "Let Katy go. You don't need her."

Pilcher hauled Katy deeper into the house and away from the door. Now neither could be seen.

"You don't want to hurt Katy," Luke called, forcing as much energy into the words as he could manage. He was still learning the limits of his new talent. "There will be nothing but pain if you hurt her. More pain than you have ever known —"

The muffled roar of a gunshot inside the house reverberated through the woods.

"Fuck," Hobbs muttered. He raised his hand to signal the officers to move in.

17

"Don't shoot," Katy Pilcher screamed from the shadows. "Please. It's me. I think my husband is dead."

"Toss the gun outside, Ms. Pilcher," Hobbs ordered.

The pistol sailed through the doorway and landed on the front steps.

"Come out with your hands up," Hobbs ordered.

Katy Pilcher emerged. She came down the steps, moving awkwardly. An officer intercepted her and pulled her to the side of the house, out of the line of fire.

But there were no more shots.

A deep silence emanated from inside the house. The officer who had taken Katy to safety shouted from his position on the side of the structure.

"She says Pilcher had some kind of seizure. He collapsed. She grabbed the pistol and shot him because she was afraid he would recover and kill her."

Hobbs looked at the shocked woman. "Are there any more guns in the house, Ms. Pilcher?"

"No," she said. "I swear it. I thought about getting one to protect myself but I didn't. I just hoped he would never find me."

She started to cry.

Hobbs gave the orders to secure the house

and moved forward. Luke watched the officer escort Katy Pilcher to a patrol vehicle. She half collapsed on the rear seat and put her face into her hands.

Luke walked to the vehicle, flattened a palm on the roof, and leaned in a little. He opened his senses, got the focus, and infused a calming note into his voice.

"Are you hurt, Ms. Pilcher?" he asked.

She raised her head, lowered her hands, and looked at him with stricken eyes. "He was going to kill me this time. Not just beat me like he did before. He was really going to kill me."

Luke reflected on the terrible energy in Pilcher's voice. "I know."

"Is he dead?" Katy whispered. "I hope he's dead. I don't care if I go to jail so long as he's dead."

Hobbs emerged from the house. He saw Luke and Katy and came toward them.

Katy wrapped her arms around her midsection and rocked. "Martin wouldn't have stopped. I know him. He would not have stopped. Ever."

Hobbs reached the vehicle. He gave Luke an unreadable look and then he turned to Katy.

"Your husband is dead, Ms. Pilcher," he said.

Katy closed her eyes. "Good. Will I go to jail?"

"No," Hobbs said. "It was a clear case of self-defense as far as I'm concerned, and I'm the one who makes that call in this town. But I need you to tell me exactly what happened in there."

"I'm not sure," Katy admitted. "I think he had a stroke or a seizure. Maybe a heart attack. He just seemed to forget that I was there. He dropped the gun and sank to his knees, clutching at his chest. I grabbed the gun and pulled the trigger."

"Did your husband have any underlying health conditions?" Hobbs asked.

Katy shook her head. "No. He never went to doctors. He didn't trust them."

"We'll know more after the coroner examines him," Hobbs said. "But no question about it — he's dead, and you won't face charges."

Katy closed her eyes. "It's finally over."

"I'll need a statement," Hobbs said. "But it can wait."

"I don't want to go back into the cabin," Katy said.

"Is there anyone you can stay with?" Hobbs said.

Katy shook her head. "I don't know anyone in town. My daughter moved to

Phoenix. Pilcher isn't her father. She hated him. She'll be very glad he's gone. So am I. Now I can go stay with Jenny. I couldn't before, you see. I knew he would follow me and maybe kill her, too."

"We'll move you to a local motel tonight," Hobbs said. He looked at the officer who had brought Katy to the vehicle. "Call the Clearwater Inn and tell Valerie we need a room for a couple of days for Ms. Pilcher."

"Yes, sir," the officer said.

Luke took his hand off the roof of the patrol car and looked at the shadowed doorway of the house. The embers of a thought he had been trying to suppress ignited.

Did I flatline him?

He had not been trying to stop Pilcher's heart today. His goal had been to render the man unconscious. But Pilcher was dead, and while that was certainly the most convenient outcome for his wife and the world in general, it left one huge unanswered question. Had he been dead before his wife pulled the trigger?

Luke nodded to Hobbs and walked to the SUV he had left on the side of the road. He could feel the cop's speculative eyes on him every step of the way. There would be no more friendly nights of poker and whiskey

21

at Hobbs's house.

He got behind the wheel of the SUV.

What had he become?

The familiar scene from his nightmares, the one in which he gripped a scalpel and walked through the blood of two dead men lying on the floor of a lab, flashed in front of his eyes.

He forced himself to focus on starting the vehicle. In the process he managed to suppress the vision. But he could not silence the voices of the two men from last night's edition of the recurring nightmare.

"Subject A is not responding. We will have to terminate."

"Wait. He may pull out of it. We can't afford another failure. He's worth a fucking fortune."

"Only if he's a success. If he does survive there will be a high probability of insanity. The client is paying for a psychically enhanced assassin, not a monster with a lethal talent."

"We can't be sure the subject will be insane if he survives. If he is we can terminate later."

"He's a failure. I'll take care of this."

"What the fuck? Stop —"

After that there were only the choked-off screams. They echoed in Luke's head as he turned into the graveled driveway of the non-descript rental house. For a moment he sat quietly behind the wheel.

The memories of his missing night seemed to be coming back slowly in his dreams. The problem was that he had no way to separate fact from fantasy. But if even some of the bloody visions were real, he could not avoid the logical conclusion: he was a psychically enhanced assassin who had killed two people, escaped, and gone rogue. And now, it seemed, he had killed again.

This town was too small for a man with a Jekyll-and-Hyde problem. It was time to move on.

CHAPTER THREE

Talia poured a glass of wine and carried it to the dining counter. She sat down in front of her laptop, slipped on her black-framed glasses, and opened the video chat.

Pallas Llewellyn and Amelia Rivers, the other two members of the *Lost Night Files* podcast team, were already in the virtual room. Ambrose Drake, the author Pallas had met in the course of investigating the Carnelian case, was also there. They were a tightly knit group.

A little more than seven months ago she and Amelia and Pallas had been summoned to an abandoned hotel in the desert with the promise of job offers. The three of them had never met until that afternoon. They had parked their cars at the dusty entrance, introduced themselves to each other, and walked through the doorway of the early-twentieth-century sanatorium turned failed resort.

She remembered thinking how deep the shadows were in the lobby. With the exception of fleeting scenes in her dreams, that was the last clear memory she could summon until she and Pallas and Amelia had been awakened by the earthquake and raging fire that had destroyed the hotel.

The quake had struck in the early hours of the following morning. She and Amelia and Pallas had been roused by the tremors of the earth, the rumble of falling debris, and the smell of smoke. They had been bound to hospital gurneys in a lab that looked as if it dated from the early twentieth century.

Working together, they had managed to escape, but in the end the fire had destroyed whatever evidence there might have been that would have given them the answers they needed. No one believed their story. The only thing they knew for certain was that they had changed. The minor psychic vibe each had possessed — a preternatural sensitivity that had seemed to be little more than especially keen intuition — had been enhanced in disturbing and unsettling ways.

Ambrose had not been with them at Lucent Springs, but he had experienced a similar episode of amnesia. He had awakened on a beach in San Diego. Like Talia and the others, he had discovered that his senses had been enhanced.

The four of them were now bound together by the mystery of their lost nights and the secrets they shared. They were not only a team working to find answers; they had become a chosen family.

"We are getting a lot of response to the Carnelian case episodes," Pallas said.

"Probably the Dark Academia vibe," Ambrose said dryly. "That particular Gothic subgenre is big in fiction these days."

"You ought to know," Talia said. "You're the author."

The podcast series covering the Carnelian case had dropped a week ago. It had brought in a lot of new subscribers as well as some interesting leads, including the one from the anonymous informant who had contacted her.

"We got lucky with the Phoenix tip," Pallas continued. "Ambrose and I talked to a woman named Charlotte Andrews. She's a fan of the podcast. She remembered that Brooke Kendrick took a psych test that sounds a lot like the one the four of us remember taking back in college."

"You were right, Talia," Amelia said. "That old test is the through line, the one connection that links all of us."

"Five coincidences is about four too many," Ambrose said. "If the people who grabbed us are working from a list of names of potential research subjects, that test has to be the source. At the time we were told that it was supposed to provide career counseling, but it looks like that was a cover for what was really being measured."

"They were searching for people who had some degree of innate psychic talent," Amelia said. "What is equally interesting is that they must have been convinced they had a way to measure an individual's paranormal profile."

"Once Ambrose suggested that the people who kidnapped us had to be working off a list, I remembered that test," Talia said. "I knew that had to be the connection."

"What made you so sure?" Ambrose asked.

Talia shrugged. "Damned if I know. It just felt . . . right."

A small but distinct thrill whispered through her. She sipped some wine and let herself take a moment to savor the positive side of her ability to find that which was lost or hidden — the flash of satisfaction that came with a successful search, at least one that did not end with a dead body. It was why she had become a librarian after graduating from college. A stint in an academic library had been followed by a string of research jobs. Admittedly, none of them had ended well — commitment issues, according to her therapist. Nevertheless, the various positions in both the private and government sectors had all involved finding answers. She had enjoyed that part. Success had always given her a nice little rush, a sensation very different from the shock that had struck that afternoon when she had located Ray Clayton in a trash bin.

Unfortunately, tonight the dark fallout from the investigation earlier that day would outweigh the small thrill she got from confirmation that the old college psych test was the source of the list.

"Okay, we have the origin point of the list, but that doesn't get us any closer to finding it," she said.

"It's a place to start," Pallas said.

Amelia's expression sharpened. "The question I keep coming back to is, why come looking for us now? It's been over a decade since any of us took that test."

"The obvious answer is that the people behind this think they need us for their crazy experiments," Talia said.

"Maybe it took this long for someone to come up with a drug that had the potential to kick our senses to the next level," Ambrose said.

"Or maybe the list got filed away and forgotten years ago and someone recently found it," Pallas added.

"Someone who is in the business of running off-the-books drug trials and doesn't mind taking the risk of kidnapping a few innocent people to use as test subjects," Ambrose said.

There was a moment of silence. No one said the rest out loud but Talia knew they were all thinking the same thing: the drug had worked.

"We need to know more about that test and the person or persons who designed and administered it years ago," Ambrose said. "Pallas and I can work that angle."

"How?" Amelia asked.

"The old-fashioned way," Ambrose said. "Start interviewing witnesses. We're going to Phoenix to follow up on the Brooke Kendrick lead. That's where she went to college."

"Good plan," Amelia said. "While Ambrose and Pallas check out the Phoenix angle, I'm going to go back to Lucent Springs."

There was another moment of silence.

Evidently Amelia could read their minds.

"Yes, I know I've been back to the hotel a dozen times since that night. And no, I've never found anything useful in the way of clues. But I'm missing something. I'm sure of it. This time I'm going to conduct interviews. I'll use the podcast as a cover. I'll tell people I'm doing advance research for a possible episode on the history of the hotel. Someone in that town knows something."

No one argued with her. This was not the first time they had speculated that one or more of the residents in the small desert community in southern California were keeping secrets. But Amelia's morbid fascination with Lucent Springs was becoming worrisome. Talia was starting to fear that her friend's obsession with the ruins of the Lucent Springs Hotel might be an unfortunate side effect of her recently enhanced senses. She knew Pallas had the same concern.

The reality was that the four of them were not yet comfortable with their new psychic abilities. They were all in the process of trying to understand how to control the new forms of perception. Each of their talents was unique and each had a profoundly disturbing aspect. Talia knew that their new sensitivity to paranormal energy, combined with the unnerving amnesia, had made each of them question their own sanity at first. They had soon learned to keep quiet about their concerns because they were not the only ones who had begun to wonder about the state of their mental health. Friends, lovers, coworkers, and families had questioned it, too.

Some of their memories were starting to return in slivers and shards in their dreams, but they were still a long way from developing a clear picture of their lost nights.

"Talia, did the fan who contacted you anonymously about a list of names ever come through with solid information?" Pallas asked.

Talia tightened her grip on her wineglass. "Not yet. Whoever sent the text seemed serious but also extremely paranoid. I'm starting to think my informant is just another overly imaginative or maybe downright deluded fan of the podcast."

"Or a full-on fraud," Ambrose suggested.

"Maybe," Talia admitted. "But it felt legit."

"It was a *text* message," Amelia reminded her. "No feelings or emotions involved."

There was no point arguing. Amelia was right. Talia swallowed some more wine.

"If there's one thing *The Lost Night Files* has proven beyond a shadow of a doubt it's that when it comes to the paranormal, there are a lot of card-carrying members of the tinfoil helmet club out there in podcast land," Pallas said.

Talia thought about the body in the trash bin. "Sometimes I wonder if I'm one of them."

"No," Amelia said, suddenly fierce. "You are not deluded. None of us are. We know that because we have compared notes. We have validated each other's experiences. We were all involuntary test subjects in someone's bizarre paranormal research experiment. We're going to find out who did this to us."

"And then what?" Talia asked. "Call in the police? Do we try to have the person arrested? Good luck proving that someone kidnapped us and gave us a drug that enhanced our paranormal senses. Do you realize how wild that sounds? It's right up there with stories about being abducted by extraterrestrials. No one will believe us. And don't get me started on how a judge or jury would react to our claims. We'd be lucky if they didn't lock us up in a psychiatric hospital."

"We'll worry about the endgame after we identify the kidnappers," Ambrose said.

"He's right," Pallas said. "Meanwhile, we're in this together . . ."

"Until we get answers," Amelia said.

"Until we get answers," Talia added.

"Until we get answers," Ambrose concluded.

It was not just the signature signoff of the *Lost Night Files* podcast — it was a solemn vow.

CHAPTER FOUR

Luke dreams . . .

. . . He stops at the doorway of the lab and looks back at the blood-splashed scene one last time. The space is illuminated with a strange blue light. An odd mix of equipment is scattered around the room. The chemistry apparatus on the long workbench looks new, but the heavy-duty gardening tools stacked against one wall are old and rusty.

He knows he should remember the details. He's a professor of history. Details are important. But he does not have time to examine his surroundings closely, because two men in white coats are sprawled on the floor in a pool of blood. Their throats have been cut. He is holding a scalpel in his right hand.

He turns and tries to decide how he will escape. He is confronted by a vast chamber lit with a violet-and-acid-green radiance. The space is crammed with luminous plants, glowing mushrooms, and curtains of thorn-studded vines. Here and there he sees flowers that look like the open jaws of snakes.

He uses the back of his hand to wipe the sweat off his forehead. The atmosphere is too warm and too humid and it is charged with a disturbing energy that threatens to dazzle his senses. Everything about the underground gardens is wrong. Colors are too intense, the light is eerie, and the plants are rustling and murmuring to each other. He senses that they are trying to decide if he is prey.

Tightening his grip on the scalpel, he sets out on the path through the gardens of hell . . .

The ding of an incoming text brought Luke out of the nightmare. For a flash of eternity he was caught in the frozen dimension that marked the border between sleep and the waking state.

He surfaced on a rush of adrenaline, swung his legs over the side of the bed, and grabbed the phone. He stared at the new message, half afraid to believe his eyes.

Today. Seattle. Address and final instructions will be sent at four thirty a.m. Cash only.

Seattle.

He had assumed that, if the informant came through, the meeting would take place in the anonymity of a metropolitan area, either Portland or Seattle. He had stationed himself in a motel that was roughly midway between the two cities.

He checked the time. It was just going on two. There would be no traffic at that hour. He had time to get to Seattle by four thirty.

He got up and crossed the room to the duffel bag and the small day pack sitting in front of the door. The duffel contained a few changes of clothes, shaving gear, a second pair of boots, and some other basics. He had been living out of it and under a new identity since he had lost an entire night to amnesia three long months ago. The pack held the essentials he would need if he was forced to run — the cash he had accumulated in a series of small ATM transactions, the pistol, and the documents required to establish yet another identity.

He knew how to disappear. He had learned the art soon after entering the foster care system. A few years spent as an analyst in the intelligence world had provided him with the knowledge he needed to fine-tune the process. You picked up a lot of useful tips interviewing bad actors for a living.

When he had been forced to vanish three months ago he had worried initially that his two years as a college professor had robbed him of his edge. He had been relieved to discover how quickly the old skills came back.

CHAPTER FIVE

Talia parked on a side street as the instructions had stipulated. She checked the time again, hitched the small pack over one shoulder, and got out of the car. Extracting the pepper spray from the pocket of her puffy, thigh-length down coat, she locked up and went briskly toward the unlit house. There were no sidewalks and no streetlights in the semirural neighborhood on the outskirts of the city. The only illumination came from a cold moon.

It was early morning — not yet six o'clock — but this was the Pacific Northwest and it was late fall, so there was no sign of dawn. She was running on adrenaline and nerves and very little sleep. The fact that there was a thousand dollars in cash in the pack put her even more on edge.

The text from the anonymous informant had come in at three thirty a.m., yanking her out of a dream involving a dead man staring up at her from the bottom of an industrial-sized recycling bin. The meeting was to take place at precisely six o'clock. The address had been sent thirty minutes ago. She had been behind the wheel of her car, waiting, when it arrived.

There was no porch light over the front door. She used her cell phone flashlight to make sure she had the right address. Her pulse was racing and she could feel a cold sweat trickling down her sides.

Following instructions, she walked along a weedy path to the rear of the small house. She was relieved to see that a light glowed weakly over the back door, as promised in the text. She went up the two porch steps and knocked twice. Hardly able to breathe, she listened intently, expecting — hoping — to hear footsteps in the front hall.

There was no response.

A crushing disappointment slammed through her. It was followed by a surge of anger. She had been conned. Okay, so it wasn't the first time a determined podcast listener had suckered a member of the team into checking out what proved to be a phony lead, but that didn't make it any less infuriating. The rush of emotions kicked up all of her senses. She was suddenly at full throttle. Currents of icy-hot anger swept through her. She wanted to scream at the trickster. *This is my life and the lives of my friends you are screwing with, you sadist.*

Damn it, she would not succumb to pointless rage. She fought a silent battle on the back porch and managed to regain control. It was her own fault. She had allowed herself to believe that this lead would pan out. It had looked so promising. After over six months of false tips she should have known better than to think this one would be any different.

And here she was standing on a stranger's back porch in the dark with a thousand dollars in her pack. A belated attack of common sense struck. She started to turn away and go back down the steps. But something stopped her — a whisper of panic, not her own. It shaded rapidly into . . . unconsciousness? Sleep? It did not feel like the echo of a recent death, but it wasn't good.

Something terrible had happened inside the little house at the end of the street. Yet another reason to get out of there. Now.

Instead, she took a breath, braced herself, and gingerly touched the door handle . . .

. . . The burn seared her senses. She yelped and yanked her fingers off the metal knob. The sudden move caused the unlatched door to swing inward on squeaking hinges. The gloom of a deeply shadowed kitchen loomed.

For a tense moment she just stood there, trying to decide what to do. There were answers to be had inside the house, she was certain of that. She needed those answers and she was willing to take risks to get them, but there were limits. She had pushed the envelope far enough this morning. She needed backup and she knew who to call. Roger Gossard owed her a few favors.

An icy frisson flickered across the back of her neck. She was suddenly, intensely aware of an unnerving chill. She knew that feeling. Someone was watching her.

It was way past time to exit the scene.

She turned quickly, intending to go down the steps and back to the car. But she froze when she saw the man blocking her path a few feet away.

For an instant shock locked her muscles and sent her senses into a chaotic tailspin. Then adrenaline splashed through her. She raised the can of pepper spray.

"Please don't use that stuff," the stranger said. "I've got enough trouble as it is. I'm not going to hurt you."

His voice settled on her like a warm summer night, soothing her senses, calming her panic. Clearly she was overreacting. The man blocking her path had made no attempt to grab her and there was no sign of a weapon. He was harmless. She lowered the pepper spray.

In the glow of the weak light over the door she could see that he was dressed in a battered leather bomber jacket, a dark T-shirt, jeans, and running shoes. A day pack similar to her own was slung casually over one shoulder. Given the deep shadows his eyes should have been unreadable. Instead they seemed to burn. *Just a reflection,* she told herself.

"Who are you?" she said.

"Another would-be buyer, like you. Evidently we were not the only customers for the list. Looks like someone else got here first and decided to make sure there were no more sales."

CHAPTER SIX

His voice whispered to her senses, reassuring her. She was feeling very calm now. That was not right. She ought to be terrified. She should be working the pepper spray for all it was worth and running for the car. What the hell was happening here?

And suddenly she understood.

She pulled hard on her senses, shook off the mesmerizing effect of his voice, and raised the can of pepper spray.

"Stop that or I will use this stuff," she said.

There was a beat of silence. She got the feeling she had surprised him.

"Okay, let's try this again," he said. "My name is Luke Rand. Who are you?"

She drew a deep breath. His voice still gave her a bit of a rush, but it was no longer hitting her senses like a riptide threatening to draw her under the surface.

On some primal level she *liked* the sound

of his voice. That was probably not good news.

"What do you know about the list?" she asked, not bothering to answer his question.

"If it's the one I'm looking for it's a list of names of people who took a certain psych test several years ago."

"The informant offered to sell it to you, too?" she said.

"And, apparently, to whoever got here first."

"The list wasn't the only thing the first buyer took." She glanced back at the door, remembering the energy on the metal handle. "Whoever it was grabbed our informant as well."

Luke Rand's eyes got a little intense. "What makes you so sure the informant didn't decide to disappear after making the first sale?"

The disturbingly soft way he asked the question rattled her nerves. She needed to stay focused.

"Just a guess," she said in her coolest tones. She could tell he knew she was lying, but he did not press her. She hurried on. "You came to the same conclusion, didn't you?"

"Yes."

"So, if the informant and the list are gone,

why are you still here?" she asked.

"I thought it would be interesting to see who else showed up."

"Right." She paused. "That was actually a pretty good idea."

"I get those once in a while."

She ignored that. "Well?"

"Well, what?"

"Has there been anybody else besides you and me?"

"No."

"You're not the oversharing type, are you?"

"No."

A moment ago she had been nervous — make that anxious. Okay, scared. Now she was getting irritated.

"I wonder how many buyers the informant lined up?" she said.

"The thing about a list is that it's easy to duplicate," he said. "Why not sell it to as many people as possible? The only thing in our favor is that the market for that particular product has to be fairly limited."

"Good point."

"I've got five grand in this pack," he said. "How much did you bring?"

Talia flexed her fingers around the strap of the pack, trying to decide what to say. She finally decided that he probably didn't intend to rob her for the cash. Like her, he was here for the list.

"A thousand," she admitted.

"You got a deal. I was told to be here at precisely four thirty. You?"

"Six."

"She was gone when I arrived."

"She?" Talia raised her brows. "What makes you so sure the seller is a woman?"

"I went into the house and took a look around while I waited. Found a short-term rental agreement dated a couple of days ago. It was signed *Phoebe Hatch.* Might or might not be the person trying to sell the list, but I'd say the odds are she's our informant."

"You just walked into the house?"

"The door was unlocked."

He did not sound concerned with the finer points of the law, and she decided that, under the circumstances, she wasn't, either.

"What did you find besides the rental agreement?" she asked, not even trying to conceal her suspicions.

"I didn't find the list."

"Why should I believe you?"

"Hell, I don't know. Maybe because I'm standing here in the backyard of a stranger's house at six o'clock in the morning arguing with a woman who is carrying a thousand dollars in a pack. You do realize that to the

45

average cop this would look a lot like a drug deal? If someone sees us and calls nine-one-one we would probably both be arrested."

"You stuck around because you wanted to identify the competition," she said.

"It seemed like the logical thing to do. Look, neither of us can afford to waste time discussing motives. Do you want to trade information? If not, I'm going to bail before one of the neighbors decides to call the police."

She glanced into the darkened kitchen. She and the rest of the *Lost Night Files* crew were desperate for answers. This was as close as any of them had come to locating the list.

"All right, I'll trade," she said. "You were here before me. You went inside. What did you find?"

"Not much. There are a few personal things. Some clothes. Some basics in the bath. But no tech. Whoever grabbed her took her phone and any other devices she might have had."

"They didn't want other buyers to look for her," Talia whispered. "Maybe they plan to murder her and dump the body."

"If they wanted to kill her, they could have done it here and made it look like a burglary-in-progress murder. It would have

46

been the simplest way to silence her. Instead they took the risk of kidnapping her. Maybe she's important to them for reasons besides the list."

"You seem to know a lot about how bad guys think."

"I'm using a technique called logic," he said.

"I wasn't criticizing you," she said quickly. "Figuring out how bad guys think is a very useful skill set."

"Thank you. I'm glad you approve. Moving right along, you have my name but I don't have yours. Care to introduce yourself?"

Her intuition sent a chill of warning. She was once again aware of an intriguingly resonant vibe in his voice. *He's trying to make me think I can trust him.* And it was working.

"Are you in sales?" she asked, deeply suspicious. "Or maybe you're a professional con artist?"

His eyes tightened. "What are you talking about?"

"Never mind. My name is Talia March. Enough about me. Got any identification?"

He hesitated and then, evidently resigned to humoring her, he pulled out a small, flat black wallet and flipped it open. She aimed her light at the California driver's license. There was a photo of Luke's hard, uncompromising face and an address in a town named Adelina Beach.

"Fine," she said. "You are licensed to drive a car. That doesn't tell me anything useful."

Without a word he flipped to another document. It, too, showed his face. The fine print identified him as a member of the faculty of Adelina Beach College.

"I've never heard of Adelina Beach College," she said.

"It's a small school in a community outside of L.A."

"Is that right? What do you teach?"

"History. Okay, my turn. What do you do for a living, Talia March?"

"I'm a member of the *Lost Night Files* podcast team. Oh, and I do a little private consulting on the side."

"You've got a *podcast*?" Luke stared at her, clearly blindsided. "What the hell?"

She steeled herself because she knew what was coming next. "We investigate cold cases that have a paranormal angle."

"Shit. Just what I needed. A podcaster chasing a ghost story."

Okay, sure, she had been prepared for the disdain and the irritation, but she got mad anyway. It had been a particularly stressful twenty-four hours, what with the body in the trash bin and now a missing informant. She was not in a good mood.

"Considering the fact that you are chasing the same list I'm after, I don't think you have any business insulting me or the podcast," she said.

"You know, we really don't have time for this argument. I suggest we save it for later."

"At the rate this conversation is deteriorating, there may not be a later. Your turn to hand over some information. Why, exactly, are you after the list Phoebe Hatch wanted to sell to us?"

"I want it because I'm pretty sure I'm on it."

"Oh." For some reason that caught her by surprise. *Should have seen it coming.*

"What about you?" he said. "Are you chasing it because you've decided it will make a good story for the conspiracy theory crowd?"

"Don't push your luck, Rand. I want that list for the same reason you do. I think my friends and I are on it."

Luke's eyes got a little sharper, hotter. "Well, now," he said softly. "You and I have a lot to talk about, Talia March. I suggest we have that conversation someplace other than here."

Compulsion shivered below the surface of the words, urging her to agree. He was right. They each had information the other needed. The smart thing to do was go somewhere private and discuss —

"Stop it," she snapped. Outrage unleashed a shot of adrenaline into her already over-hyped nervous system. "Of all the cheap tricks. History professor, my ass. You're a hypnotist, aren't you? One with a genuine psychic talent. You're trying to manipulate my energy field or something. Don't do it again."

He watched her in silence for a moment. She knew he was trying to figure out how to handle her.

"I'm not a hypnotist," he said finally. "I told you, I teach history at Adelina Beach College. That's the truth."

He had the nerve to sound offended — and maybe a little defensive. He was also irritated.

"Bullshit," she said. "Our relationship, such as it is, has gotten off to a very rocky start. Don't compound the problem with mind games. In case you haven't noticed, we are in the middle of something dangerous here."

"That's why I suggested we go somewhere else to talk," he said, his voice too even now.

"No, you want to go someplace private so that you can try to interrogate me while giving up as little information as possible. I don't work like that."

"You are not a very trusting person, are you?" Luke said.

"Nope. And obviously, neither are you. Let's get something straight. There will be no interrogation. Either we agree to a mutually beneficial exchange of information or this ends here."

"Fine. Pick a coffeehouse, any coffeehouse. I'll meet you there."

She gave that a moment's thought. "All right. I know a place that opens early and serves freshly baked biscuits as well as coffee. I'll give you the address. You go on ahead. I'll meet you there."

"You're trying to ditch me."

"Trust me, as appealing as that sounds, I am not trying to get rid of you. I want to talk to you as badly as you want to talk to me. But first I'm going to take a look around inside Hatch's house."

"I thought you were concerned with the legalities," he said.

"I have reason to believe that Ms. Hatch may be hurt or injured inside that house. It's my duty as a concerned citizen to take a look."

"Has anyone told you that you're a lousy liar?"

"Unlike, say, you?"

"Everyone has a talent," he said.

"And yours is the ability to lie?" She nodded. "Makes sense. Probably a side effect of your hypnosis talent."

"I am not a hypnotist," he said through his teeth. He exhaled. "Never mind. If you insist on going inside the house, I'll come with you."

"Why?"

"Because I don't think it's smart for you to hang around here alone. Has it occurred to you that someone else may be watching this house to see who shows up to buy the list?"

Startled, she glanced around the still-dark neighborhood. There were a lot of places where a watcher could hide.

"Damn," she whispered.

"Exactly."

Without a word she turned and went into the dark kitchen. Luke followed, closing the door behind him. He took out his phone and turned on the flashlight. She got the icy-hot sensation that signaled another shot of adrenaline hitting her bloodstream. She was alone in the house with a man she had just met, one she had no reason to trust.

She tightened her grip on the can of pepper spray.

"You're not going to need that," Luke said, annoyed.

She decided to ignore him. She opened the flashlight on her own phone.

"The blinds are closed in every room," Luke said, "but keep the light aimed low."

"If the police do show up I'm sure you'll be able to hypnotize them into thinking we've got every right to be here," she said.

She expected him to deny his talent again but he surprised her with a question.

"What makes you think I'm a hypnotist?" he asked.

He sounded genuinely curious. Intrigued. And wary.

"Something you do with your voice." Cautiously she opened her senses and moved slowly across the kitchen. "I expect it comes in handy."

He did not respond to that.

"Is your ability to manipulate people with your voice the reason you think you might be on that list?" she asked.

He was silent for a beat.

"Yeah," he said. "It is."

"Is there any practical use for your talent? Outside of doing stage shows in Vegas, I mean?"

"There was up until about three months ago," he said evenly.

"What happened three months ago?"

"It's complicated."

She glanced back at him, trying to get a read. She was very aware of him now, and not just because he was standing in the same room. She could pick up the whisper of his energy field. It was distinctive, to put it mildly. Powerful.

Focus, woman.

She contemplated the battered furnishings. The only thing that looked new was a small plant on an end table. Everything else — the sagging sofa, floor lamp, and rug — looked as old as the house.

The familiar sense of knowing shivered through her.

"Here we go," she said softly.

"What is it?" Luke asked, his voice sharpening.

"I don't know yet, but there's something hidden in this room."

Luke speared the flashlight around the space. "Are you sure?"

"Yes, I'm sure. This is what I do, Luke Rand. I find stuff. Whether I want to or not."

She aimed the flashlight at the little plant on the end table. It looked healthy and vibrant. Well-tended. A grocery store tag with a barcode stamped on it was attached.

"That doesn't fit," she said.

Luke studied the plant. "Explain."

"Everything in this house indicates that Phoebe Hatch was using it as a temporary hideout. It was never intended to be a home. But she went to the trouble of picking up a small potted plant at a supermarket. I think she was lonely. And afraid. She didn't dare get a dog or a cat, because she knew she might have to abandon the animal."

"So she picked up a cheap houseplant instead?"

"Yes," Talia said.

She sorted through the tendrils of hot energy that burned in the space. Luke watched, not speaking, as she crossed the room to the end table. She took a breath and gingerly touched the plastic pot.

Desperation and determination lanced through her senses.

"Shit," she whispered. She shook her fingers as if she had touched a hot stove. "I hate when this happens." The small, instinctive action did nothing to cool the burn.

"Now what's wrong?" Luke asked.

"Nothing."

"You really are a bad liar."

"I'll practice."

She studied the plant. There was nothing to see except potting soil and green leaves. But it concealed a secret.

She used a fingertip to poke around in the dirt. The small memory card was buried a half inch below the surface. She dug it up and blew off the bits of soil.

"Okay, I am officially impressed with your talent, Talia March," Luke said.

The pot was still hot.

"There's something else," she said. "Something just as important. Personal."

She explored the soil around the plant with her fingers. A delicate gold chain necklace with a small crystal pendant was concealed beneath the surface. She pulled it out and examined it in the light of her phone.

"I get why she hid the memory card," Luke said. "There's probably something important on it. With luck, it will be the list we're looking for. But why hide the neck-lace? It doesn't look particularly valuable."

Another exhilarating flash of knowing zapped Talia's senses.

"Trust me, it's valuable," she said.

"Now we definitely need to talk."

"Sure," she said, still riding the rush. "I'll give you the address of that coffeehouse I found earlier."

A chill stirred the fine hairs on the back of her neck.

"Stop that," she said.

"Do not," Luke warned in a dangerously soft voice, "try to lose me. I will be right behind you."

"I wouldn't dream of dumping you," she assured him. "At least not in the immediate future."

"Is that so? Why not?"

"Simple. You've got information I need. As long as you are a potentially useful resource I will not be ghosting you."

"I'm flattered, of course, but you do realize that logic works both ways, right?" he said. "You've got information I want, so I will be sticking very close."

"In other words, we are using each other." She gave him her shiniest smile. "I can work with that. Let's go get some biscuits and coffee and see what's on the memory card."

CHAPTER SEVEN

Talia took the memory card and an adapter out of her small cross-body bag and set them down on the table. "I don't mind telling you I'm a little nervous. What if it's just a list of names and nothing else?"

They were in a booth in a non-chain coffeehouse near Lake Union. The city was just waking up and people were trickling through the door in search of the homemade biscuits featured on the menu. She and Luke had given their orders to the server a moment ago and were drinking coffee while they waited for the food to arrive.

"If all we've got is a list," Luke said, "then we will track down every name on it and gather as much information as possible. We will ask questions and we will keep asking them until we've got enough data to build a storyboard that will provide us with some answers."

She pursed her lips, thinking. "Huh. That

sounds like a smart way to go forward with the investigation."

"Thank you," he said, his voice a degree or two above freezing. "I'm an instructor, remember? I like to lay things out in a logical manner."

"I wasn't trying to insult you."

"Yes, you were. Never mind. Load the damn memory card."

"Right."

She set her phone down on the table so that they could both view the screen and set about the task of importing the data from the memory card.

"There's only one item on here," she said, excitement spiking. "It must be the list. This won't take long."

A photo appeared. It was a picture of a piece of paper. But there was no list of names. Instead there were a website address and a handwritten note.

Talia March, if you find this it means they grabbed me. I think they will keep me alive for a while, but in the end they will kill me. I know too much. Please look for me. No one else will. I have listened to all of the episodes of the Lost Night Files. I know what you can do. Find me and you'll find the list.

Luke groaned. "I hate it when informants decide to go all cryptic and mysterious."

"When you run a podcast like *The Lost Night Files* you get contacted by the cryptic, mysterious type a lot," Talia said. "Most of the tipsters are frauds. Some are straight-up delusional. But once in a while you get the real thing."

Luke studied the note. "I think Phoebe Hatch is for real."

"So do I." Talia took the necklace out of her pocket. The transparent stone was warm in her palm. She could feel the faint buzz of energy that told her it had been worn by someone for a very long time — years, probably. "This was important to Phoebe. Apparently she's a fan of the podcast, so she knows that we often discuss the properties of crystals. She is aware that I might be able to use this stone to find her."

Luke studied her for a long moment, his gaze speculative. "Do you really believe that crystals have some paranormal properties?"

She slipped the necklace over her head and gave him her brightest screw-you smile. "Yep."

"I was afraid you were going to say that."

"Says the man who is searching for a list of people believed to possess psychic abilities because he has every reason to suspect that he's on said list."

"Fair point."

"There's no sense fighting it, Rand. You and I are stuck with each other until we figure out what happened to Phoebe Hatch and the list that has our names on it."

"I usually work alone."

"Not anymore." She glanced at the screen of her phone. "We need to check out this website."

"On that we are in total agreement."

He was already on his phone entering the website address. She did the same on her own phone. When the results came up she knew she was not the only one who was bewildered.

"What the hell?" Luke said. " 'Discover the Unplugged Experience. Leave the stress of modern life behind and join us on Night Island for a three-day retreat that will change your life. Come walk the garden labyrinth. You will learn to use the deep, insightful secrets of the Venner Meditation System to achieve inner balance.' Well, shit."

"You are not keen on achieving inner balance?" Talia said.

"This is a brochure advertising a retreat for people who are burned out," Luke growled. "What does that have to do with Hatch and the list?"

Talia tightened her grip on the crystal. Energy shivered in the stone.

"Everything," she said quietly.

Luke's jaw hardened and his eyes were grim but this time he did not argue.

She went back to her phone. "According to the website, 'Night Island is a privately owned island in the San Juans. It is under the control of the nonprofit Wynford Institute for the Study of Medicinal Botany. The Institute sponsors the Unplugged Experience. Access is allowed only to registered guests, and there are no more than ten at any given time.' "

"How do you make money on an operation that takes only ten customers at a time?" Luke asked.

"By charging several hundred dollars a night, probably," Talia said. She scrolled down, searching for the financial details, and stopped when she found them. "Nope. It's not expensive at all. 'The Unplugged Experience is dedicated to promoting the benefits of achieving harmony and balance in daily life.' There's a lovely mission statement."

"Forget the mission statement," Luke said. "I found some reviews. The Unplugged Experience has been operating for about six months. Evidently it hasn't been a big success. No one seems thrilled by the meditation and labyrinth walking. One reviewer calls Clive Venner, the guru in charge, 'a run-of-the-mill grifter with a New Age hustle.' Says the System is just a worn-out collection of old-fashioned breathing and meditation exercises. But people do rave about the vegetarian cuisine."

Talia looked up. "Really? So the food is good?"

"Apparently. If you're vegetarian. One guest notes that 'the homemade sourdough bread and mushroom pâté are to die for' and another says that, 'whatever you do, don't miss the chocolate crème brûlée.' "

"Interesting." Talia went back to her phone.

"What are you doing?" Luke asked, his voice sharpening.

"Trying to make a reservation," she said. "I want to see how hard it is to book the Experience. Oh, wow. Not hard at all. I can get a room as early as tomorrow. Probably because it's off-season. At this time of year tourism in the San Juans slows down. Hang on."

"Stop, damn it. We need to talk about this."

"In a minute. I'm making a reservation for three days, starting tomorrow."

"That," Luke said evenly, "is a very bad idea."

A shiver of cold energy charged the atmosphere. She glared.

"I warned you not to try to manipulate me," she said.

"I'm not —"

"Yes, you are. I realize you're pissed. It's okay to be annoyed with me. A lot of people find me annoying."

"No shit. I wonder why?"

"For your information, I'm not feeling all warm and fuzzy toward you right now, either."

"I'm crushed, of course."

"I'm not joking, Rand. I don't care if you're irritated. It's not okay to try to manhandle my aura or whatever it is you're doing. If we're going to work together there will have to be rules. Rule number one is that you are not allowed to mess around with my energy field. Is that clear?"

He studied her for a long time, his eyes half-closed. She knew he was once again trying to decide what to make of her and how to deal with her.

"Think of us as temporary allies," she suggested in an effort to be helpful.

Luke blinked.

She smiled, satisfied. "There. See how

easy that was? Now I suggest we stop wasting time. If you don't like my plan to go to Night Island, can I assume you have a better one?"

"Yes."

"I'm listening," she said, trying to sound encouraging. It wasn't easy, because she was pretty sure he did not have a better idea.

"I will book the Unplugged Experience," he said evenly. "Alone."

"Forget it. You don't have the right vibe."

"What's that supposed to mean?"

She finished entering her credit card details, hit the submit button, and put the phone down on the table. "No offense, but you just don't look like the meditation retreat type. No one will believe you booked a tech-free experience that consists of breathing exercises, labyrinth walking, and vegetarian cuisine."

"I can fake it. Pay attention, Talia. I've got a few rules, too. Rule one is that you are not going to that island on your own."

"It's not like I'll be walking into a mysterious Gothic castle on a remote island. The retreat is sponsored by a legitimate non-profit organization."

"Do you have any idea how many non-profits are smoke-and-mirrors operations designed to provide cover for bad actors?"

Luke asked.

"I won't be alone. There will be other guests and a staff and a daily ferry service."

Luke glanced at his phone, frowning. "A chartered ferry service, apparently."

"So?"

"We're not talking about the state ferry system. A charter operation runs on demand. It has to be booked in advance."

"Listen to me, Luke Rand. A woman has been kidnapped, but we can't go to the police, because we have absolutely zero proof. At best they would let us file a missing persons report. You read her note. She thinks her life is in danger, and that retreat is the only lead we've got."

"I told you, I'll check out the island," he said.

"Not on your own. I'm going, too. What's this all about? I thought you had seen the light."

"What light? Are you referring to that oncoming train?"

"We agreed that we would work together."

"We agreed to exchange information. That's different."

"No, it's not." She turned to watch the server approach with a tray. "Oh, good, here comes breakfast. Wait until you taste the biscuits. Perfect texture. They use real butter and they make sure to keep it very cold. That's one of the secrets, you see."

"I'll make a note of that," he said.

"I sense sarcasm."

"Probably because you're psychic."

CHAPTER EIGHT

Luke Rand was alive. Not only that, he appeared to be stable.

The assassin sat behind the wheel of the rental car and studied the photo on the phone. There was no doubt. The man who had appeared at Hatch's house and was now having coffee with the podcast woman was the failure from the last round of experiments. The fact that he had survived was amazing; that he was not insane was even more astounding.

The assassin hit send and texted the photo with a single comment.

Instructions?

There was a pause. The assassin knew the individual who had just received the picture verifying the identity of the buyer was taking a moment to process the shock — but only a moment.

The instructions came through a short time later.

Terminate

With pleasure.

The excitement that accompanied the anticipation of the kill was phenomenal. The only thing that surpassed it was the rush that came in the aftermath of a successful hit.

CHAPTER NINE

"So, you have a problem with podcasts that focus on the paranormal but you don't doubt the reality of paranormal energy and psychic talents?" Talia asked around a mouthful of biscuit slathered in butter.

She was going back to that topic? Luke reached for his coffee mug and gave himself a beat to compose his response. The process of trying to get a handle on Talia March was turning out to involve a steep learning curve. He had known her for less than two hours and he was already losing ground.

"I have a problem with podcasts that sensationalize the paranormal," he said, going for his seminar tone.

Talia aimed her knife at him. "*The Lost Night Files* does not sensationalize the paranormal. We don't operate like that ridiculous *Anomalies Report* blog."

He paused the coffee in midair. "*Anomalies Report?*"

"I'm not surprised you aren't aware of it. It's a low-end operation. Small audience. But talk about sensationalizing the paranormal. It covers crap like those so-called energy vortexes in Sedona, astral travel, and Area 51 stuff. Real junk science."

"You sound like you read the blog."

"I check it out occasionally," Talia admitted. "Mostly because it pulls in some information from the dark web."

"That interests you?"

"It's a resource *The Lost Night Files* desperately needs. I'm competent when it comes to navigating the surface web, but I'm not a pro, and I'm a total amateur when it comes to the dark web. I've been trying to find a virtual assistant with that kind of expertise but I haven't had any luck so far. Probably because we can't afford to pay really good money."

"Yeah, that might be a reason."

"My point is, unlike the *Anomalies Report* blog, *The Lost Night Files* conducts serious investigations of cold cases that appear to involve genuine paranormal elements," Talia said. She continued to point the knife at him. "We focus on real psychic phenomena. We don't do ghosts and hauntings. Well, not unless they are somehow related to the case."

"I'll take your word for it."

"Don't you dare pat me on the head."

"I haven't touched you," he said.

"I was speaking metaphorically. I would think a history professor would realize that." Talia lowered the knife. "But I'm going to let this particular incident of head-patting go, because I don't want to waste time arguing."

"Good plan," Luke said.

A fragile truce settled on the booth. He told himself he'd dodged a bullet — or, in this case, a knife. Metaphorically speaking.

He went to work on the two biscuits he had ordered and watched Talia munch hers. The woman ate with appreciation and enthusiasm. He decided to put those attributes into the plus column. He was still working on the pros and cons of Talia March — currently there seemed to be more cons than pros — but it was surprisingly pleasant to share biscuits and coffee with a woman who made no secret of enjoying her food.

He had to admit the biscuits were good. Hot and tender. He buttered the second one and spooned honey over it.

For the past three months he had been eating for fuel, not for pleasure, but here he was, savoring the best biscuits he had ever eaten — in the company of a woman he had no reason to trust. A woman who had set off a thousand alarm bells when she had recognized his talent and proceeded to resist it. That was a first. Obviously he still had a lot to learn about camouflaging his new abilities.

The really disturbing twist was that, in spite of the risks and the unknowns involved, it was a relief to discover that Talia was not only aware of his talent but could resist it, at least at the level he had used on her. She hadn't panicked. She had been annoyed. True, she had not witnessed his Mr. Hyde side, but at least he now knew that he did not have to be careful around her. He could relax. A little.

The fact that she had some ability to ward off his talent might present a problem in the future, but right now he did not have to think about that. He just wanted to study the woman on the other side of the table.

There was something sleek and feline and intriguingly unpredictable about Talia March. Her dark hair was pulled into a tight knot at the back of her head. The severe style emphasized her strong profile and green-gold eyes. She radiated a magnetic energy that made him want to get closer and test the boundaries.

This was not good news.

It was one thing to discover that he was attracted to her physically — something of a shock, given his depressing lack of interest in sex during the past three months — but not a problem. He could deal with physical attraction. What ought to worry him was that she aroused another, far more dangerous reaction — curiosity.

Obviously she had a few control issues. Again, not a problem. He had control issues, too.

She also had a strong measure of a true paranormal talent.

"How did you figure out where Hatch hid the memory card and the necklace?" he asked around a mouthful of biscuit.

Talia dusted crumbs off her fingers and reached for the mug of coffee. "I'm psychic, remember?"

"So am I. But I would not have been able to find those things in the plant pot. Talk to me, Talia. We're on the clock now. If we're right about what happened to Phoebe Hatch, we're dealing with a kidnapping."

She drank some coffee and looked as if she was considering how much to tell him. After a moment she set the mug down.

"I've always been good at finding stuff that has been lost or hidden," she said. "Including information. The ability made me an excellent librarian and researcher. I always considered it a form of intuition."

"Go on."

Talia's eyes became stark and unreadable. "A little over seven months ago something happened. Now I'm very, *very* good at finding stuff. Especially dead bodies."

He watched her for a moment. "You're serious, aren't you?"

"Yes." She exhaled slowly. "On the plus side, my new talent has allowed me to make some money doing crime scene work for a private forensics firm here in Seattle. You'd be surprised how many people are interested in finding bodies."

"No," he said. "I'm not at all surprised. But I get the impression that you don't like the work."

"No, I don't. Among other things, Roger Gossard, the forensics psychologist who hires me to consult, looks at me like I'm Wednesday Addams, or maybe her mother, Morticia. He always makes sure I conveniently disappear before the police show up."

"Annoying."

"Not as annoying as the fact that I don't sleep well for a few days after I find a body."

"Nightmares?"

"And sometimes anxiety attacks." Talia's dark brows rose. "How did you know?"

"Because I've been having a few night-mares myself for the past three months." He drank some coffee, trying to decide how much to tell her. "Something happened to me a while back, too. Three months ago, to be precise."

A great stillness came over Talia. She watched him with unblinking eyes. "By any chance did you suffer a bout of amnesia?"

"I did."

This was dangerous territory, but theirs was a transactional relationship. To get information from her he had to give a little in return.

"How much time did you lose?" she demanded, suddenly very urgent.

"About a day and a half. When I woke up I was hallucinating." He thought about his trek through the blood pool and the gardens of hell. No need to go into details. "I saw things. Impossible things. I don't know how much was real."

"Where were you when your head cleared?"

Time to finesse his story. "On a street in downtown Seattle."

That was reasonably close to the full truth.

She shut her eyes briefly. When she opened

them again there was grim understanding in her gaze. "Join the club. I know four other people, including myself, who went through similar experiences. Amelia and Pallas and I woke up in Lucent Springs, California. Ambrose Drake came to on a beach in San Diego. We've concluded we were all involuntary participants in someone's bizarre experiments."

"Someone who is working off that list we're after."

"Yes."

He stuffed the last of a biscuit into his mouth. "Do the four of you remember where you were just before the blank spots in your memories?"

"Ambrose recalls getting into a car at the airport. It was supposed to take him to a writers' conference. Amelia, Pallas, and I went to an abandoned hotel outside of Lucent Springs. We thought we were being hired to assist in a renovation project. We walked into the lobby, and that's the last thing we remember clearly until early the next morning, when we were awakened by an earthquake and a fire. We barely made it out alive."

"Was there anyone else around?"

"No. We woke up on hospital gurneys in what looked like an old lab. We didn't have time to take notes. We barely escaped the fire."

"That sounds a little too familiar."

Talia frowned. "The earthquake and fire?"

"No, the lab scene." *Enough,* he thought. He had already said too much. "At least I think there was a lab. I told you, I was hallucinating. I don't have any sharp memories until I came fully awake on that street in Seattle."

"What was your last memory before the amnesia hit?"

"I was doing some research for a paper I planned to write for a small history journal. I had an appointment with a source who claimed to have some interesting documents that related to my subject. I knocked on the door of a hotel room in Portland. It opened. And that's the last thing I remember."

"You said you taught history at Adelina Beach College."

"That's right."

Talia held her coffee mug in both hands and studied him over the rim. "I've done some research for a couple of historians. What's your area of expertise?"

"I teach a course titled 'Investigating the Paranormal.' "

"What?" Talia set the coffee mug down hard. Her eyes widened. "You're kidding."

"No. Mostly it's a history of government efforts to create psychic spies, but I cover other areas of paranormal research, too."

"I didn't know there were any serious academic institutions still offering classes in parapsychology."

"Most of the big schools shut down their departments in the latter half of the twentieth century. Adelina Beach College closed its research lab, but by then the library had acquired an extensive collection of literature related to the paranormal. The school has maintained it because it has historical research value. But the only class offered is the one I teach."

"I see." Talia thought about that. "I'll bet it's popular."

He almost smiled. "It is. There's a waiting list every quarter, and not because I'm such a riveting lecturer."

"People are fascinated with the paranormal."

"Yes."

"With a voice like yours I'll bet you are a very good speaker," she said. "So why aren't you in Adelina Beach teaching that class?"

"I took a sabbatical three months ago." The conversation was becoming a little too one-sided again. Time to flip the script.

"How did you discover the existence of the list?"

"My friends and I started wondering why we were chosen as test subjects. We decided we probably hadn't been selected at random. That's when we concluded that whoever was running the experiments had to be using a list."

"What made you so sure that you weren't randomly selected?"

"Because we all had one thing in common," Talia said. "Psychic-level intuition. What about you? Could you do that hypnotic trick before your lost night?"

"It's not a trick," he said. "And it's not hypnosis." He tightened his grip on the mug handle, not sure why he was allowing her to irritate him so easily. He usually had better control. True, he hadn't had a lot of quality sleep lately, but that was not a good excuse. Something about Talia March was getting to him. That had to stop. "For most of my life it was just a knack for reading someone's voice."

Talia watched him with undisguised curiosity. "Define *read.*"

"It was a lot like being able to analyze body language, I think. Once I had a sense of what was going on beneath the surface I could . . . talk to people who were upset.

Get them to calm down." He paused. "Or persuade them to answer questions."

"Did your ability have any practical applications?"

He shrugged. "It got me assigned to an intelligence unit after I joined the Marines. I finished college in the military. That's where I took the psych test, by the way. When I got out I was recruited into one of the government intelligence agencies. Worked as an analyst. Got an advanced degree in history online and started teaching at Adelina Beach."

"How do you use your talent in your work as a history professor?"

"I let the local police know that I was available for hostage and crisis negotiation. I'm pretty good at that kind of work."

"And now?" Talia pressed. "After your lost night?"

"Like you, I can do everything I used to do with my talent, but I'm a little stronger now."

"Uh-huh."

It was clear she was not satisfied with that answer. The glint in her eye warned him that she was going to push harder. Luckily, her phone rang, distracting her.

She glanced at the screen and groaned.

"This day just keeps getting better and better."

She picked up the device and took the call. "Hi, Dad."

Luke breathed a small sigh of relief and drank some more coffee.

CHAPTER TEN

"What's the matter?" Trevor March said. "You sound tense."

"I'm not tense." Frantically she tried to switch gears and get into her cool, confident, and, above all, *stable* adult daughter mode. The daughter who had completely recovered from her hallucinatory experience in the desert and no longer needed a therapist. "You caught me at a busy moment, that's all."

"You're busy? At seven forty-five in the morning? Are you getting ready to go to work?" Parental approval suddenly infused Trevor's voice. "So you finally landed a real job? About time."

Talia drummed her fingers on the table and glared at Luke, who pretended not to notice. "I'm still doing some consulting and developing the podcast brand."

"Those don't qualify as real jobs and you know it. You're still in a downward spiral.

You need to go back into therapy."

Time to try to turn the tables. "Is there a reason you're calling at this hour, Dad?" she asked, projecting concern into her voice. "Is everything okay on your end?"

"We're fine. Did you follow up on any of those leads I sent you?"

So much for the effort to redirect the conversation.

"Not yet." No point mentioning that she had dumped the contact information he had emailed to her straight into the trash folder. Sure, one of Trevor's business pals might be willing to repay a favor or two by finding a mind-numbing job for her, but she had other plans for her life — just as soon as she discovered the truth about her lost night.

"Talia, I've told you before that you're wasting your time trying to start your own consulting business and that podcast thing is a dead end. You've got to get serious about your future."

"Dad, why did you call me so early in the morning?"

"I called to wish you happy birthday, of course."

"Oh, right. Thanks. I forgot."

"I called early because I wanted to touch base with you before the car service arrives."

"You're on your way out of town?"

"The kids are on a school break, so we're off to the Maui house," Trevor said.

"You're not going to Aspen?"

"It's too early for Aspen."

"Of course. I knew that." *Not.* She had never been to Aspen in her life.

"We use Aspen for the winter break," Trevor continued. "Say, why don't you join us for a few days there this year?"

The prospect of spending a few days in the bosom of Trevor's second family did not bear thinking about. Her half-siblings, aged five and seven, were not a problem but they were destined for a very different world than the one in which she lived. They were enrolled in an expensive, exclusive school that was preparing them academically and socially for the rarefied atmosphere of the social circles inhabited by the offspring of wealthy hedge fund managers and successful tech entrepreneurs.

The real issue was Trevor's second wife. Isabel was polished, stylish, and beautiful in a high-maintenance blonde way. She was also a year younger than Talia. On the rare occasions when she was obliged to deal with her husband's daughter from a previous marriage she was always gracious. Talia did her best to respond in kind, but she knew both of them found the family get-togethers uncomfortable.

"Thanks for the invitation, but I never learned to ski," Talia said. *Because you were always too busy making money to take Mom and me on vacations.*

"Forget the skiing." Trevor chuckled. "Aspen is about making connections. And that's reason enough for you to join us this winter. I'll make sure you meet the right people."

"I've got a lot going on at the moment, Dad. Finished a consulting gig yesterday and the podcast is getting some traction."

"I've told you, you're wasting your time with that podcast. No way you're going to generate serious cash with a platform like that. The audience for the woo-woo stuff is too small."

"You've mentioned that."

"Don't expect me to finance it," Trevor warned. "I'm not going to pour any money down that drain."

"I wouldn't dream of asking you to help finance the podcast, Dad. I know how you feel about it."

Trevor grunted. "Working as a freelance assistant doesn't cut it, either. No benefits, no future."

It wasn't Trevor's fault that he was under

a misconception about what, exactly, she did as a consultant these days. She had thought it best not to go into the details. If he found out she was working as a psychic who specialized in locating the dead he would start looking for a way to get her committed to a psychiatric hospital for observation.

"I like to call it consulting work, Dad."

"Call it whatever you want — you're wasting your time. At your age you should be on a clearly defined career path. Your future is slipping away."

"Thanks for reminding me." *I'll get right on that, just as soon as I find out who stole a night of my life and used me in an illegal and dangerous experiment.*

"I'm serious about this, Talia. You've had more than seven months to recover from that incident in Lucent Springs."

"Seven months and twelve days." *Not that I'm counting.*

"Whatever. My point is that you need to get your act together. Look, I've got to go. Isabel says the car is here. Think about what I said."

"I will."

"Happy birthday."

The call ended before she could say thank you. Talia took the phone away from her ear and put it back down on the table.

"Sorry about the interruption," she said. "That was my father."

"It's a little early for a phone call. Everything okay?"

"Oh, yes, fine. Dad and his family are on their way to Hawaii. He wanted to get the happy birthday phone call out of the way before they left for the airport."

"Today is your birthday?"

"Uh-huh. My mom will check in next, but she will probably just send a digital birthday card, because she and Ron are on a world cruise. She says it's a pain trying to figure out the time zone stuff for phone calls and video chats. Just as well. I don't need another lecture on getting my act together."

"Do your parents know about your psychic investigation work?"

"Nope. Trust me, it's better that way. They didn't believe me when I tried to tell them what happened during my lost night. They think I did some drugs with friends and hallucinated the whole thing. If I told them I was convinced that I now have a knack for finding dead bodies they would panic. Again. They mean well, but I don't need the stress."

"I understand," Luke said.

"Families. Can't live with them, can't live

without them."

Luke nodded and drank some coffee.

"Do you get helpful lectures, too?" she asked.

"No."

"Count yourself lucky."

"I'll do that."

She got the ping that told her she had missed something. "I just screwed up, didn't I?"

"No."

"Where is your family?" she asked, deciding to face the situation head-on.

"There are some distant relatives in Oregon, but I've never met them. My parents were killed in a boating accident when I was thirteen. I went into the system." Luke paused. "It would be more accurate to say that I was in and out of the system."

"Foster care?"

"I spent some time on the streets. Managed to get through high school. Joined the Marines the day I graduated."

"Married?" she asked, wondering why she cared.

"Came close a couple of times but it never happened."

"Kids?"

"No."

No family. Foster care. Time spent living

on the streets. And he'd gone through the trauma of a lost night without a support group. She tried to steel herself against the wave of sympathy that was welling up but she could not stop the tears from gathering in her eyes. She blinked hard and then reached for a napkin.

Luke looked at her, alarmed. "Are you okay?"

"Yep." She dabbed at her eyes and crumpled the napkin. "Allergies."

"You are not a good liar."

"I'll work on the problem."

"Not until you tell me what is going on here. Why the tears?"

"Okay, you want to know the truth? I had a sudden urge to give you a hug. Don't worry — I squashed it."

He stared at her, stunned, but he recovered swiftly. "Good. That's good. The last thing I need is your sympathy."

"Right." She straightened and squared her shoulders. "I get the point. You're not a hugger. I don't know what came over me. You're a real loner, aren't you?

Luke's eyes got cold. "I don't need therapy, either."

She fired up her brightest, shiniest go-to-hell smile. "Noted."

Apparently he did not know what to do

with the smile.

"What about you?" he asked.

"I may not have a close-knit family, but I do have one. I'm not a loner. I've got some very good friends."

"The podcast crew?"

"Yes." She narrowed her eyes. "They are the kind of friends who would come looking for me if I up and vanished, especially if I was last seen in the company of a known non-hugger."

"I'll keep the threat in mind," he said, totally serious.

She groaned. "That was sort of a joke."

"I know." His brows rose. "I'm also aware that you were only partially joking. Your friends really would come looking for you if you disappeared."

"Absolutely."

"And you would look for them if they vanished."

"Yep."

"Anyone else in the picture who might feel obligated to search for you?" he asked.

"You're asking if I've got a significant other in my life. The answer is no. I haven't had a serious date in over seven months."

He nodded in an understanding way. "You haven't dated since the amnesia spell."

"Tried it a few times. It didn't go well.

Turns out dates do not want to hear about amnesia or a psychic talent for finding bodies. Real conversation stoppers."

"What about before the amnesia event?"

"I was seeing someone on a casual basis but it ended after my lost night."

There had been nothing casual about the affair with Quinn Elwick, at least not on her side. Her therapist had told her it was time to commit and she had been determined to try. For two months she had gone about the business with a spreadsheet, the guidance of her therapist, and half a dozen well-reviewed relationship advice books. But things had fizzled, just as they always did. She knew she had only herself to blame.

Luke appeared satisfied in a perverse sort of way. "You scared him off."

"Yep. I made the mistake of trying to tell him about my lost night. He concluded I was delusional. I have to admit, sometimes I wondered if he was right."

"Did you consult a doctor?"

"Amelia, Pallas, and I went to an emergency room the morning we escaped the hotel. We got a diagnosis of 'transient global amnesia.' Apparently it's not as uncommon as one might think, and it sounds better than the other option."

"A psychotic break."

"Right," she said. "What about you? Did you consult a doctor when you woke up on the streets and realized you'd lost nearly two days?"

"No."

"Why not? Weren't you worried that you might have had a medical crisis of some kind? A seizure maybe?"

"I did some research online," Luke said. "I decided there wasn't much a doctor could do for me. I didn't think I could even get one to believe me."

Once again, she sensed he was telling her the truth, but not all of it. Maybe he had avoided a medical diagnosis because he was afraid he would wind up going down a long, endless road of useless, expensive tests or be advised to consult a psychiatrist. She didn't blame him, but her intuition told her there was something missing from the tale.

"You were probably right," she said, "but I'm a little surprised you didn't pursue that angle first. Pallas and Amelia and I went to an emergency room immediately. We wanted to make certain we hadn't been assaulted."

"Sounds like a reasonable move."

He did not offer any more information about his own situation.

"Must have been tough waking up alone," she said, trying to probe gently around the edges of his story without alerting him. "At least Amelia, Pallas, and I had each other. Our memories are either missing or fractured, but we've been able to validate each other's experiences. That has been comforting during the last few months."

"I'm sure it has."

"Didn't you question your own memories? Wonder if you had hallucinated the whole thing?"

Amusement sparked briefly in his eyes. "Save your energy. I'm sure you have many skills, Talia March, but faking a trust-me-I'm-your-new-best-friend-you-can-tell-me-anything vibe isn't one of them."

"Right. Something tells me that trying to be friends with you would be a lot of hard work, anyway. I'll get to the point. What aren't you telling me about your lost night experience?"

He watched her in silence for a long time.

"When I came to I discovered I had picked up an object during the missing hours," he said finally. "Something that made me realize I had spent time in a medical setting."

"Really?" Excitement splashed through her. She leaned forward. "That's great. We've been trying to find some hard evidence. What have you got?"

"Nothing you can use on your podcast," he said. "Just one of those little gadgets they use to check a person's oxygen levels. The kind you clip on your finger."

"Oh, right, a fingertip pulse oximeter." She sat back with a small sigh. "Interesting, and as you said, it does help verify that you were in a medical setting, but it's not useful as proof. A lot of people have those gadgets at home."

"I told you, it's nothing you can use on your podcast," he said, his tone hard, flat, and firm.

Maybe a little too hard, flat, and firm. He was shaving the truth again. But she knew a locked and bolted door when she ran head-first into one. Time to back off a little. She could be subtle.

"Your pulse oximeter is a bit like the gurneys at the Lucent Springs Hotel," she said in a warm voice that suggested she had believed every word of his story. "Useful for confirming our memories, but not the kind of proof we could take to the police."

That stopped him for a beat. "You said there was a fire. Did the gurneys survive?"

"They were badly charred and twisted, but they were made of metal, so yes, they did survive."

"Couldn't you use those as evidence to

show to the local police?"

"Turns out the Lucent Springs Hotel once served as a tuberculosis sanatorium, so the authorities wrote them off as vintage relics from the old days."

"I see. I'd like to hear more about your experience."

"We should definitely compare notes," she said, going for an encouraging tone.

"Some other time. Right now we've got priorities. Let's get back to the problem of Phoebe Hatch and the list. You are not going to that island on your own."

She gave him another sparkly smile. "I am aware that you are not about to let me chase the list on my own. You want it as badly as I do."

"You don't know what you're getting into."

"Neither do you."

"But at least I bring some practical skills to the table," he said.

"That annoying little hypnotic thing you do? I'm not sure how useful it will be."

"You'd be surprised. But I was not referring to my annoying little talent." He patted the pack sitting on the bench next to him. "I've also got a gun."

She brightened. "Why didn't you say so? In that case, maybe it's not the worst idea in the world for you to accompany me to Night Island. Go ahead and make a reservation for yourself."

"I'll get right on that," he said, his tone making it clear that he had not been waiting for permission.

"Separate cabins," she added quickly. As soon as the words were out of her mouth she felt the heat rise in her face.

"Separate cabins," he repeated.

His tone was matter-of-fact, as if he had never even considered sharing a cabin. So why had the possibility occurred to her?

He went to work on his phone. She watched him for a moment, opening her senses a little. The power and heat in the atmosphere around him probably should have alarmed her. Instead, it gave her a little zing of awareness. It wasn't like any other zing she had experienced, but after brief consideration she decided it was a good zing. On a zing scale of one to ten, it felt like a solid eleven or twelve. She was suddenly glad that she would not be going to Night Island on her own.

He looked up abruptly. She realized she had been gazing at him much too intently. *I wasn't staring. I was just trying to get a read on him.* But that was not the whole truth. She wanted more than a read, a lot more.

She realized she was intrigued by a man she could not trust, one who was keeping secrets, a man with his own agenda.

"I booked the three-day package," he said. "Starting tomorrow. The site says we will be picked up at ten a.m. by the private ferry service at a dock a few miles north of Seattle."

"What are you going to do until then?"

"Find a hotel, take a shower, drink a lot of coffee, and do some research. I want to know more about that island and Clive Venner, the guy running the Unplugged Experience. And then I need to get some sleep."

"I agree that it would be a good idea to get more information before we head for Night Island." She paused, thinking. "We also need to share the data. Why don't you go ahead and find that hotel room, take your shower, and then come over to my apartment to do your research? We can work together. No sense duplicating our efforts."

He appeared, if not actually amused, at least mildly entertained. "You want to keep an eye on me, don't you? The invitation to work at your place is your not-so-subtle way of making it clear that you don't trust me to share data."

"I was just trying to be practical."

"It's okay, I haven't decided if I can trust you, either, so I agree we should work together on the research. Give me your address. With luck I will be able to find a hotel that will let me check in early. When I'm settled I'll come over to your place."

She sat back, suddenly uncertain. This was what came of acting on impulse — serious buyer's remorse. She had just invited a stranger into her home. What was she thinking?

"Allies, remember?" Luke said, as if he had read her mind.

No, she thought, *he's not a total stranger. He's one of the lost night people. One of us.*

Her apartment building had very good security. The front desk was staffed twenty-four hours a day. Luke would be on camera from the moment he appeared at the entrance. She was taking a risk, but it was a calculated risk.

Her phone pinged, startling her out of her misgivings. New email. She glanced at the screen.

Happy Birthday! Click on the link to read the message.

"That will be my mom's card," she said. She picked up the phone, slipped out of the booth, and grabbed her jacket. "See you later."

"Your address," Luke reminded her. "And phone number."

"Oh. Right."

They went through the process. When they had each other's details safely stored on their phones, she turned to leave. But she paused.

"The front desk staff will give me a call when you arrive and then send you up in the elevator," she said, trying to sound helpful. Gracious.

Once again he looked amused. "In other words, there will be a record of my visit, and camera footage as well."

She raised her chin. "Exactly. And your phone is now on my list of contacts."

"Having second thoughts about spending the rest of the day together?"

"No," she said. She was having second, third, and fourth thoughts, but she knew she was not going to change her mind. "We are working this investigation as a team."

"What about later?"

"Later?"

"Will you be going out with your friends to celebrate your birthday this evening?"

The question threw her off-balance. "No, my circle of friends got very small after my lost night episode. The only people I hang with now are the members of the podcast crew, and they are currently scattered up and down the West Coast. So no, I won't be partying tonight. I'll be packing for the trip to the island and then I'm going to get some sleep. See you in a couple of hours."

"All right."

It wasn't until she was out of the restaurant and in her car driving home to her apartment tower that she realized she had stuck Luke with the breakfast bill. She decided not to worry about it. He could use some of the cash in his pack to pay for the biscuits and coffee.

CHAPTER ELEVEN

An hour and a half later she was waiting at the door for Luke.

She was expecting the knock because the concierge had just phoned to notify her that he was on his way up to her apartment, but for some reason the knowledge that he was standing right outside in the hall sent a splash of edgy energy across Talia's nerves. It was the kind of feeling she got just before a storm rolled in over Seattle — anticipation and a thrilling frisson of excitement, spiked with a hint of danger.

She stood on tiptoe to peek through the peephole. Sure enough, Luke was out there. He was wearing a fresh shirt and trousers, his hair was neatly combed, and he had shaved. He would have looked as if he was arriving for a date — if it wasn't for the pack slung over his shoulder, the duffel bag, and the attractive yellow and white box he was carrying.

If he was planning on spending the night, he could think again, she vowed silently.

She opened the door.

"Hi," she said. Cool, smooth, and businesslike.

"Hi," he said.

He stood there looking at her in a politely expectant way. She went blank, trying to figure out what she was missing. Finally she came to her senses and hastily stepped back.

"Come in," she said.

"Thanks."

He crossed the threshold and stopped. The intimate, sensual zing of awareness that she had experienced earlier in the restaurant was a thousand times more intense here in her territory. Luke was not especially tall, nor was he bulked up with gym-engineered muscle, but he somehow managed to suck up all the oxygen in the space. She was suddenly not sure what to do with him.

So much for cool, smooth, and businesslike.

She had been a serial dater most of her adult life — commitment issues, according to her old therapist. This was not the first time she had invited a man into her apartment, but she had never allowed one to spend the night. It was time to deal with the duffel bag.

"The hotel wouldn't let you check in early?" she asked, trying for subtle.

"What?" He followed her gaze to the duffel. Understanding struck. "Right. The hotel gave me an early check-in, but I didn't want to leave anything behind. I've been living out of this bag and the pack since the amnesia event. Keeping it close at hand has become a habit."

It was her turn to get hit with a jolt of understanding. "They are your go bags, aren't they? You don't know who you can trust and you don't know if the people who ran the experiment on you are searching for you. You're ready to disappear at a moment's notice."

"That pretty much sums up my life for the past three months."

"Believe me, I understand," she said. "You can leave your things on the floor next to the door. I'll take your jacket. Did you park on the street or in a garage?"

"My hotel is only a few blocks away. I decided to walk." He set down the duffel, pack, and the pretty box and handed her his jacket.

"Good idea." She took the jacket. "Parking is hard to find in this neighborhood, and very expensive."

Now she was babbling. *Get a grip, woman.*

His leather jacket was infused with the heat of his body and a faint scent that was all male and all Luke Rand. She realized she was trying to take a surreptitious sniff and gave herself a mental slap. *Don't go there. Don't even think about going there. You do not need the complications.*

She pulled herself together, hung up the jacket, and waved Luke toward the long dining bar that separated the kitchen from the living room. "Why don't you set up there with your phone? The coffee will be ready in a minute."

"Sounds good," he said. He collected the yellow and white box and headed for the dining bar. "Out of curiosity, do you have any idea why Hatch charged you a lot less than she charged me?"

"Probably because she is a true fan of *The Lost Night Files.*" Talia went into the kitchen and took the coffeepot off the burner. "I think she contacted me directly instead of one of the others because she feels a certain kinship with me. Something to do with my talent, maybe."

"Makes sense," Luke said. "The only thing I picked up from her texts was the fact that she was scared."

"Now we know that she had good reason."

"She planned to run but she intended to

105

go off the grid, so she needed cash," Luke said. He angled himself onto one of the barstools and braced a foot on the floor. "She was going to disappear."

"But someone grabbed her before she could execute her plan." Talia poured two coffees and set one mug on the bar in front of Luke. She glanced at the yellow and white box and saw the name of a bakery. "I see you brought a snack for yourself. Good idea. I don't have much in the way of food on hand at the moment. I was planning to do some grocery shopping this afternoon, but I don't need to stock up now, since I'll be gone for a few days. I'll be using up what's left in the refrigerator today."

Luke glanced at the baked goods box as he reached for the mug. "That's for you."

"Me?"

Startled, she stared at the box as if it had just materialized out of thin air. She removed the lid and smiled when she saw the half dozen cupcakes inside. Each was decorated with mounds of yellow frosting and the words *Happy Birthday*. An unfamiliar warmth whispered through her.

"Thank you," she said. "I can't remember the last time anyone brought me a birthday cake."

"It's not a birthday cake," Luke said. "Just

a half dozen cupcakes. No way to know how long they were sitting in the case at the bakery. They're probably from yesterday. I wouldn't be surprised if they're stale."

"Let's find out." She picked up one of the cupcakes and prepared to take a bite.

"You just ate two biscuits a couple of hours ago," Luke said.

"This is just a taste test." She took a bite of the cupcake and grabbed a paper napkin to wipe the frosting off her mouth. "Not stale at all. Try one."

Luke selected a cupcake and took a healthy bite. He chewed, swallowed, and then nodded, evidently satisfied. "Nope, not stale."

She watched him reach for a napkin. He had nice hands. Strong hands. Competent hands. She had never paid much attention to a man's hands before today.

"It was very thoughtful of you to take the time to pick up the cupcakes," she said.

"The bakery was across the street from the hotel. Convenient."

She wrinkled her nose. "Tell me the truth. Did I look pathetic this morning when I got the phone call from my dad and the e-card from my mother and then informed you that I wouldn't be celebrating my birthday tonight because my only close friends are all out of town?"

"No. You looked fierce. You made it clear you could not have cared less that no one was going to show up with a cake and presents."

She sighed. "I knew it. Pathetic."

"Okay, maybe a little. But you hid it well."

"Thanks. That makes me feel better. Let's get to work."

At five o'clock that afternoon, Luke put down his phone, got to his feet, and walked across the living room to stand in front of the glass door that opened onto a small balcony. He contemplated the view of the Space Needle framed by glassy towers.

"Either the Unplugged Experience is an innocent operation run by a high-minded nonprofit whose only goal is to explore the medicinal potential of plants, or . . ."

"Or it's a cleverly disguised cover for an illegal enterprise engaged in kidnapping people and running experiments on them with weird drugs that are designed to enhance an individual's natural psychic talents," Talia concluded.

"Maybe both," Luke said thoughtfully. "Think about it. The Unplugged Experience provides a convenient way for supplies to be brought in and for people to come and go from the island without drawing the attention of the authorities. Routine activity is also a good cover for providing security to ensure curiosity seekers don't sneak in."

Talia glanced at her notes. "We know the island was purchased by a private trust in the nineteen fifties and administered as a botanical research facility for several years. The research was halted in the nineteen seventies. The trust maintained control of the island until about eight months ago, when it was purchased by the Wynford Institute for the Study of Medicinal Botany, a private corporation."

"It was the Institute that invited Clive Venner to establish the Unplugged Experience on the island," Luke continued. "Until that point Venner had been a low-level player in the meditation-and-mantras business. Why did the Institute select him?"

"I sense suspicion."

Luke turned away from the city lights. "Yes. You do." He checked the time. "I should head back to the hotel. We both need sleep."

"We both need dinner, too," she said on impulse. "You're welcome to stay. Nothing special. I've got a lovely head of cauliflower in the refrigerator and some sourdough bread that won't last until we get back. We didn't finish off the cupcakes at lunch, so we've got dessert."

Luke looked at her for a beat, evidently flummoxed. She knew she had caught him by surprise.

"Sounds good," he said. He stopped, apparently searching for something more to say. "Thanks."

"No problem." She got up and went around the end of the dining bar and into the kitchen. "Wine?"

"That sounds good, too." He watched her take a bottle out of the small wine cabinet. "About our trip to Night Island."

She went to work with the opener. "What about it?"

"It will be obvious that we know each other. We need a cover story."

"That occurred to me." She got the cork out of the bottle. "I've got a plan."

He groaned. "Of course you do. Let's hear it."

She poured two glasses of wine, set one in front of him, and gave him a triumphant smile. "Couples therapy."

There was a short beat of silence. Luke did not take his eyes off her.

"Okay," he said, "I did not see that coming. How does couples therapy work as a cover?"

"Simple." She sipped some wine, pleased with her own cleverness. "We're a couple. We've been having problems, so we went to a therapist who suggested the Unplugged Experience on Night Island. We need to get away from the tech and learn to focus on our relationship."

Luke watched her, not blinking for a long moment. Then he swallowed some wine and lowered the glass. "We booked separate cabins. How does couples therapy explain that?"

"Easily." She set her glass down and opened the refrigerator. "Our therapist does not want us to be distracted by sex. We are supposed to remain celibate during our stay on the island so that we can concentrate on the deeper aspects of our relationship. Obviously, separate cabins are the best way to make sure we don't, you know —"

"Get distracted."

"Right." She took the cauliflower out of the vegetable drawer. "I think my couples therapy excuse solves all of our problems when it comes to explaining why we know each other and why we are not sleeping in the same cabin."

"Has anyone ever told you that you have an interesting imagination?"

"Occasionally." She set the head of cauliflower on a cutting board, opened a drawer, and selected the large vegetable cleaver. "But mostly people tell me that I have a tendency to be too controlling. It's probably true. I'm not the spontaneous type."

Luke watched her whack the cauliflower into bite-sized pieces.

"Ever tried spontaneity?" he asked.

She thought about her long history of failed romances and brought the knife down on the helpless vegetable with a good deal more force than was necessary. A large chunk of cauliflower flew off the board and landed on the floor.

"Once in a while," she said, bending down to retrieve the fallen veggie. "It doesn't go well for me."

When she straightened she saw that Luke was watching her with very close attention, a mix of wariness and amusement glinting in his eyes.

"What?" she said.

"Would you mind aiming that very large knife in a different direction?"

She realized she was gripping the handle of the cleaver much too tightly. She winced. "Sorry. It's been a long day. I get a little tense when the subject of spontaneity comes up."

"I noticed."

"I've been under a lot of stress lately."

"You aren't the only one."

She glanced at him, once again registering the grim line of his jaw and the preternatural aura of awareness that charged the atmosphere around him. The phrase *battle-ready tension* came to mind.

She opened a cupboard and selected some spices — cumin, paprika, coriander, and turmeric.

She poured some olive oil into a bowl, added the spices and some salt, and whisked the ingredients together.

"How does spontaneity work for you?" she asked.

"Results vary between your average doomsday scenario and the apocalypse," he said.

"Same with me," she said.

Luke drank some wine and looked thoughtful. "Seems to me booking a stay on Night Island to look for a kidnap victim qualifies as a spontaneous decision."

"Nope. That was based on reason and logic and a lack of options. It's the only move we can make, given the information available."

"True."

"My regrettable spontaneous decisions usually involve my personal life," she said.

"Relationships."

"Same." He watched her toss the cauli-flower chunks in the olive oil and spice mixture. "What are you making?"

"Roasted cauliflower. I'll serve it with some tahini dipping sauce."

"I don't think I've ever had that."

"Vegetarian comfort food."

CHAPTER TWELVE

He could get into the concept of vegetarian comfort food for dinner, Luke decided, especially if there was someone to share it with. Someone interesting. Someone like Talia March. *Forget it. There isn't anyone else like Talia March out there in the known universe. She's one of a kind.*

He stopped on the sidewalk across the street from Talia's apartment tower and looked up, mentally counting floors until he reached the twentieth. The lights glowed in the windows of her apartment. When she had ushered him out the door a few minutes ago she had mentioned that she planned to pack. That was probably what she was doing at that very moment. Packing for Night Island wasn't going to be a problem for him. Everything he needed was on his phone or in the duffel and the pack he was carrying.

That, he decided, did not say much that was positive about his current lifestyle.

He had a brief fantasy of calling Talia to see if she would come out onto the balcony to wave goodbye. A dumbass fantasy.

He turned away from the warmly lit windows of the apartment on the twentieth floor and kicked up his senses a little, a technique that, during the last three months, had become automatic whenever he found himself in an unfamiliar environment.

He started walking the five blocks to the hotel. The rain had stopped, leaving a sharp chill in the air. The still-damp streets reflected the lights of the shop fronts and passing cars. There were other people on the sidewalk, coming and going from the neighborhood bars and restaurants. He wondered which of the local eateries and watering holes were Talia's favorites.

Focus, Rand.

He summoned up some willpower and concentrated on the mission to Night Island. He and Talia were in agreement on that course of action. It was not just their only solid lead, it felt like a damned good lead. If the situation looked different when they were on the ground tomorrow they could take the ferry back to the mainland and try to find another angle to pursue.

There was no question but that the new owner of Night Island, the Wynford Institute for the Study of Medicinal Botany, raised a lot of red flags. On the surface it seemed to be a legitimate nonprofit, but if there was one thing he had learned during his time in the intelligence sphere, it was that when it came to entities like privately controlled research operations, appearances were frequently deceiving.

The first shock of the ice knife struck just as he stopped at an intersection to wait for a light. It felt as if a blade had been driven into his chest. The force of the blow did not take him down, but he staggered back a couple of steps and dropped the duffel. Automatically he glanced down, expecting to see the hilt of a knife sticking out of his chest.

There was no blade, but the pain began to spread. He was growing colder.

Heart attack.

No. Someone is trying to kill you. Better do something about it.

Instinct and intuition took over. He pulled hard on his new talent, trying to push back on the icy sensation in his chest. The cold immediately retreated. That settled it. He was dealing with psychic energy.

The invisible knife of glacial ice struck again. This time the cold expanded rapidly inside him, chilling his lungs, making it hard to breathe.

He channeled the adrenaline washing through his bloodstream, concentrated, and got a fix on the frequency of the powerful wave-lengths of ice coming at him. He focused, sending out subtle destabilizing currents in carefully calibrated pulses. He had never tried to flatline such energy before, but the technique turned out to be no different from the one he used to manipulate an agitated aura.

The ice knife in his chest vanished as suddenly as it had struck. He could breathe freely again. The driver of one of the stopped vehicles gunned the engine and roared through the intersection, defying the red light. Horns blared. Brakes screeched.

Luke turned quickly but the car carrying the assailant disappeared around a corner and was gone.

He waited a moment, running through scenarios and possibilities. They all ended with the same conclusion, which, in turn, left him with only one logical option.

He took out his phone and made the call. Talia answered on the first ring.

"What is it?" she asked, her voice laced with tension. "What's wrong? Are you okay?"

"How did you know that something was

wrong?" he asked, distracted. He could not remember the last time someone had displayed so much anxiety about his well-being.

"Answer my question," she snapped. "Are you all right?"

"Yes. I'm fine. Calm down."

"Don't tell me to calm down, damn it. Tell me what happened."

He tried to come up with a subtle way of describing the situation. And failed.

"Someone just tried to kill me," he said.

"Oh, my God. But you're okay?"

"Yes. Listen, Talia, this puts a twist on things."

"This is where you tell me it wasn't some random act of street violence, isn't it?"

"There was nothing random about it. We have to assume that whoever just tried to murder me is connected to the kidnapping of Phoebe Hatch."

"Oh, shit."

"That's my take on things, too."

"You did say that someone might have been watching her house today to see who else showed up to buy the list. Looks like you were right. Did the attacker use a knife or a gun?"

"There's another angle to this thing. Whoever tried to kill me used energy to try to take me down."

There was a short silence from Talia's end.

"I don't understand," she said after the pause. "Some sort of weapon? Like a Taser?"

"No. Psychic energy."

Another short pause.

"Is that even possible?" she asked.

It wasn't disbelief he heard in her voice, he decided. He was picking up curiosity tinged with skepticism. At least she didn't think he had imagined the attack. She was just trying to find a rational explanation for how it had gone down.

He thought briefly about explaining to her why he was so sure that the would-be killer had been able to focus paranormal energy and use it as a lethal weapon but decided that would be a really dumb idea. This was not a good time to tell her about his Mr. Hyde problem. It was unlikely that there would ever be an opportune time. *Well, see, they were trying to create psychic assassins in this secret lab and evidently I was a failure. Went rogue and murdered a couple of people. Or something.*

"Trust me, it's possible," he said. "It felt as if someone plunged a knife made of ice into my chest."

"That's . . . horrifying." Talia paused again before continuing in a gentle, soothing tone.

"Do you think you might have had an anxiety attack? Difficulty breathing and tightness in the chest are common symptoms. I've had a few myself."

"Talia, listen to me. It was not an anxiety attack. It was a psychic drive-by."

"Okay, calm down."

That was more than a little irritating.

"Excuse me?" he said. "You're telling me to calm down? I seem to recall recently getting a lecture from someone informing me that it was a bad idea to tell a person to calm down."

"You're right. I apologize. Did you see the person who attacked you?"

"No." He summoned up his memories. "I think the attacker was in a car at the intersection. The passenger side door was facing me. I couldn't see the person behind the wheel. By the time I realized where the wavelengths were coming from the vehicle was gunning it down the street. Nearly hit a couple of other cars."

"You know, viewed from a certain perspective, this can be seen as good news."

"The fact that I survived? Yes, that does strike me as good news. Listen, Talia —"

"Well, that, too. What I meant was, an attack on you means we are on the right track."

He tightened his grip on the phone. "It also means I will not be spending the night at my hotel."

"You're going into hiding?"

"No, I am not going into hiding. Someone found me tonight. It follows that they are aware of you. I will be spending the night at your place."

She took a moment to process that. "All night?"

"No, only until midnight when I turn into a pumpkin. Yes, Talia, all night. From now on, we stick together."

"Okay, okay, there's no need to get sarcastic. Uh, what about on Night Island?"

"Let me put it this way: your cover story about our couples therapist recommending separate cabins is out. See you in ten minutes. Do not open the door to anyone else."

He ended the call before she could respond and headed back toward Talia's apartment tower. One thing was clear: he was not the only psychic assassin on the planet.

That begged the real question. *Did someone send you to terminate me? If so, why?*

The answer was obvious. *Because I'm a failed experiment. I went rogue.*

And now he had dragged Talia into the line of fire.

CHAPTER THIRTEEN

Shivering from the toxic cocktail of bio-chemicals unleashed by the combination of focusing at full power followed by a failed kill, the assassin dumped the rental car in a parking garage and hurried toward the safety of an anonymous hotel room.

It was difficult to believe that the target had been able to repel the strike. Rand was a lab mistake. A fucking failure. The fact that he had not gone down tonight was disturbing.

Taking Rand out should have been a simple, straightforward job — maybe not quite as easy as terminating the homeless men who had served as target practice, but still, a routine hit.

Using the homeless men as targets had allowed the assassin to calibrate the new paranormal power and run some basic experiments. Psychic talent, it turned out, had to be fine-tuned. When used as a weapon it required practice to work out range and limitations. There was a learning curve.

Upon reflection it was obvious that Rand had been too far away tonight. But distance was not the only problem. There had not been sufficient time to acquire a solid fix on the right wavelengths. Next time would be different.

CHAPTER FOURTEEN

Energy stirred Luke's senses. It wasn't the ice-cold sensation he had experienced last night when he was attacked in Seattle. This was different. Primal. Vital. For a nanosecond it raised the ghost of a dream. In the next instant the memory vaporized into nothingness.

He leaned against the railing of the small chartered ferry and watched Night Island, a natural fortress of forbidding rock crowned by a dark, seemingly impenetrable forest, draw closer. Another frisson of awareness flashed through his senses. It was gone in an instant, but it was accompanied by an adrenaline spike. There was something important about Night Island. He and Talia were not wasting their time.

"Where is the lodge?" Talia said. "I don't see any buildings — just a dock."

She was right. There was a cabin cruiser tied up at the dock and a van parked nearby, but there were no other indications that the island was inhabited.

"The lodge and cabins are probably up there at the top of the cliffs," Luke said. "We can't see them because of the greenery."

"The island looks very rugged, doesn't it?" she said.

The uncertainty in her voice made him glance at her. She was standing next to him, bundled up against the damp November chill in a down jacket, scarf, and wool cap.

He thought about the night he had spent in her spare bedroom surrounded by the trappings of her podcast studio — a high-quality microphone and a stand, a computer, headphones, a desk, and a chair. The walls were covered with enlarged photographs of the ruins of the Lucent Springs Hotel. Arrows and labels were neatly arranged to indicate the various spaces and rooms — lobby, ballroom, old sanatorium lab. It looked like a crime scene storyboard, which, he reflected, was exactly what it was.

There was a notebook on the desk filled with details about a recent series of episodes involving a murder at a sleep clinic. He had paged through it before climbing into bed. It was clear he was not the only one obsessing over a lost night. The realization that he was not alone in his quest had finally hit home.

He had slept surprisingly well, right up until the dream struck.

He had slammed awake, pulling himself out of a dreamscape in which he gripped a scalpel and walked through the blood of the two dead men on the floor. He sat on the edge of the bed for a long time, wondering if he had called out or made some noise that might have awakened Talia. He relaxed a little when he heard no sound from her bedroom. No footsteps in the hall.

He had eventually gone back to sleep. The next time he had awakened it was to the aroma of freshly brewed coffee. After showering, shaving, and dressing he had walked cautiously into the main room and sat down at the dining counter. He hadn't been sure of what to expect by way of a morning greeting.

Talia had seemed — not exactly anxious — but uncharacteristically unsure of herself as she poured coffee and placed the mug in front of him. When he met her eyes he knew she had heard him during the night.

"Sorry," he said. "Bad dream."

"I understand. I've had a few myself."

"Did I scare you?"

"No."

"I scared you." He grimaced. "I can tell."

"No, damn it. You did not scare me."

"Then why are you watching me as if I might leap over the counter and attack you?"

She planted both palms on the counter. "I'm not afraid of you. I'm just not sure what to do with you. I'm not accustomed to having a man sitting here in my kitchen at breakfast."

He stared at her, trying to analyze the new data. "Huh."

"Exactly. Huh." She took her hands off the counter and turned to yank open the door of the refrigerator.

"Why not?" he asked before he could stop himself.

She swung around. "For the same reason that I never spend the night at a date's apartment. It's a bridge too far. I know it's ridiculous, but that's just how it is. I've got issues when it comes to relationships, okay?"

"What kind of issues?"

"Commitment issues."

"No problem." He relaxed. "I've got commitment issues, too. Now that's settled, let's move on to more important stuff. What's for breakfast?"

"You're very good at compartmentalizing, aren't you?"

"Just trying to lighten the atmosphere."

She gave him a steely smile. "It's not working."

"All right, let's deal with the elephant in the room. Do you think you'll be okay sharing a cabin with me on Night Island? Because if there's going to be a problem, we need to discuss it now."

"Don't worry, I won't have a panic attack. I only get those when I find dead bodies."

He watched Talia's profile now as the ferry drew closer to the island. He was not sure what to make of the troubled look in her eyes.

"Having second thoughts?" he asked. "You can stay on board and go back to the mainland."

She shot him a glare that would have done credit to a basilisk.

"Right," he said. "We're both getting off the ferry."

"It's not as if we've got a better lead, is it?"

"No," he said. He had a sudden urge to put his arm around her shoulders, draw her close, and reassure her. He reminded himself he had known her for a little more than twenty-four hours and that they were working an investigation. It wasn't as if they were lovers, or even good friends, for that matter. They were allies. Besides, she had been right

— he was not the hugging type. "If it makes you feel any better, my intuition tells me that this is where we need to be."

She reached inside her coat. He knew she was touching the crystal in Hatch's necklace. "Mine does, too."

"Are you getting anything off the crystal?"

"The vibe is stronger than it was on the mainland, but it's distorted." Talia frowned, concentrating. "It's as if there's some other energy in the atmosphere around here that's interfering with the currents."

"Any idea what that indicates?"

"Nope. This is the first time I've experienced this kind of static."

He and Talia were not the only people on the ferry who were bound for the Unplugged Experience. An hour and a half ago when they had arrived at the pickup location on the mainland they had found three others waiting. None of them had appeared enthusiastic about spending a few days living the tech-free life. All three had been on their phones, determined to make one last connection with the plugged-in world before going into unplugged exile.

Oliver Skinner had the edgy, can't-stay-off-his-phone vibe of a tech worker who had grown up on a diet of high-octane video games and energy drinks. Marcella Earle, aggressively friendly, might as well have had BORN FOR SALES tattooed on her forehead. It had come as no surprise when she had introduced herself by handing out business cards indicating she specialized in Seattle real estate.

The third individual, Jasper Draper, got Luke's vote for the guest who most regretted signing up for the Unplugged Experience. He explained that he had a travel blog and that he had decided to do a feature on the fad for tech-free getaways.

"None of us actually left our phones at home," Talia said. "Do you think the staff will try to confiscate them?"

Oliver Skinner, standing nearby, looked at her. "From my cold, dead fingers."

"My sentiments exactly," Jasper Draper said. "I'm a journalist. I need my phone."

Marcella Earle looked at her phone and groaned. "Don't worry, they won't bother to grab our tech. No service."

Talia took her phone out of the pocket of her coat and checked the screen. "You're right. Well, I suppose that's not a surprise."

"Fuck," Oliver said.

"Shit," Jasper muttered.

The ferry bumped gently against the wooden dock. Luke watched a man dressed in jeans and a flannel shirt climb out of the van and come forward to handle the lines. He waved at the ferry pilot and then greeted the passengers as they trooped off the vessel.

"Welcome to Night Island," he said. "My name is Nathan Gill. I'm a guide for the Unplugged Experience. Prepare for three days that will refresh, renew, and restore your inner balance."

"Translated," Oliver Skinner said, "that means prepare for the most boring three days of our lives."

"And probably a lot of kale," Jasper Draper grumbled. "But at least there will be booze, according to the brochure."

"An excellent collection of wines and top-shelf liquors," Nathan assured him cheerfully. "Don't worry about a diet of kale. Octavia Venner is a magician in the kitchen. You'll be eating vegetarian, but I think you'll enjoy it."

Talia brightened. "I'm really looking forward to the cuisine. The online reviews were very enthusiastic about the chef. I'm excited to try the mushroom pâté and the risotto."

Luke managed, barely, to hide a smile. The other guests stared at Talia as if she was from another planet.

"Got a feeling it's going to be a very long three days," Marcella Earle said.

CHAPTER FIFTEEN

The energy in the atmosphere was getting stronger. Maybe it varied depending on where you happened to be on the island, Talia thought. Or maybe the currents got more powerful after dark.

She opened the door of the small, rustic cabin and paused on the threshold, taking in the night. The evening was surprisingly warm, considering that it was the end of November — not tropical island warm by any means, but the temperature was higher than normal in the Pacific Northwest at this time of year. She would not need her down coat or knit cap for the walk through the gardens to the lodge. The lightweight parka she had tossed into her bag at the last minute would do.

Here and there the lights of the guest cabins could be glimpsed through the maze of heavily overgrown plants that surrounded the lodge. The nearby forest was a looming darkness that blended seamlessly into the deep black of a night rendered starless by a thick cloud cover. Luckily the path to the lodge and dinner was illuminated. The stepping stones emitted a subtle blue light.

She slipped into the parka and stepped outside the cabin. A little shock of awareness arced across the back of her neck when she turned to lock the door. The sensation was different from the one she had felt a moment ago. This vibe stirred her senses in another way. There was a disconcertingly intimate quality to it. It was not the first time she had experienced it. Earlier that morning while preparing breakfast she had identified the cause. Her intuition was telling her that Luke was nearby.

She had never reacted to the presence of any other man in this way, and that was more than enough to make her turn to the universe for an answer to the question that leaped to mind: *Why this one, universe?*

The universe responded with a dose of common sense. *One night in your spare bedroom does not a relationship make.*

She turned on the step and watched Luke make his way toward her, his duffel bag in one hand, the pack slung over his shoulder. He was following one of the stone paths that wound through the lush foliage.

"I'm not an expert when it comes to gardening," he said, shoving a broad leaf out of the way, "but these plants look like they haven't been trimmed, pruned, or cut back in a long time. It's amazing that you can still see the stepping stones."

He wore the battered leather jacket, trousers, and black pullover that he'd worn on the ferry. Outwardly he appeared relaxed, but she was getting to know him, and something about the way he moved told her that he was on high alert.

"The plants do seem to be flourishing, don't they?" Talia said. "And it's so warm here compared to Seattle. What's up with all the energy in the atmosphere?"

"Probably a storm on the way," Luke said.

Talia reached out to touch a long, sword-shaped leaf. "I don't recognize any of these plants. Some of them, like the ferns, look familiar but . . . different."

"Don't forget this whole island was a botanical research laboratory in the twenti-eth century and now it's under the control of the Wynford Institute for the Study of Medicinal Botany," Luke said. "There must have been a lot of experiments over the years. These plants are the result."

Talia shivered. "Don't know about you, but the word *experiment* makes me nervous these days."

"That makes two of us. The others didn't seem to notice the energy — at least, they didn't comment on it."

"We didn't say anything, either, except to each other."

"True," Luke said. "But I'm wondering if the sensation is more intense for us because of our enhanced senses."

"Sounds logical."

Luke held out his hand. "If you'll give me your key I'll put my things in your cabin."

So we're really doing this, Talia thought. Last night she had told herself to think of him as a houseguest. Separate bedrooms. But tonight they would be sleeping in the same room. Yes, there was a cot in the cozy cabin in addition to the bed, but still — the same room.

She gave him the key and watched him open the door and drop the duffel inside. He kept the pack slung over one shoulder. When he relocked the door and turned around, the cool, withdrawn look was back in his eyes.

"I know this isn't ideal," he said. "But we don't have much choice."

"I agree. We need to be adults about this. Allies, remember?"

He drew a deep breath and exhaled slowly.

"Right. Allies. With luck, I won't have any dramatic dreams, but if I do, wake me, okay?"

"Okay." She paused. "Same goes for me. If I seem to be having a bad dream, just give me a little shake."

"Deal."

They started along the path through the gardens, heading for the lodge.

"Did you notify the Venners that you won't be using your cabin?" she asked, trying to find a neutral topic.

"No. I'll do that in the morning."

She slanted him a quick, searching look. "You're afraid I might kick you out of my cabin, aren't you? In which case you would need a place to sleep."

"If you kick me out I'll sleep on your doorstep," Luke said. "I don't want you to be on your own, especially at night."

"Got it. Don't worry, I won't make you sleep on the doorstep. I assume we have a plan for pursuing our search for Phoebe Hatch?"

"I'm working on one," Luke said. "Later tonight I'm going to take a look around the Unplugged Experience office. I noticed it at the main lodge today when we checked in."

"I'll come with you."

"Not a good idea."

"It's our only available idea. You don't want me to be alone at night, remember?"

Luke's jaw tightened but he did not argue.

"Besides, you need me," she added. "I'm the one who can find things."

There was a short silence.

"You're right," Luke said after a moment. "Like I said, I'm used to working alone."

"That does not come as a dazzling revelation. But you had better get accustomed to having a partner, because we're in this together until we get answers. Consider yourself a temporary member of the *Lost Night Files* team."

"My dreams of fame and glory are coming true at last."

"Stick with us, pal, and we'll make you a star."

Chapter Sixteen

"Remember that all things are connected. The Venner System is designed to teach you how to open yourself to the reality of this truth. As you move through the Unplugged Experience you will discover your personal link to the universe. The secrets of establishing your inner peace will be revealed."

Clive Venner listened to the sound of his own voice and wondered if the audience was as bored by it as he was. The small crowd gathered in front of the fire for the after-dinner drinks was starting to get restless. Probably wishing they could get on their phones. He didn't blame them. It wasn't like there was anything else to do on the fucking island.

He wondered which guests would be leaving on the noon ferry tomorrow. He was tempted to board it himself. But the terms of the agreement he and Octavia had signed were strict. They had committed to not leaving the island for the duration of the contract. If they bailed before the end they would forfeit the money the Institute was depositing in their bank accounts every month, and it was a *lot* of money.

Oliver Skinner was the first to get up. He went to the table where a variety of after-dinner liqueurs and small pastries had been set out. Marcella Earle followed him.

This was not good. Clive reminded himself that he had a job to do. The guests were supposed to be paying attention to his spiel. He needed to inject some energy into the welcome pitch. The problem was that he had been using the same script since the start of the gig, six months ago. It was similar to the one he had worked with for nearly four years in various locations. He needed new material.

Just one more month until the contract was completed. One more month. There was so much money waiting. He would never have to run another con. He could retire to a real island, the kind that had palm trees, beaches, and warm seas. Just one more month.

". . . You will discover the secrets of true mindfulness — not the weak versions that have been made popular by apps and podcasts," he continued. "The Venner System is a very different method of centering yourself. You will train your mind to be in the moment — not just for a short break, but all the time. You will discover that this practice will provide you with deep, restful sleep and the ability to concentrate. But most of all it will give you a deep, abiding sense of inner balance . . ."

Three of the guests who had arrived that day fit the standard retreat profile, Clive thought. In addition to Skinner, the tightly wound tech worker, and Earle, the intense real estate agent, there was Draper, the jaded travel blogger. It was the couple that had booked separate cabins who raised a red flag. There was something off about them. The claim that their couples therapist had recommended two cabins didn't ring true. He had been running cons and scams his whole life. His survival instincts were well honed.

He reminded himself that Rand and March were not his problem. He was in charge of maintaining the aboveground illusion. As far as the outside world was concerned, he was just another smooth-talking meditation and mindfulness instructor running a retreat for the overstressed, the overanxious, and the overworked. What happened underground, stayed underground.

All he had to do was keep his mouth shut, enjoy a few short-term liaisons with some of the more attractive female guests when the opportunity arose, and take the money when the gig was completed.

One more month.

". . .You will begin your quest to find your best self tomorrow morning," he continued. "I will awaken you with the gong. Together we will walk the labyrinth path in the gardens before breakfast. And now I bid you all a night of dreams that enlighten and expand your inner universe."

He rose from the meditation cushion, trying not to let the stiffness in his knees and hips show. The loose-fitting, pajama-like trousers and long-sleeved shirt provided good camouflage, but he had to face the facts — there was no graceful way for a man his age to get to his feet after sitting cross-legged on the floor for extended periods of time, cushion or no cushion. Tomorrow he would start using a chair.

A movement in the arched opening between the lobby and the small dining room made him glance across the rustic space. He saw Octavia. She was drying her hands on a kitchen towel. He knew she had been observing his lackluster performance. It was her fault the script had gotten old. She was the one who had written it.

The script wasn't the only thing that was showing its age, he thought. Octavia was in her midthirties now, no longer the ethereal young beauty who had started out as an adoring acolyte and lover and had eventually become his business partner.

She had ceased believing he was a serious meditation and lifestyle guide a long time ago and demanded a cut of the profits. There was no getting around the fact that she was a damned good cook. As one of the online reviews said, "Go for the tech-free experience, stay for baked polenta with cheese and the salted chocolate caramel tart." Food, it turned out, was a bigger draw than the prospect of living without a phone for a few days. Who knew?

So, yes, Octavia had brought in the business, but at the end of this gig he would no longer need her.

He put his palms together, bowed to the small group, and left the firelit lobby, heading for the cabin he and Octavia shared. He would pour a large glass or two of whiskey. The free booze and the money were the only reasons he was still on the island.

The trek through the gardens to the cabin gave him chills, as usual. The damned plants gave off an eerie glow after dark. The technical word for it was *bioluminescence,* according to Keever, the assistant gardener, but it was creepy. The weird light had gotten stronger during the past two months. The atmosphere was gradually warming and the storms were more frequent.

Octavia was convinced the changes were caused by whatever was happening underground. He had dismissed her theories at first, but now he was sure she was right. He reminded himself that whatever the Institute was up to down below was not his business and not his problem.

One more month.

CHAPTER SEVENTEEN

The plants were getting scarier. Unpredictable. Dangerous. But it was the fungi that worried him the most.

Eddy Keever clutched the vintage flashlight-shaped device and hurried through the radiant underworld jungle. He took great care not to step off the glowing stones of the path. He had a healthy respect for the plants down here in the old lab.

Forget healthy respect. He was terrified of the specimens.

When he had accepted the offer of employment as an assistant gardener he had been told that the plants and fungi were the same species as those in the conservatory but had been genetically modified by decades of exposure to the violet and green radiation that emanated from the walls and ceiling of the underground tunnels.

The plants, especially the fungi, had fascinated him at first. The position as assistant to the Night Gardener had offered him the opportunity to continue his work with mushrooms. After the string of disasters that had ruined his life, the job with the Institute had seemed too good to be true. And, of course, it was.

But he knew too much now. He had to get off the island and disappear. He could no longer pretend that his boss's undeniable brilliance excused the fits of rage, the strange experiments, and the insistence on secrecy. He was pretty sure now that the Night Gardener was certifiably insane.

Back in the twentieth century the underground gardens had been cultivated as a clandestine botanical experiment run by the government. But at some point the project had been abandoned. The lab had been shut down. The specimens had been left untended. They should have died. Instead, they had flourished.

Nature had found a new niche, and, as nature always did, it had taken over, establishing a self-sustaining ecosystem. Now, years later, the bizarre mushrooms, snakelike vines, creepers, leaves, and fronds choked the main tunnel and some of the side corridors. The path through the greenery was still clear, thanks to the energy in the stones, but he wasn't sure how much longer that would be true. In the end, nature was always stronger than any human-made barrier that was intended to control it.

The Night Gardener had laughed at him when he had asked if any of the plants were carnivorous. He had been assured that, while the soil had the same natural composting properties as the surface gardens and could absorb the nutrients of dead insects or the occasional rat, the plants were not meat eaters.

But he no longer believed that. Two weeks ago he had seen the remains of the dead test subject in one of the mushroom forests. Forty-eight hours later there had been nothing left except bones. Ultimately, they would disappear, too.

Now there was another test subject in the lab. The woman had been drugged into a state of semiconsciousness. The Night Gardener claimed the subject was suffering from a rare disease and had volunteered for the experimental treatment. It was her only hope, the Night Gardener said. Maybe. But Keever was pretty sure that if things went wrong the underground gardens would once again devour the evidence.

How long before the specimens made the leap from composting the dead to capturing and devouring live human prey?

Forget the fucking contract. He had to get off the island. When the noon ferry left tomorrow, he was going to be on board.

Relief slammed through him when he emerged from the underworld gardens and stepped into the conservatory. This would be the last time he had to make the trek.

He closed the vault door, locked it, and gave himself a moment to overcome the disorientation that always hit him when he returned to the surface. When he felt steady he made his way through the glass-walled jungle, following the glowing stone path. He entered the air lock. The door hissed shut behind him. The key device pinged. Black crystals illuminated. There was a muffled thunk as the large bolts of the outer door slid aside.

He went outside into the labyrinth gardens, pausing to lock the door. Night had fallen hours ago. The grounds were illuminated thanks to bioluminescent greenery and the glowing stones of the path, but the lodge was dark and there were no lights in the windows of the cabins. He remembered that the guests for the new session of the Experience had been expected on the noon ferry. He wondered how they would react if they learned about the dangerous world down below. Some would no doubt be curious or even thrilled, just as he had been at first. They would probably view the old lab as a twisted version of Alice's Wonderland. The smart ones would pack and escape on the next ferry. That was exactly what he intended to do.

He shoved the key into the leather tool belt draped around his waist. Tonight was the last time he would need it to access the conservatory and the underground lab. The realization brought another rush of relief. He would miss his mushrooms, though. If he could have published the results of his studies he would have become a legend in botanical circles. But his work with the fungi wasn't worth his life.

He hurried along one of the dimly lit footpaths that wound through the labyrinth gardens. The guest cabins scattered about the grounds were marked by porch lights, but for the most part they were obscured because of the tall, thickly packed plants. The specimens up here were not dangerous, but he suspected it was only a matter of time before the forces at work down below reached the surface.

He was taking a shortcut behind cabin number seven when he saw the figure dressed in dark clothes prying open a rear window. He came to an abrupt halt, more bewildered than alarmed. It took him a few seconds to realize that he was watching a burglary in progress.

This was not his problem. His only goal was to get off the island and as far away as possible.

He started to move on down the path, but it was too late. The figure turned and saw him.

The invisible, ice-cold knife struck with stunning force. He could not move. He could not breathe. He had never been so cold. He would not have believed such cold existed. His blood was freezing in his veins.

He was vaguely aware that there was something wrong with his heart. He sank to his knees and tried to call for help, but it was too late. He fell into the depths of the frozen sea.

For a heady moment the assassin savored the intoxication of the kill. There was nothing like the thrill that came with having the power of life or death.

But in the next beat reality descended. Decisions had to be made. Move the body or leave it there in the bushes? On the plus side, there would be no indications of violence. Cause of death would look like a heart attack or a stroke. Reasons not to move the body included the possibility of accidentally depositing some trace evidence. Best to leave the dead man where he was and let him be found by chance when someone happened to pass by the rear of cabin number seven.

The assassin turned back to the window with a sense of regret. It would not be a good idea to carry out the plan now. It would take time to recharge. Every kill was exhilarating, but they were also exhausting. It would not be smart to confront the target at less than full power.

The assassin took a moment to close the window with gloved fingers and then faded into the shadows. There would be other opportunities. Besides, half the fun was toying with the target before the kill. Making the hunt a game of cat and mouse delivered the biggest rush of all.

CHAPTER EIGHTEEN

Talia watched, impressed, as Luke did something creative to the lock on the door at the rear of the lodge. It was obvious he'd had some experience with breaking and entering.

She made a note to interrogate him about his extremely vague past. But the questions would have to wait. It was after midnight, and what they were doing was illegal and probably dangerous. They both needed to focus.

She followed him into a hallway and waited while he closed the door and switched on a penlight. Her senses were jacked up. She could literally feel the silence and the emptiness inside the lodge. She was aware of something else as well — the whisper of energy that told her Luke was running hot, too.

"The office is halfway down this hall," Luke said quietly.

"Where did you learn how to pick locks?" she whispered.

"YouTube."

"Oh, right."

He worked more B and E magic on the door of the office. Once inside, he closed the door and swept the penlight around the small space. There were a couple of battered metal filing cabinets, a desk equipped with an ancient mechanical calculator, a typewriter, and a landline phone.

"Talk about a time warp," Talia whispered. "No computer. No printer."

"And no high-tech security system, because modern tech doesn't work here on the island," Luke said. "That's a good thing for us, because it means that if there are any records to be found they will be in paper format. No need to try to guess passwords."

"Hard to imagine running a modern business without tech," Talia said. "What, specifically, are we looking for?"

"Anything that points to a money trail would be helpful."

"You're a traditionalist when it comes to investigations, I see."

"Absolutely," Luke said. "It always comes down to money and power. You take the desk. I'll check the file cabinet."

She focused on the vintage metal desk, opening her senses to the energy around it. There was a little heat around one of the drawers. She crossed the room and went to work.

It didn't take long to find the source of the energy: a notebook of lined pages divided into columns.

"I've got a business ledger that goes back to the opening of the Unplugged Experience six months ago," she said. "It's mostly a record of supplies and provisions that have been ordered."

"These file drawers are almost all empty," Luke said. "Just a few folders, including one that contains a record of bookings for the past six months."

Talia turned a page in the ledger. "The Unplugged Experience may not be a moneymaker, but the Institute for the Study of Medicinal Botany is pouring money into it. Chef Octavia gets a generous budget for the restaurant end of the business."

"Are you talking about the cook?"

"Octavia Venner is a *chef.* That saffron and parmesan risotto we had at dinner tonight was brilliant, to say nothing of the sourdough bread. It was obviously baked here on the island, and it was the best I've ever had. And don't get me started on the

156

watercress and endive salad. I'm going to beg Octavia for the dressing recipe."

"I doubt she'll give it to you. She looked sullen tonight. I got the feeling she is not a happy camper."

Talia winced. "Yep, I got that feeling, too. But chefs are notoriously temperamental. They're artists, and they have to work under a lot of pressure."

"I'll take your word for it. Anything else of interest in that ledger?"

Talia studied the entries. "Well, I think I now know why Chef Octavia is wasting her time cooking for a low-rent operation like the Unplugged Experience."

"What did you find?"

"She and Clive Venner are making a lot of money working for the Institute. There's a record of the monthly deposits into their bank accounts."

" 'Accounts' plural?" Luke asked sharply. "There's more than one?"

"Yes. Separate accounts, one for Octavia and one for Clive. They are each getting hefty CEO-category salaries, Luke."

"Interesting. I wonder if the Unplugged Experience is just an old-fashioned money laundering operation."

"We didn't come here because of a run-of-the-mill business scam. We're here because Phoebe Hatch found something that linked Venner and the Unplugged Experience to that list we're chasing."

"Right," Luke said. "So the next step is to take a look around Venner's quarters. I'll do it tomorrow morning when he leads the first meditation class."

"There aren't many guests here this week," Talia said. "Venner is bound to notice that you're not in the audience."

"You'll have to cover for me. Tell him I overslept or that I got sick on the organic food we ate tonight."

"I refuse to let you blame your fake illness on Chef Octavia's risotto."

"Think of something else, then," Luke said. "We've seen enough. Let's get out of here."

She watched him drop a file folder back into a drawer. Energy pulsed around the folder.

"Wait," she said. "I think that file might be important. What's in it?"

"Records of recent bookings. Why?"

"I don't know," she admitted.

"There's no time to go through it here. I'll take it with us."

When he opened the front of his leather jacket to tuck the folder inside, the beam of her flashlight glinted briefly on dark metal.

He had told her he had a pistol, but this was the first time she had seen it. For some reason it came as a shock to realize that it was no longer stowed in his pack.

"What if one of the Venners notices the missing paperwork?" she asked.

"Why would they bother to look at a file of registered guests? Don't worry, I'll replace the folder tomorrow."

They made their way back down the hall to the rear door and moved outside into the night. Talia took a deep breath, letting the invigorating energy of the gardens envelop her. The leaves of a nearby plant sparkled as if dusted by tiny crystals. The sky was one-o'clock-in-the-morning-with-a-low-hanging-cloud-cover dark, but the greenery looked as if it was bathed in silver moonlight.

"The bioluminescence of these plants is beautiful," she said. She caught a large, fan-shaped leaf, held it out of her way, rounded the corner . . . and came up hard against Luke's unyielding back.

"Oomph."

Moving fast, he snagged her with one arm, pulled her close to his side, and put his hand across her mouth. It all happened before she realized it *was* happening. She froze, aware that he was watching something very intently. She followed his gaze and peered through the jungle of luminous greenery. Glimpses of pale fabric appeared and disappeared in the choked undergrowth. The sleeve of a loose-fitting shirt. A trouser leg. And then she heard the humming.

She and Luke were not the only ones abroad on the garden path tonight.

CHAPTER NINETEEN

Luke took a couple of seconds to consider the options. Under other circumstances he would have preferred to gather more information before confronting the individual who was ahead of them on the path, but time was running out. He and Talia needed answers.

Speaking of Talia . . .

It occurred to him that he was holding her captive, imprisoned under his arm, his hand across her mouth. In the shadows her eyes glittered with impatience. She wasn't struggling; just waiting for him to release her.

He took his hand off her lips and let her go. She nodded once, letting him know she had seen the person on the path. He started forward, making no effort to silence his footsteps. Talia kept pace with him.

There was a sharp snap as a twig or small branch was nipped off. Someone was using a pair of pruning shears at one o'clock in the morning.

Snap. Crack. Crunch.

He rounded the corner first. Talia followed. They both stopped at the sight of the ethereal figure in white — white trousers, a white shirt, and white sneakers. Her pale blond hair was clipped in a casual twist that left a few tendrils free to bob around her very pale face. She held the pruning shears in one gloved hand.

"Good evening," she said, turning to meet them. Her voice went with the Tinker Bell persona — light and musical. "What fun to run into other people who enjoy the gardens at this hour. I usually have them all to myself. You must be new on the island."

"We checked in for the Unplugged Experience today," Talia said. "I don't recall seeing you in the lodge earlier."

"No. I do my work at night."

"You're an employee here?" Luke asked.

"You could say that." The woman smiled a secretive smile. "But I don't see my work as a job. It's a calling. Now, you must excuse me. The night is getting on, and I still have plants to prune. They grow so quickly here on the island."

She started to walk away along the path of blue-lit stones.

"Wait," Talia said quickly. "Who are you?"

"What?" The woman giggled. "My apologies. I didn't introduce myself, did I? I'm the Night Gardener."

She floated away and soon vanished into the depths of the gardens. Without a word, Luke grabbed Talia's hand and followed. The path led to the entrance of a massive glass-and-steel conservatory. They arrived in time to watch the Night Gardener move inside. The metal door clanged shut behind her.

Evidently aware that she was being watched, she smiled one last secretive smile and raised the shears in an airy wave before she turned and disappeared into the luminous plants that crammed the interior of the conservatory.

Talia watched closely, but the walls of the structure were made of thick, heavy glass, the sort used in banks and other high security settings. The kind of glass that could stop a bullet. The result was a somewhat distorted view of the jungle inside.

Luke went to the steel door and tried to open it. "Locked," he announced. "I don't think there's a YouTube video for this." He ran his fingers over a steel plate set with small black crystals. "It looks old, but I've never seen anything like it."

Talia peered into the glass hothouse. "What's your take on the Night Gardener?"

"She is either stoned to her back teeth or living in another reality," Luke said. "Maybe both."

"Yep, that was my assessment, too." Talia abruptly became aware of the energy shivering through Phoebe Hatch's necklace. She reached up to touch the crystal with her fingertips. *"Luke."*

He glanced at her. "What?"

"Phoebe's necklace is sending a stronger signal. There's still a lot of static, but the current is definitely more powerful."

Luke contemplated the steel door in front of them. "We need to get inside the conservatory."

"I think so," Talia said. "But I gotta tell you, it gives me the creeps."

"This whole damned island has that effect on me."

The fierce edge on the words surprised her. "What, exactly, is your definition of a creepy vibe?"

He was silent for a moment, studying the distorted view of the interior of the conservatory. "There were times today when the energy here felt . . . familiar."

That stopped her cold. She caught her breath.

"Well, shit," she said softly.

"Yep."

"Do you think you've been here before?" she asked. "Is this your Lucent Springs?"

"If this was the scene of my lost night, all I can tell you is that I have no clear memory of it."

"But the energy feels familiar."

"Sometimes."

"What now?"

"We go back to your cabin," Luke said. "I want to take a closer look at those papers I found in the file cabinet, and then we need some sleep."

"All right."

CHAPTER TWENTY

It had probably been a mistake to tell Talia that the energy on Night Island had a familiar feel. The less she knew about his lost night, the better. The last thing he wanted to do was try to explain two dead bodies, the scalpel, and his status as a not-so-failed experiment. The problem was that it was getting too easy to talk to Talia. He needed to be more cautious.

The trek back through the gardens took them along a path that was different from the one they had used earlier in the day. The stepping stones wound through banks of massive, luminous ferns, past Marcella Earle's cabin and the one that had been assigned to Oliver Skinner. Both were dark. No surprise. It wasn't as if there was anything in the way of after-hours entertainment on Night Island.

Unless you were the Night Gardener.

They were about to pass behind cabin

seven, the one that Luke was supposed to be using, when he sensed the shock that struck Talia. In the next second he heard her take in a quick, sharp breath. She stopped.

"Shit," she whispered. "Shit, shit, *shit*. I hate when this happens."

"What?" he asked, searching for the source of the threat.

Talia gazed at the wall of green that bordered the path.

"Pretty sure someone died behind those ferns," she said.

Luke took out the penlight he had brought with him and eased aside some of the heavy fronds. He was getting to know Talia well, he realized, because he didn't question her conclusion.

The dead man sprawled, facedown, on a bed of crushed ferns. He looked to be in his late thirties. He was dressed in gardener's clothes. A leather belt studded with gardening implements was wrapped around his waist.

"This night just keeps getting more and more interesting," Luke said. "Here, hold the flashlight for me."

CHAPTER TWENTY-ONE

Talia aimed the flashlight at the dead man and watched Luke search the body. The swift, efficient way he went about the task told her that this wasn't the first time he had done that sort of thing.

"What are you looking for?" she said.

"Something that might tell us why a man who looks like he was in good physical condition dropped dead out here in the middle of the night."

"Any sign of injury?"

"No. None."

A chilling possibility struck. "Luke, what if some of these plants are poisonous? Maybe you should leave him alone. Get away from those ferns. We'll wake up the Venners and let them handle this situation. They're in charge here."

"He looks like he worked in these gardens. He would have known if there were dangerous plants in the vicinity. Also, the lodge has been in operation for nearly six months. If guests were getting killed by poisonous plants, someone would have complained online." Luke paused and sat back on his heels. "Huh."

She saw that he had extracted an object that looked like a flashlight from the pocket of the dead man's tool belt.

"Find something?" she asked.

"Maybe." He got to his feet and slipped the object inside his jacket. Then he paused and pinned her briefly with his heated eyes. "Are you all right?"

She folded her arms around her midsection and focused on her breathing. "I'm great."

"You're not great."

"This is my second dead body this week," she said coldly. "And the week's not over. I'm having a little trouble processing, okay?"

She groaned. She should not be snapping at Luke. It wasn't his fault that she had happened across a dead man.

"Sorry," she muttered.

"Are you going to — ?" Luke asked.

"Pass out? No." She made herself start down the path that led to the Venner cabin. "Let's wake up management."

CHAPTER TWENTY-TWO

A short time later, management, in the form of Clive and Octavia Venner, stood on the path aiming flashlights at the body. They were not alone. Clive had alerted Nathan Gill, who had grabbed a first aid kit. He was now crouched beside the dead man, checking for a pulse.

Marcella Earle had been awakened by the commotion and had come outside in a bathrobe to see what was going on. She had shrieked at the sight of the body. That, in turn, had brought Oliver Skinner and Jasper Draper to the scene.

It occurred to Talia that the only one who was not there was the Night Gardener.

"It's Eddy Keever," Octavia said. She stared at the body, transfixed. "The assistant gardener."

There was more than shock and dismay in her demeanor, Talia thought. Something about her posture and the way she was looking at Keever sent a message of dread and maybe a whisper of panic.

"No sign of injury," Nathan Gill said.

"Overdose," Clive declared. "We knew he was using. The Institute should have let him go weeks ago."

"It's not that easy to find employees with his particular skill set who are willing to commit to life here on the island for extended periods of time," Nathan pointed out quietly.

"Can't blame people for not wanting to work here," Oliver Skinner muttered. "I'm already bored."

Marcella took a step closer to get a better look. "Last year I came across a body while I was showing a house in Seattle. My clients freaked out. Killed the sale, of course."

"Are you sure he died of an overdose?" Jasper Draper asked.

"Hard to say." Nathan got to his feet. "Could have been a heart attack or stroke."

"He looks too young for a heart attack or stroke," Marcella said.

"Aneurysm, maybe," Jasper Draper offered. "One thing's for sure, this will add some interest to the blog post I'm going to do when I get back to civilization. I can see the headline now. 'The Unplugged Experience Provides a Killer Retreat.' "

No one laughed.

"That's enough," Nathan said. He picked up the emergency kit. "I'll get the stretcher and a blanket from the storage locker at the lodge. We'll put the body in Keever's cabin until the ferry gets here tomorrow." He looked at Clive. "I'm going to need some help with the stretcher."

Clive looked alarmed. "My back —"

"I'll give you a hand," Luke said quietly.

Nathan's eyes tightened. He nodded once and hurried away toward the lodge.

Talia looked at Octavia. "Someone should notify his next of kin."

Octavia shook her head. "We'll have to leave that up to the Institute. Eddy didn't provide any emergency contacts on his employment form. The gardens were the only things he cared about — well, specifically the mushrooms. He was very helpful when it came to harvesting the ones I use in the kitchen. He said there were a lot of poisonous and hallucinogenic varieties on the island."

Talia and Marcella looked at each other. Neither said a word, but Talia had a feeling they both would be skipping the mushroom pâté in the future.

"The Night Gardener will have her hands full looking after these gardens and the conservatory on her own," Luke said.

He might as well have lobbed a small grenade at the Venners. They stared at him with classic deer-in-the-headlights expressions.

Clive recovered first. "You met Pomona Finch?"

"Is that her name?" Talia asked. "She introduced herself as the Night Gardener."

"Pomona is what people used to call eccentric," Octavia said. "But she has an amazing affinity for the plants. Keeps odd hours. She works nights and sleeps days. I'm surprised you met her. When she's awake she is usually inside the conservatory. She's obsessed with the experimental specimens she's cataloging."

"Why didn't we see her at dinner?" Talia asked.

"She doesn't eat with the guests," Octavia said. "She doesn't like people and she doesn't appreciate good food. Mostly she eats those awful energy bars. She tells me when she needs more and I order a supply for her. We see very little of her. As I said, at this hour of the night she's usually hard at work inside the conservatory. She doesn't like to be disturbed during the days."

Clive grunted. "Eccentric, like Octavia said."

Marcella glanced at the body. "Did Keever work nights, too? Is that why he was out here in the gardens at one in the morning?"

"Yes, Finch insisted that he work nights," Octavia said. "She said it was the best time to tend to the plants. Something about their energy."

Clive fixed Luke with a suspicious gaze. "What were you and Ms. March doing out here at one in the morning?"

"The separate-cabins thing wasn't working for us," Luke said. "Don't rat us out to our couples counselor, okay?"

Jasper and Oliver snorted, amused. Marcella rolled her eyes. Clive scowled, clearly unsatisfied with the answer.

"You were *both* out here?" he pressed. "Why weren't you in one of your cabins or the other?"

"See, this is the problem you get when there are no phones in the cabins," Luke said. "There was a misunderstanding about time and location. The result was that I was on my way to Talia's room and she was on her way to mine. We met somewhere in the labyrinth. We had just decided to go to her cabin to spend the rest of the night when we ran into the Night Gardener. The next thing we know we're practically stumbling over Keever's body."

"Nothing like a dead body to ruin a guy's sex life," Jasper said.

No one snickered. He shrugged.

Luke took Talia's arm. "Gill will be back with the stretcher soon. I'll take you to your cabin and then give him a hand with the body."

He urged her quickly along the path. She kept silent until they were at the door of the cabin and she could be certain they would not be overheard.

" 'The separate-cabins thing wasn't working for us'?" she said, shoving the key into the lock of her cabin door. "Really? That was the best excuse you could come up with to explain why we were out in the gardens tonight?"

"I thought it sounded reasonable under the circumstances," Luke said. "It fit with our cover story."

She groaned and pushed open the door. He was right. Letting the others think that they had been unable to follow the couples counselor's instructions to avoid the distraction of sex was the most logical explanation for their late-night garden tour. But for some illogical reason it irritated her. She reminded herself that her nerves were already on edge.

"Okay, forget it," she grumbled. She

moved inside the cabin, flipped the light switch, and turned to face Luke. "Nothing we can do about it now. We've got bigger problems."

"I admire your mature, professional approach to the crisis," Luke said. He slipped the folder out from under his jacket and gave it to her. "Take this. See you in a few minutes. Lock the door until I get back. I don't think the killer will make another move tonight, but no sense taking chances."

She clenched the folder. "Killer?"

"Eddy Keever did not die of natural causes."

She took a breath. "Murdered?"

"Yes."

"I was afraid you were going to say that. But there were no signs of violence."

"If I'm right, he was killed by paranormal means."

Stunned, she stared at him. "What — ?"

"Later," Luke said. "I need to help Gill deal with the stretcher. This is a good opportunity to get a look at Keever's cabin. I'll be back as soon as possible. Meanwhile, like I said, lock the door and don't open it for anyone except me."

"You need to get over this bad habit you have of giving me orders. But yes, understood."

She closed the door in his face, shot the bolt home, and crossed the small room to the table. She dropped the folder on the table and opened one of the miniature liquor bottles. It was turning into a very long night.

CHAPTER TWENTY-THREE

The trek back to Keever's darkened cabin was made mostly in silence. Evidently Nathan Gill did not feel obliged to offer any thoughtful Unplugged Experience meditations on the subject of death. That was a relief.

Inside the cabin they set the stretcher with its blanket-covered burden on the narrow bed. Luke stepped back.

"Did you know him well?" he asked.

"No." Nathan studied the body for a moment. "None of us did. The Institute hired him off-site and sent him here. We were told he would be working nights like Pomona Finch."

Luke surveyed the cabin as he followed Gill to the door. There wasn't much to observe. The rustic space had a shabby, mildly cluttered, lived-in look. There was a small plastic baggie of what looked like dried, crushed mushrooms and a bong on the table.

"Looks like Keever found a way to relax after a hard night's work in the conservatory," he said.

Nathan glanced dismissively at the smoking apparatus. "Trust me, you would be looking for some distraction, too, if you were stuck on this island for a few months."

"I notice you're sticking it out," Luke said.

"What can I tell you? The money is very, very good. And during the late summer and early fall there was other entertainment available. You'd be amazed by how many attractive women are interested in private mindfulness sessions."

CHAPTER TWENTY-FOUR

"Do you really believe that Keever was murdered by paranormal means?" Talia sank down on the end of the bed, sipped some brandy, and studied the cabin wall that was less than three feet away. Her frazzled senses were settling down, but she was still getting occasional icy chills across the back of her neck.

"Yes," Luke said.

She would not have thought it possible for him to move even farther into the cold, remote dimension she was starting to think of as the Luke zone, but he somehow managed to make that happen.

He carried the glass of whiskey she had poured for him across the cramped space to the wall where his jacket and shoulder holster hung on a hook. Reaching into a pocket, he took out the small, flashlight-shaped object he had found on Keever's body.

He sat down beside her, close but not touching. The bedsprings squeaked under his weight. He swallowed some whiskey. She got the feeling he was giving himself time to work out how much to tell her. That did not bode well, she decided.

She looked at the object in his hand. It was about an inch and a half wide and some five inches long. A ring of what looked like black beads or crystals was embedded at one end, where the bulb would have been in a real flashlight. It looked futuristic in a vintage sort of way — like a prop in an old science fiction film.

She straightened, kicked up her senses, took a breath, and gingerly reached out to touch the object. A tingle of energy zapped across her senses. She yelped and instinctively yanked her hand away from the gadget.

"It has a paranormal vibe," she said in wonder. "Do you think it's a weapon?"

"I have no idea."

"I got a small shock from it, probably because it was on Keever when he died." She shook her fingers in an attempt to ease the singed feeling. "Maybe it's some kind of paranormal gardening tool that he used in the conservatory."

"Such as?"

"I have no idea. I don't garden. But we know the plants around the lodge are not what anyone would call normal. I don't think those inside the conservatory are, either."

Luke tightened his grip on the device. He was so close she could feel the heat of his body and sense the energy charging the atmosphere around him. He turned the object in his hands, examining it closely.

"It's important," he said. "The question is, why?"

Belatedly she realized that the heat of Phoebe Hatch's crystal had intensified when she touched the gadget. She took a breath and put a fingertip on it again.

She got another little jolt from the strange device, but she felt something else. The crystal pulsed. She knew that particular vibe.

"I don't have any idea what that thing is, and the sensations I'm picking up are muddied because it is associated with Keever's body," she said. "But I think that gadget has been close to Phoebe, and . . . recently."

Luke watched her, his eyes sharp. "Anything else?"

"We may be able to use it to find her. But before you ask, I have no idea how to do that."

"We know it's got a connection to the conservatory because it was in Keever's tool belt," Luke said. "What's more, Nathan Gill wasn't just looking for signs of an injury when he checked Keever's body tonight. He was searching for something. Maybe it was this device."

"If it's valuable, why didn't the killer take it when he murdered Keever?" Talia said. She paused. "Assuming the killer is male."

"At this point we can't make any assumptions," Luke said. "There are three other women on this island besides you. Octavia Venner, Pomona Finch, and Marcella Earle. But getting back to your questions, it's possible the killer was not after this gadget. Maybe the goal was to silence a guy who had seen something he shouldn't have seen. It's also possible the murderer panicked and didn't take the time to stop and search the body."

"Or didn't know about the gadget? Maybe Keever was involved in some risky side hustle. Drugs or blackmail. That would explain murder."

"I'm sure of one thing," Luke said. "Nathan Gill is more than just a guide for the Unplugged Experience."

"What do you mean?"

"He's not here on the island because he

wants to help people learn to meditate. He indicated he's working the gig for the money and the occasional fling with a guest. But I think there's more to it. He tries to keep a low profile, but you saw him tonight. He's the one in charge here on the island, not Clive Venner."

She contemplated the wall for a few seconds. "That raises some interesting questions."

"Yes, it does."

"Gill knows we found the body," she said. "Maybe he'll assume we took that gadget. What if he thinks we murdered Keever?"

"There's not much we can do about Gill's conclusions. We need to keep moving forward."

She kept her attention on the wall of the cabin. "Before we can do that, I need to know something, Luke."

He exhaled slowly. "You want to know why I'm so sure it's possible to kill with paranormal energy."

"Yes."

There was a long silence.

"I know it's possible because I'm sure I could do it," he said. "In fact, I think it is what I was created to do."

CHAPTER TWENTY-FIVE

Shocked, she turned her head to stare at him. "Bullshit."

"I don't have any solid memories of my lost night but I sometimes hear voices in my dreams." Luke got to his feet and began to prowl the narrow space in front of the bed. "Two men talking. The first one says, *'Subject A is not responding. We will have to terminate.'* The second one says, *'Wait. He may pull out of it. We can't afford another failure. He's worth a fucking fortune.'* The first man says —"

A chill raised the fine hairs on the back of Talia's neck. "Go on."

"The first man says, *'Only if he's a success. If he does survive there will be a high probability of insanity. The client is paying for a psychically enhanced assassin, not a monster with a lethal talent.'* " Luke stopped at the window and looked out into the night. "They argue a bit more and then —"

185

"What?"

"The two men scream," Luke said. He gripped the edge of the window frame with one hand. "Not for long."

She dug her fingers into the bedding on either side of her thighs and forced herself to breathe with Pilates control. "That does sound . . . problematic."

"Yes, it does, doesn't it?" Luke said.

He spoke in an unnervingly cool and detached manner. He was in professorial mode. But there was something else going on beneath the surface. Fear? Pain? Horror?

She pulled herself together and tried to focus. She needed answers. "Do you remember anything else?"

"In my dreams I see two men in white coats on the floor. They are both dead. Their throats have been cut. I walk through their blood."

"That is awful."

"It gets worse," Luke said. "I told you that when I came fully awake I realized I had an object on me that indicated I had been in a medical setting."

"A fingertip pulse oximeter."

"That was true, but I had something else, as well. A scalpel."

Ghostly fingers trailed a path down Talia's spine. She reminded herself that she had known this man for only a couple of days. She forced herself to sit quietly while she processed the story.

"You say you see these scenes in your dreams?" she asked.

"Yes. But I'm sure they are real memories, Talia, not just images from a nightmare."

The tension in the small confines of the cabin was a physical force, a gathering storm. Talia did not move. She watched the taut line of Luke's shoulders as he studied the darkened gardens and knew that she was looking at a man who was trying to maintain his balance while walking along the edge of an invisible cliff.

Comprehension struck with the force of a small bolt of lightning.

She snapped her fingers. "So that's it."

Luke turned his head to look at her. "What?"

"You're afraid that whoever drugged you and somehow enhanced your paranormal senses turned you into a version of Frankenstein's monster," she said.

He closed his eyes very briefly. When he opened them they glittered with stark certainty. "More like Dr. Jekyll and Mr. Hyde."

"You're serious, aren't you?"

He nodded once.

She drew a steadying breath and straightened her shoulders. "All right, let's think about this."

"Trust me, Talia, it's all I think about these days."

"I mean from a logical perspective. How would you go about killing someone with psychic energy?"

"Maybe put them into a coma and . . . keep going."

"Keep going?"

"Until everything shuts down, including the heart," he said.

The ice-cold certainty in his voice stole her breath for a moment. She knew then that he had been dealing with his Jekyll-and-Hyde fears ever since his lost night.

"And I thought I ended up with a depressing talent," she said.

Luke did not respond. He watched her.

"Are you absolutely sure you could stop someone's heart?" she said, trying to choose her words with exquisite care.

"You're asking me if I've ever killed anyone with my talent," he said, emotionless now.

She cleared her throat. "Yes."

"Maybe."

She frowned. "You don't know for sure?"

Luke turned back to the bioluminescent

gardens. "Given our situation, you have a right to the truth, and the truth is I don't know if I killed anyone with my talent."

"Tell me what happened."

"In my other life as a history professor I did some hostage and crisis negotiation for the local police department. I was good at de-escalation."

"Because of your original talent."

"Yes. But shortly before Hatch contacted me about the list, I was called to a crime scene. A man named Pilcher had been stalking his wife. He tracked her down in the small town where I was living until now. When I arrived on the scene he was holding his wife at gunpoint, threatening to kill her. I used my new talent to get him under control. I was trying to render him unconscious. He collapsed. I don't know if I stopped his heart, because his wife grabbed the gun and put a bullet in his head."

"But you're sure you could have killed him, aren't you?"

"Yes."

"How does your talent work? I know I think of it as hypnosis, but you told me it isn't that, at least not exactly."

He turned to look at her again, his eyes fierce and cold. "Once I have the fix on certain wavelengths in a person's voice I can project counterpoint currents with my own voice. I essentially jam the signal. That sets up a kind of psychic dissonance that the brain can't handle. It shuts down, taking the vital organs with it. I'm sure that if I pushed hard enough I could kill someone the way Keever was killed tonight."

She threw her arms out wide, exasperated. "Well, don't."

He stared at her as if she had switched to another language, one he did not even begin to comprehend. " 'Don't'? Is that all you can say?"

"Luke, you're overthinking this. I can pick up a gun and shoot someone in cold blood. But I'm not going to do that. Okay, I would shoot someone to protect myself or someone else if there was no alternative and if I actually had a gun. But we're talking about seriously extenuating circumstances. Life or death. My point is, you've got a talent that can be used as a weapon, but you're the one in control of your ability. You're not Jekyll and Hyde."

"What makes you so sure of that?"

"Two reasons." She held up a single finger. "One, you didn't kill me when you found me at Phoebe Hatch's place."

"Why the hell would I have done that?"

"A sociopathic assassin would have figured

it was the logical thing to do, especially after I found the memory card, because at that point you no longer needed me. I became excess baggage. In fact, you made it clear you considered me a problem, remember?"

"That is not the same thing as wanting you dead."

"It is for a sociopathic killer." She held up a second finger. "Two, you brought me cupcakes for my birthday."

He looked at her in disbelief. "That logic is a little weak, don't you think?"

"Nope. I've known you long enough to conclude that you are irritating, stubborn, and obsessed with finding out who stole a day and a half of your life. I can deal with all that, because I share those personality traits. But an assassin wouldn't have picked up a box of cupcakes because he felt sorry for me on my birthday."

"You're an expert on assassins?"

She groaned. "Never mind. Tell me about the scalpel."

"What about it?"

"Why would you use a scalpel on those two men in white coats if you could kill with your psychic talent?"

Luke hesitated. She could see that he was mentally recalibrating events. "At that point I probably didn't know what I could do with my talent. It would have been instinctive to pick up a weapon."

"I would have thought that under those circumstances your intuition would have kicked in and you would have discovered your new ability. That's how it happened with me. I didn't know I could find dead bodies until I accidentally discovered the first one."

"The bottom line is that I was holding a scalpel, Talia, and those two men had clearly been killed with a blade."

"You said you walked through a lot of blood."

"Yes."

"Was there any blood on the scalpel or on your clothes?"

That stopped him. He seemed to focus on the middle distance, as if trying to summon up his memories. After a time he shook his head.

"I can't remember," he said slowly. "Why can't I remember?"

"Excellent question. Blood has enormous symbolism in dreams and visions. If you had used that scalpel there would have been a lot of blood on the blade, your hands, your clothing. I think that would have made an even stronger impression than the memory of the blood on the floor."

Luke went silent again but she knew he was trying out the new version of events she was offering. Energy heated his eyes. And maybe hope.

"When and how did you discover what you could do with your new talent?" she asked after a moment.

"I can't remember those first few hours, but when I woke up on a street in Seattle, I knew I had to get lost until I could figure out what had happened to me. I picked up a few things at a shelter and then found a doorway. That first night some doper tried to steal my stuff. I tried to talk him out of it using my old ability. But instead of calming down and going away quietly, he dropped to the ground, unconscious. I realized then that if I'd kept up the pressure I probably could have killed him."

"But you didn't."

He hesitated. "No."

"You said you were Subject A."

"Right."

"Why not just 'the subject'?"

Luke's eyes tightened. "What?"

"It sounds like the people conducting the experiment had to distinguish you from someone else. If you were the only subject in the lab, why would they label you A?"

"Who knows what those guys in the white

coats were thinking?"

"There were three subjects in the experiment in Lucent Springs," she said. "Amelia, Pallas, and myself. There were two subjects in the experiment that took place in Carnelian. So, yes, I'd say there's an excellent possibility that there were two in the experiment in which you were involved. Maybe more."

Luke thought about that for a moment. He did not relax completely but she thought some of his tension dissipated.

"Maybe," he allowed.

"We're wasting time," she said. "Enough about you. We need to focus on finding Phoebe Hatch."

"You're right," he said, decisive and controlled once again.

"Huh."

Luke glanced at her. "Now what?"

"I'm the one who finds stuff, remember?"

"So?"

"So it occurs to me that I found Keever's body within a few yards of your cabin."

"Yeah, that occurred to me, too," Luke said.

"Probably a coincidence. If he was leaving the conservatory he would have passed by the back of your cabin."

"Where a killer with psychic talents just

happened to be hanging around, spotted Keever, and decided to get rid of him?"

"When you put it like that, probably *not* a coincidence," Talia admitted.

"I'm going to set up the cot," Luke said.

"I thought you wanted to study those papers you took from the file drawer in the office."

"Tomorrow," Luke said. "Paperwork always takes a lot of time. We both need sleep."

He unlatched the folding cot and opened it. There was barely room for it to fit between the bed and the front door.

Talia eyed the thin mattress and the worn bedding. "It doesn't look very comfortable."

"I've slept in worse. If I dream, wake me."

"Same."

A short time later she crawled into bed wearing the flannel pajamas she had packed to deal with the chill she had expected to encounter on the island. The pajamas were, she reflected, the least sexy nightwear in her wardrobe. For some reason she regretted the sartorial choice.

Luke emerged from the bathroom wearing a T-shirt and his cargo trousers. He went to where his holster hung on the wall hook and took out the pistol. She watched him carry the gun across the room and slide it under the cot.

He glanced at her. "Something wrong?"

"No," she said quickly.

He turned out the light. She listened as he unzipped and removed his trousers and got into bed.

Silence fell.

She had known about the gun, she reminded herself. But for some reason it came as a shock to realize he had been carrying it all day and was now sleeping with it under his cot. Within easy reach.

"Do all history professors carry guns?" she asked.

"Can't speak for all of them, but I started carrying one after someone grabbed me and made me Subject A in an experiment that gave me a potentially lethal talent."

"But you carried a gun before that, didn't you?"

"I told you I was in the military and later in the intelligence world, Talia. The kind of work I did can't be done with a computer or a phone. I have to hear the voices I'm trying to read in person. That means I spent a lot of time in some dangerous places."

"Makes sense."

"Do all podcasters carry pepper spray?"

"They do if they've got a history of being kidnapped, drugged, and used as a subject in an illegal experiment."

"Makes sense," Luke said. "Are you okay?"

"No anxiety attack yet, if that's what you're worried about," she said, irritated. "But stay tuned."

CHAPTER TWENTY-SIX

She did not have an anxiety attack during the night.

Talia was still marveling at that the next morning as she stood at the breakfast buffet, trying to decide if she wanted two slices of the polenta, feta cheese, and eggs casserole or two eggs Florentine.

Under the circumstances, she thought, the fact that she had slept rather well was astonishing, considering what she had been through recently. Maybe she had simply been too exhausted to succumb to anxiety. But she suspected the reason she had enjoyed a panic-free night had a lot to do with the knowledge that she was not alone.

Luke had apparently slept soundly, too. If he had experienced any nightmares, he had not awakened her with them.

She settled on the polenta, cheese, and eggs dish and was reaching for a serving spoon when the storm struck with startling force.

A metal object clattered on the floor behind her. She turned quickly and saw Marcella Earle lean down to retrieve a fork.

"Sorry," Marcella said. "Caught me by surprise. I didn't know there was a storm due today."

"Neither did I," Talia said.

But strictly speaking, that was not true, she thought. She had awakened from a restless sleep with the feeling that fierce energy was gathering in the atmosphere. It was as if Night Island was a giant magnet that was attracting the forces of nature.

She had attributed the premonition to her imagination, but now she wondered if her psychic side had picked up the wild currents of wind and rain a couple of hours before they had materialized. *Something wicked this way comes.*

She glanced out the window, wondering if Luke had been caught outside when the deluge hit or if he had made it into Keever's cabin first.

Oliver Skinner grunted. "This is what comes of being cut off from the internet. You can't even get the fucking weather forecast." He helped himself to the last croissant on the tray. "I don't know about the rest of you, but I've had it with the Unplugged Experience. First a dead guy in those creepy gardens last night and now a storm? Forget it. The food's good but it's not worth the weirdness. I'm leaving on the noon ferry."

Octavia appeared from the kitchen. She had a tray of replacement croissants in her hands and a forbidding glare in her eyes. "There are no refunds for bad weather conditions."

"Who cares?" Oliver stuffed half a flaky croissant into his mouth. "I just want off this island."

"I'm with you," Marcella said. She shuddered. "That dead body last night was just too much. And now this awful weather. I'm leaving today, too."

Jasper Draper spoke up from the coffee and tea bar. "I'll be surprised if anyone gets off this island today. I'm told the tides around here are tricky enough in good weather. What do you want to bet the ferry cancels?"

As if on cue, Clive Venner emerged from the hallway that led to the office. "I just got off the phone with the charter people. There won't be a ferry run today, and maybe not tomorrow, either. There's an atmospheric river moving in, and Night Island is directly in its path."

"Fuck," Oliver muttered.

Marcella groaned. "Seriously? And here I was wondering how things could get worse."

"Things can always get worse," Oliver Skinner assured her.

Marcella glared at him.

Clive cleared his throat. "I think that, under the circumstances, we will cancel morning meditation."

"Oh, hey, that's a great idea," Jasper muttered.

Clive scowled. As far as Talia could see, the expression had absolutely no impact on Jasper.

"I urge you all to enjoy your breakfast," Clive continued. "There are cards, books, and board games in the lobby. Allow yourself to slow down and relax in front of the fire. Open your mind to the power of nature and remember that all things are connected."

He turned and went back down the hall. Octavia watched him leave, her jaw tense, her posture rigid.

Talia tried a smile. "The risotto last night was absolutely amazing, Chef. In fact, everything you've served us has been incredible. Any chance you might write a cookbook one of these days? *Recipes from the*

Unplugged Experience?"

"No," Octavia said.

She set the tray of croissants on the table and disappeared into the kitchen.

Talia sighed, selected one of the fresh croissants, and sat down at a table. Marcella joined her.

"So much for trying to flatter the cook," Marcella said. "Save your breath."

"Chef," Talia said, buttering the croissant.

"What?"

"Octavia is obviously a talented chef. We are fortunate to be eating her creations."

"The food is excellent," Marcella agreed. "But as Oliver said, it's not worth hanging around this island. Now that I know I can't get off today and maybe not tomorrow, either, it's all I can think about."

"How did you hear about the Unplugged Experience?" Talia asked.

"A friend of mine who is a real foodie recommended it. Mind you, she had never tried it herself, but she said there were a lot of rave reviews for the food online. Also, she thought I could use the meditation practice. I've been seriously overstressed lately. But I don't think meditation will work for me. Just thinking about having to sit still for a half hour makes me nervous. I'm glad Venner canceled the session today."

"I'm with you," Talia said. "I'd rather eat Chef Octavia's food than meditate."

Marcella picked up her coffee. "Did your couples counselor really suggest that you and your partner book separate cabins?"

"Luke isn't —" Talia stopped. Luke *was* her partner — just not in the sense that Marcella meant. Regardless, there was a cover story to maintain. "Yes, it was the therapist's idea."

Marcella chuckled. "And you paid good money for that advice, I'll bet."

"Don't remind me."

"Obviously the separate-cabins thing didn't work out."

"Nope."

"Must have been awful stumbling over that body last night." Marcella shuddered. "Especially in those gardens. There's something strange about the plants on this island. I'm no botanist, but they don't look normal to me."

Jasper plunked a plate of eggs Florentine down on the table and took a seat. He forked up a bite and looked at Talia. "Where's your partner this morning?"

"Yeah," Oliver said, taking a chair. "What happened to Rand? Did he decide to sleep in?"

Talia surveyed the dining room and decided the coast was clear. She cradled her cup in both hands, leaned forward, and lowered her voice.

"Do you want to know the truth?" she said. The others watched her intently. "He went out early this morning to try to find some cell coverage. He's a desperate man without his phone."

"He's not the only one," Jasper said, wolfing down another bite of his eggs Florentine.

Oliver grimaced. "The storm probably caught him by surprise. Good luck to him. He'll be drenched by now."

"I'm a little worried, to be honest," Talia said. "I hope he doesn't wander off into that forest."

The others nodded in a somber, understanding way.

"If he finds a place where he can make a call, tell him I'll pay good money for the information," Jasper said.

"Same," Oliver added.

"Count me in, too," Marcella said.

Talia drank some coffee, pleased with her story. Luke was wrong. She was a very good liar.

Nathan Gill materialized in the arched opening that separated the dining room from the lobby. "Rand is wasting his time. He won't get a signal anywhere on this island. But he could easily get lost if he leaves the gardens and wanders into the woods. He wouldn't be the first person to disappear on this rock."

Marcella frowned. "Are you serious?"

"There's a reason why we tell the guests not to go outside the grounds," Nathan said. He looked at Talia, his eyes cold. "But I doubt if you need to worry. I'm sure Rand is too smart to do something stupid like hike into the woods just to find some cell service."

"Way too smart," Talia said.

"Let's hope so," Nathan said.

Marcella spoke up. "Say, that's your cabin cruiser tied up at the dock, isn't it?"

"Yes," Nathan said. "But before you ask, the answer is no. I can't take you off the island in the cruiser for the same reason the ferry can't dock here. The weather is bad and the water is too rough."

He turned and went toward the hallway that led to the rear door. Talia watched him until he was out of sight, recalling Luke's observation about the man. *What's more, Nathan Gill wasn't just looking for signs of an injury when he checked Keever's body tonight. He was searching for something.*

"So much for projecting positive energy," Marcella said in low tones. "I'm starting to feel like a prisoner on this island."

"You can say that again," Jasper said. "But speaking of positive thinking, I've got a title for my blog post on the Unplugged Experience. 'My Vacation on the Real Devil's Island.' "

Chapter Twenty-Seven

The body was gone.

Luke stood in Eddy Keever's small cottage, rainwater dripping off his plastic poncho, and contemplated the empty bed.

The missing body was not the only thing that had changed since he had last been here. Someone had conducted a thorough search of the cramped space. The old mattress sat at an odd angle on the rusty bedsprings. The contents of the drawers had been rifled through. The corner of the worn, braided rug was flipped up as if someone had raised it to check the floorboards. The door of the small medicine cabinet in the bathroom stood open.

Luke took a moment to prowl the cabin, trying to get a feel for the man who had lived in it. He found a sophisticated assortment of academic tomes and a handful of out-of-date journals — all devoted to botany. Scraps of paper tucked into two of the journals marked pages with articles written by Edward H. Keever, PhD. The subject of each was the symbiotic relationship between fungi and plants.

There were other records of Keever's past stored inside a battered suitcase, including divorce papers dated five years earlier that indicated he'd had an inept lawyer. There was also a printout of a terse email informing him that he was being fired from his job as a professor in the botany department of a small college for unspecified reasons.

Keever had been an academic whose life had apparently fallen apart. Somehow he had wound up as an assistant gardener on Night Island.

Something about the way the cabin had been torn apart sent a message of desperation and frustration. The fact that the baggie full of dried mushrooms was still sitting in plain sight meant the intruder had not been interested in drugs.

Luke unzipped the pocket of his cargo trousers and took out the small, flashlight-shaped device. He thought about the quick but methodical way Nathan Gill had searched Keever's body while pretending to look for signs of injury.

"Is this what you were looking for, Gill?" he said to the empty room. "Why did you take the body?"

Gill would probably be at the lodge eating breakfast with the others. There might be time to take a look around his cabin.

Luke went back out into the rain- and wind-tossed garden. The latest downpour was over but the next wave was fast approaching. The cloud cover was heavier than it had been earlier, cloaking the island in a surreal twilight.

He turned a corner and stopped when he caught sight of the conservatory. He changed his mind about searching Nathan Gill's cabin. Time to wake up the Night Gardener.

He followed the winding path through the maze of towering plants and stopped at the entrance to the glass-walled building. Yes, the island was sunk deep in gloom, but it was midmorning, so there should have been no sign of the eerie bioluminescence that he and Talia had observed last night. The plants inside the conservatory, however, glowed with a pale radiance. He got the uneasy feeling the vegetation was stirring in reaction to the energy of the storm. It was as if it was drinking in the currents of power that charged the atmosphere.

If this was any other place besides Night Island he would have lectured himself severely about his overactive imagination. But this *was* Night Island. Death by paranormal means happened here. Bodies went missing.

He was about to move past the steel door and follow the stone path that would take him around the conservatory when he heard a tiny, muffled ping. For a couple of seconds he wondered if he had stumbled into a location where he could get connectivity.

He moved into the limited shelter provided by the overhang above the conservatory entrance and took out his phone. Nothing. The device might as well have been a rock.

Another ping. Louder this time. The sound was coming from one of his cargo trouser pockets. He retrieved the gadget he had found on Keever's body. The pinging was stronger now, more frequent.

It was as if he was holding a directional indicator of some kind, he decided. He turned slowly on his heel. When he faced the steel door, the pinging became a constant hum. The circle of crystals set in the front end flashed with dark energy. He heard a low rumble from within the steel door, the sound of heavy bolts sliding aside. There was a click. The gadget went quiet in his hand.

Not a directional indicator, he decided. The gadget was a key.

He tried the door. It opened. A wave of humid air scented with the earthy smells of a hothouse rolled out.

This was getting interesting, but first things first. He was here to talk to the Night Gardener.

Luke closed the door and aimed the device at the lock. The pinging started. The black crystals pulsed. There was another rumble as the bolts inside the steel door slid home.

He stood there for a few more seconds, trying to decide how to move forward.

Priorities, Rand. Priorities.

Pocketing the gadget, he made his way around the conservatory and saw the cabin on the edge of the gardens. The overgrown plants loomed around the small structure as if guarding it — or, perhaps, waiting to consume it.

Not surprisingly, the shade was pulled down in the front window. There was no Do Not Disturb sign on the door, but there might as well have been. Visitors were not welcome.

He went forward and rapped sharply on the front door. "Wake up, Ms. Finch. I need to speak to you. It's important."

When he got no response he tried again, pounding on the door.

"Wake up, Ms. Finch. It's about your conservatory."

No one came to the door. Either Pomona Finch was a very sound sleeper or else she was ignoring him.

It was time to dispense with the social niceties. He tried the door and was startled to discover that it was not locked. He opened it a scant inch or two and spoke through the opening.

"Ms. Finch? I'm Luke Rand. We met last night. I need your help. A woman's life is in danger."

A deep sense of emptiness whispered in the atmosphere. It was accompanied by a dank, musty smell, as if the cabin had been closed up for a long time. He eased the door open farther, allowing a shaft of gray storm light into the space. He was braced to find a body or an unconscious woman. There was neither.

The disturbing sense of emptiness grew stronger. He gave it a moment but he could not shake the growing certainty that no one had lived in the cabin for a very long time.

He walked slowly through the main room and the bath. There were no sheets or blankets on the bed. No clothes in the closet. No toiletries. No personal possessions. No signs that a meal had been eaten in the cabin. No coffee mugs in the small sink. The layer of dust told him that if Pomona Finch had ever spent time here, it was long ago.

If he had not met the Night Gardener last night he would have had a hard time believing she existed.

He closed the door and went back along the path that led to the front of the conservatory. The gadget in his trouser pocket gave another muffled ping when he went past the entrance, but he ignored it and kept going. He needed to get back to the lodge; back to Talia.

Things had gotten complicated, but a plan of action was taking shape.

CHAPTER TWENTY-EIGHT

Talia wasn't aware that her pulse was beating too fast and her anxiety level was climbing toward the red zone until Luke appeared on the covered porch in front of the lobby. Through the windows she watched him remove the plastic rain poncho and shake off the water.

Relief slammed through her. She struggled to conceal it, as well as the ridiculous impulse to fling herself into his arms and yell at him for having turned her into a nervous wreck.

She and the others were scattered around the lobby. A cheerful fire burned on the massive stone hearth. Opting not to make a fool out of herself, she got to her feet and went through the arched opening into the dining room. She poured a mug of coffee and returned to the lobby.

Luke opened the front door and moved into the room. He stopped short when he realized that Marcella, Jasper, and Oliver were staring at him with varying degrees of hopeful expectation.

"Something wrong?" he asked politely.

"I'm afraid I let the secret out," Talia said. The energy around him and the heat in his eyes told her that he had discovered something important in the course of his explorations.

"Since when is private meditation a secret on this island?" Luke said, turning to hang his poncho on a wall hook.

He unzipped his leather jacket but he did not remove it. Talia remembered watching him tuck the pistol into the concealed holster before leaving the cabin.

"Forget the meditation story," she said. "I knew no one would believe me if I told them you had gone out into the storm to meditate, so I said that you were searching for a cell connection."

"Ah." Luke ran his fingers through his damp hair. "That explains the mood of the room."

"No luck, I assume," Marcella said, sounding resigned.

"Afraid not," Luke said. "It was a long shot."

"We got more bad news while you were out," Jasper Draper grumbled. "The ferry

215

was canceled. There's no escape from Night Island today."

Oliver Skinner looked up from the game of solitaire he was playing on the card table. "To prove that things can always get worse, we were informed there's a good chance the ferry won't be operating tomorrow, either. The storm system, we're told, will persist for a while. The term *atmospheric river* was used."

"I'm not surprised the ferry isn't running," Luke said.

Talia walked across the room and handed him the mug of coffee she had just poured. "This is probably a good opportunity for all of us to practice positive thinking."

"Fuck positive thinking," Marcella said. She got up to select a volume from the small bookcase on the far side of the lobby. "Every book here is about the power of mindfulness, or yoga, or meditation, or herbal remedies. I'd kill for a good murder mystery."

"We've already got a dead body cooling in one of the cabins," Oliver said. "Don't know about you, but one's enough, as far as I'm concerned."

Marcella winced. "You're right. Poor choice of words on my part." She selected a book and went back to her chair.

216

Luke glanced around. "Speaking of the power of positive thinking, where's our local guru?"

"He and Chef Octavia are in the office," Talia said. "Morning meditation was canceled along with the ferry."

Luke's expression sharpened. "Where did Gill disappear to?"

"He probably went back to his cabin to meditate on the power of nature," Oliver said. "You know, like you were supposedly doing. Maybe he's got a secret cell phone connection."

Luke looked at Talia. "How long ago did he leave?"

"About fifteen minutes ago." Talia gestured toward the dining room. "The eggs Florentine are gone, but there is still some of the polenta, feta cheese, and eggs casserole left. The feta is made from real sheep's milk, by the way. It's not the cow version."

"I take it that's a good thing?"

"Yep. Also, you're in luck, because I saved a croissant for you."

"Thanks," Luke said. He picked up a plate and helped himself to the last of the polenta casserole. He added the croissant and a slab of butter and sat down at a table.

Talia refilled her coffee and took a chair

across from him. She reminded herself that the guests scattered around the lobby could overhear whatever she said. "When you're finished I thought we could take one of the board games back to the cabin and kill time until lunch."

"Sure," Luke said, forking up a large bite of the polenta dish. "Sounds like a plan."

"The excitement never ends here on Night Island," Jasper Draper sniped from the other room. "Personally, I think I'll take a bottle of whiskey back to my cabin and get drunk."

The door of the office slammed open. Clive Venner's angry voice boomed the length of the hall.

"One more fucking month," he raged. "That's all. You can damn well stick around for four more weeks. We signed a contract, remember? Focus on the money, you stupid bitch. It's the score of a lifetime for both of us. Just one more month."

Heavy footsteps thudded on the floorboards. A moment later the rear door of the lodge opened and slammed shut.

Talia realized she and Luke were not the only ones staring at the entrance of the hallway. The other guests were equally riveted.

"I guess that does it for positivity practice today," Marcella said.

CHAPTER TWENTY-NINE

"Keever's body disappeared?" Talia stared at Luke, stunned. "Why would anyone move it?"

There had been a brief lull in the storm after Luke finished breakfast. They had used the opportunity to grab a board game and make it back to her cabin before the next squall line struck.

The cloud cover seemed darker than ever. She could have sworn that the plants in the gardens had grown taller, the leaves more massive, in the past few hours. The vines growing up the walls of the cabin were starting to obscure the windows, cutting off a lot of what little light was available. Claustrophobia was gnawing at the edge of her awareness.

"There aren't many reasons for moving Keever's body," Luke said. "The obvious one is to make sure it doesn't make it back to the mainland and into the hands of the authorities."

Talia caught her breath. "No body, no questions."

"When you think about it, there's no reason why Keever's death has to be reported."

"But we all saw the body."

"The only thing Jasper Draper, Oliver Skinner, and Marcella Earle care about is getting back to the mainland," Luke said. "Reporting Keever's death is not their problem. They'll leave that to management."

"Who won't have to be bothered if there's no body." Talia paused, thinking through the logic. "Jasper and Oliver and Marcella won't be a problem for Nathan Gill. The Venners probably aren't, either. But you and I are. He doesn't know that, though."

"We have to assume he does know it," Luke said. "The missing body isn't the only news. Keever's cabin was searched, but not for the drugs. They are still there. And here's the next headline: no one is living in the Night Gardener's cabin."

"Meaning?"

"It's empty," Luke said. "There's no indication that anyone has stayed there for a long time. No towels. No clothes. No sheets for the bed. A layer of dust on everything. It had the smell a room gets when it hasn't been opened up in a long time."

Talia sank down on the side of the bed. "This is so weird. If Pomona Finch isn't living in that cabin behind the conservatory, where does she live?"

"Damned if I know," Luke said. He sprawled in the room's single chair, his legs outstretched, a fresh pair of socks on his feet. His boots were sitting in front of the small heater, drying out. "Probably inside the conservatory. That place is big, and there's a jungle inside. You could conceal an entire camper van in there. The more interesting question is, why did Venner lie to us about the Night Gardener's sleeping arrangements?"

"He and Octavia have been living here for six months," Talia said. "By now they've probably learned a few things about whatever is going on here and they know not to talk about it."

"Judging by that argument we overheard, Octavia has had enough. Maybe she's ready to walk before the contract is up."

"If she leaves, Nathan Gill can forget trying to keep the Unplugged Experience going as a cover. Her cuisine is the only thing that makes Night Island even moderately appealing. People are certainly not going to pay for Clive's washed-up meditation chatter."

"No," Luke agreed.

Talia studied the vines on the other side of the window for a moment and then touched the glass with her fingertips, trying to remember how high the snakelike greenery had been the day before.

"I swear, those vines were just starting up the window yesterday," she said. "They are at least a couple of inches taller this morning. I can't believe how quickly plants grow in these gardens. It's like they are on steroids. It doesn't feel natural."

"Nothing about this damned island feels right. Whatever happened here occurred decades ago. Those old botanical experiments must have altered the local ecosystem. And who knows what the Wynford Institute for the Study of Medicinal Botany is screwing around with now?"

Talia touched the crystal pendant at her throat. The vibe was still there; still strong. Still murky. She turned to face Luke. "I was sure we were close to finding Phoebe when we arrived on the island, but now it feels like we're trapped in the garden labyrinth. Going in circles."

"About that," Luke said quietly. "We may have an exit strategy."

He got up, reached into one of his cargo pants pockets, and took out the flashlight-shaped object.

"Something interesting happened this morning when I went past the entrance of the conservatory," he said. "I heard a few pings and the crystals illuminated. The next thing I know, the door unlocked."

"It's a key?"

"Yes."

Adrenaline hit Talia like a tonic. "We have to get inside."

"Agreed. But I think our odds of finding a way in without being noticed will be better if we wait until this evening after dinner. Meanwhile, I'd like you to use your talent."

She nodded, resigned. "You want me to find Keever's body."

"No, I don't think it would give us any more information than we've already got."

"Okay, that's a relief. What am I looking for?"

"Keever was stuck on this island for what must have been six very long months. Unlike the Venners, he was working closely with the Night Gardener and he was a trained botanist. There's a chance he made notes or kept a record of what he and Finch were doing in the conservatory."

"Assuming Gill didn't find them when he

searched Keever's cabin."

"Assuming that, yes."

"What if someone sees us?"

"I don't think anyone is paying attention to Keever's cabin," Luke said.

CHAPTER THIRTY

Octavia was going to fuck up the score of a lifetime. What was wrong with the bitch? Back at the start she had wanted the payoff as much as he did. Now she was threatening to walk.

Clive sank into a chair, hoisted the bottle, and took a long swallow. The whiskey hit him with a soothing warmth. Some of the anxiety that had been eating at him all day melted away.

He hated the damned island as much as Octavia did. When they had signed the contract Gill hadn't said anything about the weird plants and the freaky weather and the scary Night Gardener.

Gill hadn't mentioned the boredom factor, either. That was the worst of it, Clive decided. It hadn't been so bad at first when bookings had usually included at least a couple of attractive females who were eager to learn the secrets of the Venner version of tantric sex. But reservations had plummeted in October and now it was November. Bookings were down to a trickle. December would be even worse.

The last month of the contract was going to be miserable, but come January he would be free. The money would be waiting for him. Octavia could do whatever she wanted after that. But he could not let her leave now. Gill had made it clear the entire contract would be voided if either of them left the island before the end date.

Octavia had become a problem. Thanks to a handful of online reviews celebrating her cooking, she had made the mistake of concluding that she was the star of the show. That was bullshit. She would be nowhere without him. He was the talent. Under other circumstances he would have been delighted to see her leave, but he could not let her jeopardize the whole project, not when they were so close to the endgame.

Clive drank some more whiskey and wondered if Gill had heard the argument in the office. According to the Institute, he was on site to handle any security problems that might arise with the guests, but Clive knew that he was also there to make certain the employees stayed on task. If Octavia really did pack her bags and get on the next ferry,

227

Gill was not going to be happy. He was already quietly furious because Keever had dropped dead of a heart attack. *Or something.*

Who knew what was going on inside the conservatory and underground? Clive thought. All he and Octavia had been told was that the Institute was conducting top secret botanical experiments for an intelligence agency and that some of the plants were poisonous. Gill, the Night Gardener, and Keever were the only ones allowed inside the big glass house and the underworld. Now Keever was dead. Had he threatened to leave? Had Gill murdered him to keep him from breaking the contract? That seemed more than a little extreme. Keever had appeared harmless.

If Gill had murdered Keever, how had he done it? Poison, maybe.

The thought of Gill sent a shiver down Clive's spine. After a moment he got up, lowered the window shades, and locked the door. Octavia would not be coming back to the cabin tonight. She would spend the night in the old housekeeper's room in the lodge, just as she always did whenever they had one of their quarrels. So damned temperamental.

He had to talk to her, convince her not to leave.

The rattle of the doorknob startled him so badly he dropped the whiskey bottle on the threadbare rug. Panic kicked up his pulse. He started to sweat. He was suddenly glad he had thrown the bolt on the door.

He forced himself to take a couple of deep breaths, picked up the bottle, and set it on the small table.

"Just a minute," he called.

He crossed to the window and twitched the curtain aside. When he saw who stood on the front step he relaxed. He opened the door.

"What are you doing here?" he said.

CHAPTER THIRTY-ONE

The plants were more agitated than usual tonight.

It was as if they were aware of the storm on the surface, Pomona Finch thought. Maybe that was precisely what was happening. She wondered if they had a way of pulling the violent energy down through the rock and steel that insulated the underground lab. There was so much she did not know about the amazing specimens that thrived in the vast gardens beneath the surface of the island. So much to be discovered.

She set the Bunsen burner aside, picked up the canister of herbicide, and went to the doorway of the lab. A thrill of excitement hit her when she contemplated the seemingly impenetrable wall of greenery. The horticultural jungle sprawled throughout the human-engineered tunnels. There was no telling how extensive the gardens were. Some sectors were so choked with vegetation they had become impassable. In other regions the plants were simply too dangerous.

The only thing that made it possible to navigate the underworld gardens was the narrow path set with slabs of radiant crystal. The plants had an aversion to the blue light that illuminated the stones and the interior of the lab.

The vegetation thrived on its own version of day and night. Days were marked by a violet radiance that emanated from the walls and the ceiling. The light changed to acid green during the artificial night. The bizarre atmosphere was enhanced by the bioluminescence of the vegetation, which varied from species to species and hybrid to hybrid.

The plants were certainly active now. The leaves and vines rustled and whispered. A thrashing noise could be heard in the areas where the more aggressive species flourished. The atmosphere was getting hotter and more humid.

Six months ago, when she had begun her work on Night Island, the underworld had been comfortably warm. But recently the temperature had been rising. So had the humidity. The changes had been imperceptible at first, but now they could no longer be ignored. The atmosphere in the underground gardens felt like a tropical rainforest. She was convinced that the dead bodies were the problem. They acted like a powerful fertilizer.

She would have to be firm with Nathan Gill. He could no longer use her gardens as a convenient dumping ground. He needed to find another way to get rid of the failures, mistakes, and problems.

She used a towel to mop the perspiration off her forehead and took a moment to savor the sights, smells, and sounds of her personal wonderland. There were times when she could not believe her good luck. She was here, standing on the brink of discoveries that could lead to a Nobel Prize, because an unknown individual at the Wynford Institute for the Study of Medicinal Botany — a nonprofit she had never heard of — had found her name on a list of people who had taken a certain psych test back in college. If not for that test she would still be stuck in a commercial lab running tests on plants destined to end up in face creams and lipsticks.

But now, thanks to the Institute, she was destined to change the world. In the future her name would be known and revered by every researcher, every professor, and every student of botany. Her work would be credited in scientific papers and textbooks for centuries to come.

In exchange for the amazing opportunity all she had to do was ensure that the Institute fulfilled its government contract. Apparently some alphabet soup agency in the intelligence sector needed a couple of psychically enhanced individuals who possessed the ability to terminate bad guys without leaving any evidence. No big deal. Every government employed assassins. She was simply doing her patriotic duty. Besides, the project had proven surprisingly interesting, because it aligned with her own research objectives.

The rustling and the whispering and the thrashing were definitely growing louder. The bioluminescence of the rainforest appeared brighter, too. The storm on the surface was apparently gaining strength.

She started to turn and go back to the lab bench but stopped when she saw the tendrils of green snaking around the edge of the doorframe. It was as if the vines sensed food inside the lab. She smiled. Really, the plants were like mischievous little children at times, always trying to sneak a cookie. Until yesterday she had been able to assign the task of keeping the greenery out of the lab to the assistant gardener. But now that Keever had dropped dead she would have to take care of the job herself.

"Oh, no you don't," she said. "Naughty, naughty."

She aimed the sprayer at the invading tendrils and pulled the trigger. There was a hissing sound as the vines withered beneath the onslaught of the powerful chemicals.

The attempts to invade the lab were new and somewhat worrisome. Six months ago, the blue radiance infused into the walls, ceiling, and floor had acted as a strong barrier, just as the light of the crystal stepping stones did outside. But lately the vegetation, especially the fungi, seemed to be developing some resistance to the energy.

Luckily, the herbicide still worked well. She had found the formula in the old notebook she had been given at the start of the project. Her quarters were inside the lab. She did not want to wake up one day and find herself imprisoned in a cage of protein-hungry vines or discover mushrooms growing in the bedding.

She started to lower the canister but changed her mind when she noticed that the aboveground roots of the walking palm growing on the left side of the lab entrance were closer to the threshold than they had been yesterday. She took a moment to give the entire doorframe an extra dose of the herbicide. No sense taking chances.

When she was finished she returned to the workbench. She was about to pick up the Bunsen burner when something made her glance at the door of the locked room on the far side of the lab. She saw the face peering out at her through the narrow opening that had once held a pane of glass.

The new test subject was awake again. She appeared to have some resistance to the sedative, probably because of her parapsych profile. Time for another dose.

Really, it was one thing after another on this project, but it would all be worth it when she flew to Sweden to accept the Nobel Prize.

CHAPTER THIRTY-TWO

"What do you think?" Luke asked.

"You're right," Talia said. "He hid something in here, and we know it wasn't the key to the conservatory, because he was wearing it on his tool belt when he died."

They were standing inside Eddy Keever's cabin. The door was closed, but the dull gray light of the storm seeped through the tattered shades.

Talia tightened her grip on one of the botany journals that contained a paper written by Keever and took a moment to focus, picking up the unique currents that had been deposited by the dead man. She shivered as another frisson sparked across the back of her neck. Working with the psychic echoes of the dead always put her nerves on edge. At least she wasn't trying to find a body.

"Got it," she said quietly. She put the journal down on the table and turned to examine the room. Pale pools of energy were splashed around the small space. "He was scared, Luke."

"And maybe planning to run? That could explain why he was murdered."

"There's some static because of the heavy paranormal currents here on the island." Talia concentrated, trying to sort out the currents crisscrossing the room. "Makes it hard to sort out the ones I'm searching for."

Luke touched her shoulder. "Are you okay?"

"I'm dealing with the residual energy of a man I know is dead. Feels a bit like conducting an autopsy. But don't worry, I'm not going to faint. I've done this before, remember?"

"Doesn't mean it gets easier."

"No, it doesn't."

She was very conscious of the reassuring warmth of his hand. Having a companion to share the experience with, one who understood how paranormal energy could rattle the senses, made the situation more tolerable. But something else was going on, too, a connection of some kind.

"Hmm," she said.

"What?"

Experimentally, she focused on the heat and weight of his hand and discovered that she could suppress some of the static that was clouding the reading.

Luke started to lift his hand.

"No," she said. She reached up and trapped his hand on her shoulder.

He did not argue or ask questions. He kept quiet and waited.

With the worst of the static partially blocked, her own anxiety was easier to contain and control. She raised her senses another notch.

The patterns of the strongest currents stood out in colors that were beyond the spectrum of normal eyesight. They were sharp and intense and they led to the old, long-unused fireplace.

"Whatever it is, he hid it over there," she said. "The hearth, I think."

Luke took his hand off her shoulder and crossed to the fireplace. He probed the bricks with his fingers. It did not take long to find one that was loose. He pulled it out and set it aside.

They both looked at the dark opening. Luke took out his flashlight and aimed the light into the shadows. The beam glinted on metal. He reached into the recess and pulled out the object that had been hidden behind the brick.

"A camera," he said.

"I wouldn't have thought a digital camera would have worked on this island."

"It's not digital," Luke said. "It's an old-school film camera with a roll of film inside. No high tech involved. But also no way for us to see the photographs until we can get back to the mainland and find a developer. Damn, you are really good at this finding thing."

He meant it sincerely, she realized. There was genuine admiration in his voice and in his eyes. He was not looking at her as if she was a member of the Addams family.

"Thanks," she said, surprised by the warm sensation that infused her from head to toe.

"We found what we came here to find. Let's go."

She could feel the energy charging the atmosphere around him. He was riding a rush. She understood because she could feel the adrenaline cocktail that followed a successful search hitting her system, too. The camera was important. It had to be. Keever wouldn't have gone to the trouble of hiding it unless it held a few secrets.

"I can put the camera inside the pocket of my jacket," she said.

Luke handed it to her and opened the door. The rain was falling steadily again. She pulled up the hood of her coat and followed him out into the storm.

They hurried along one of the garden paths. When they turned a corner Talia caught a glimpse of the conservatory. The plants inside were glowing as if it was the middle of the night.

Her senses were fizzing and flashing thanks to adrenaline and the wild energy of the storm and because of Luke. He was no longer touching her but she could not stop thinking about that moment of intimate connection back in Keever's cottage when he had put his hand on her shoulder and helped her suppress the static.

They made it into her cabin a second before the squall hit. Luke got the door shut, shot the bolt, and stripped off his dripping plastic poncho. She retrieved the camera and set it on the table, and then she shrugged out of her parka. For a moment she stood there, clutching the jacket, and watched Luke hang his things, including the holstered gun, on the wall hooks.

When he turned around she realized she had been staring at him through her rain-splattered lenses. Embarrassed, she yanked off the glasses and set them on the table next to the camera.

Luke took her parka without a word and hung it beside his jacket. Then he sat down on the one chair and stripped off his boots and socks. She sank onto the edge of the lumpy bed and removed her own soaked footwear.

She tried to ignore the tension that seethed in the small space, but it was impossible. There was a fierce, primal, deeply sensual quality about the energy charging the atmosphere. She tried to find a label for the sensations igniting her blood. Passion? Lust? Hunger? Need?

When Luke straightened in the chair, he looked at her with eyes that burned. "We probably shouldn't get too excited about the camera. For all we know the pictures may be scenic views of Night Island."

"No," she said. "Whatever is on that roll of film is important. I'm sure of it."

Luke's mouth kicked up in a grimly satisfied smile. "Yeah. I'm sure of it, too."

She hesitated. "Thanks for not asking me to find Keever's body."

"Like I said, not much point. Also, we don't have time to waste on a search that doesn't promise to yield any useful answers."

Without thinking about it, she reached up and touched the crystal in Phoebe Hatch's necklace. Luke watched in silence, waiting for her verdict. She shook her head and lowered her hand.

"The vibe is still strong," she said. "Phoebe is alive and I'm sure she's somewhere here on the island, but we're no closer to finding her. Whenever I try to get a focus I feel like I'm looking down into a whirlpool. Phoebe is at the bottom. I have no idea how to interpret that visual."

"With luck we'll know more when we get into the conservatory tonight."

"I hope so."

Luke watched her with a speculative expression. "Back in Keever's cabin, when I put my hand on your shoulder —"

"Yes?" she said, trying to maintain a cool edge. *You're a professional.* But she was suddenly a little breathless.

"I got the impression that the physical contact helped you work through the background static."

"Yes, it did."

"Makes sense," Luke said. He frowned a little, serious and thoughtful. Professorial. "The physical connection may have allowed us to combine forces. I think I was able to reinforce your aura so that you were free to concentrate on the search."

Outrage zapped through her. So much for her romantic fantasy. It was depressing, not to mention annoying, to discover that yes, he, too, had sensed the connection between them in Keever's cabin, but no, it hadn't hit his senses with the same wave of sensual heat. She was an adult — she could deal with rejection. But she did not have to put up with an academic lecture.

"Stop right there," she said. "We are not in a classroom, Professor Rand, and I am not in the mood to listen to your theories of paranormal physics. Save it for your next seminar."

His eyes tightened at the corners. "You're pissed."

"Whatever gave you that idea?"

"I'm psychic," he said. "Also, you're looking at me as if you'd like to kick me to the curb — or, in this case, out into the rain."

She crossed her arms. "It's an interesting thought."

He prowled toward her, deliberate and intense. Instinctively she took a step back. That was as far as she could go in the small space.

Luke stopped in front of her, so close she could feel the heat of his body and breathe in his scent.

"Do you want me to tell you what I was really thinking when I put my hand on your shoulder back there in Keever's cabin?" he said.

His voice was freighted with a compelling intimacy. This was the sound of raw desire, she thought.

She managed to catch her breath. "I'd love to hear what you were thinking back there in Keever's cabin, so long as it doesn't involve a lecture on metaphysics."

"I was thinking that I wanted to take you to bed and make you come so hard you would never forget me."

It wasn't poetry, but her intuition told her that he meant every scorching word, and it sounded infinitely more exciting than the date who only looked up from his cell phone long enough to ask, *My place or yours?*

Belatedly she reminded herself that she was not the spontaneous type. She made a stab at logic.

"The effect on your senses may have been caused by the energy of the storm and the weird atmosphere here on Night Island," she said.

"Now you're the one giving the lecture," he said. "Forget the explanations and just answer one question for me."

"What?"

"Did thoughts of having sex with me cross your mind when we touched back there in Keever's cabin?"

She drew a deep breath and prepared to

take the leap into the dark.

"Yes," she said. "Thoughts of that sort did occur."

"You will notice I'm not touching you now."

"So?"

"I still want to take you to bed and make you come so hard you won't be able to forget me."

Nope, she did not need poetry. She needed Luke. She uncrossed her arms and wrapped them around his neck. "I am still having thoughts of going to bed with you."

With a groan he pulled her hard against his chest. His mouth came down on hers, fierce, exciting, demanding, and infused with a primal hunger. An unfamiliar exhilaration dazzled her senses.

The world outside the cabin went away. She had never before experienced raw, elemental passion, but she quickly concluded it was one of those things you recognized when you were swept into it.

They fell onto the bed, tangled up in each other. She was vaguely aware of the squeaks of the aging springs, but she ignored them, because Luke was sprawled on top of her, his mouth shifting from her lips to her throat.

"You smell so good," he whispered.

"So do you." She threaded her fingers through his damp hair. "Wild. Like the storm."

He got her pullover off and then his mouth was on her breasts. She managed to strip him to the waist and flatten her hands on his chest. He stroked her slowly all the way down to the damp heat between her thighs. When he found her core with his fingers she shivered and strained against him, needing more.

He leaned over her, his eyes burning. "I knew it would be like this."

She clenched her fingers into the sleek muscles of his shoulder. "Did you?"

"Right from the start. Hang on. I've got some condoms somewhere at the bottom of my duffel."

He rolled to the side of the bed. She braced herself on her elbow and watched as he leaned over to unzip the duffel. When he turned back to her a moment later he rested one leg across the inside of her thigh, gently pinning her.

"We are going to be perfect together," he said.

"Maybe not perfect, but that's okay," she said. "Not a problem. Really."

His eyes gleamed with wicked laughter.

"Why are you expecting less than great results?"

"I didn't pack my vibrator," she said.

"That's okay, I've got good hands."

He kissed her again before she could say anything else.

She twined one leg around his and reached down to grasp the rigid length of his fierce erection. Knowing that he wanted her so intensely gave her a euphoric sense of her own power.

The tension inside her escalated swiftly. She was already wet and aroused and shivering with anticipation.

He was right, she thought. He did have good hands. He used them to trigger her first climax. It took her by surprise. She was still glorying in the thrill when he eased himself deep inside her. Instinctively she tightened around him.

"Yes," he said, his mouth very close to her ear. "Like that. Perfect."

His voice pulled her back into the vortex.

The winds howled around the cabin and the vines slapped the windows. Lightning cracked and thunder rolled. She knew the elemental forces of nature were laying down the soundtrack for her memories of this time with Luke.

When her second climax struck it took

her breath. She could not even cry out. But there was no time to contemplate that astonishing fact, because Luke was surging into her one last time, his whole body granite-hard.

"Talia."

She wrapped herself around him and he held her as if he would never let go. She told herself it was enough, but Luke was right — she was a lousy liar.

CHAPTER THIRTY-THREE

The violent forces of the storm dissipated sometime later, leaving behind a steady rain. Talia sat up on the side of the bed, the quilt wrapped around her, and watched Luke emerge from the bathroom. He was in his trousers and a fresh T-shirt. His hair was still damp from the shower. There was a satisfied energy about him, and he startled her with a quick, sexy grin.

"No vibrator?" he said. "No problem."

She dissolved into laughter, got to her feet, grabbed some clothes, and headed for the bathroom.

"You sound way too smug," she said.

"I do, don't I?"

She turned to look at him through the doorway. "I will admit you confirmed one of my initial observations about you."

"Yeah? What was that?"

"Back at the beginning I told myself that you possessed very competent hands."

249

Luke's brows rose. "Merely competent?"

"New data has been received. I can now upgrade the analysis to excellent. Quite possibly the greatest of all time."

"GOAT. Wow. Be still my heart. Is there an award?"

"Maybe."

She closed the bathroom door and turned on the shower.

Fifteen minutes later, she walked out of the steamy room dressed in jeans and a pullover. Her hair was once again in a snug bun. She found her glasses on the table and put them on. It took her a beat to realize something was missing.

"Where is the camera?" she asked.

"I put it back in your parka," he said. "I don't want to take a chance and accidentally leave it in the room when we go to lunch."

"Good idea." She glanced at the wall clock. "Speaking of lunch, it's almost noon. When I asked Chef Octavia about the day's menu this morning she said something about a Comté and leek quiche. I'm starving."

"I'm hungry, too." Luke appeared somewhat surprised by that realization. "Guess we both worked up an appetite."

Talia started to respond, but a nerve-icing

scream stopped her cold.

"What on earth — ?" she gasped.

"Sounded like a woman," Luke said. He was already reaching for his holster and pistol. "Octavia or Marcella."

"Or the Night Gardener, Pomona Finch," Talia said, cramming her feet into her still-damp boots.

Luke shrugged into his jacket and opened the door. "The scream came from some-where near the lodge."

The shrill cry had ceased but it seemed to echo endlessly through the gardens. Talia pulled on her parka and followed Luke out into the dripping gardens. They raced along the path that led to the lodge. They were not the only ones responding.

"What's going on?" Jasper shouted from a nearby path. "Who's screaming? Marcella? Is that you?"

"No," Marcella shouted. "I think it was Octavia."

Talia rounded a corner a few steps behind Luke and saw Oliver Skinner standing in front of the lobby entrance. He was not alone. Marcella was with him.

"What the fuck is happening around here?" Oliver rasped. "I just want off this island."

"You aren't the only one," Marcella said.

Jasper appeared, breathing hard. "Did the scream come from inside the lodge?"

"I'm not opening that door," Marcella said. "There's no telling who or what is in there."

Luke went up the porch steps, opened the lobby door, and stepped inside. He reappeared almost immediately. "There's no one here. The scream must have come from the Venner cabin."

No one objected when he led the way around the lodge. Talia and the others fell into step behind him.

Octavia was on the front steps of the cabin she shared with Clive. She was sobbing, her arms wrapped around her waist.

Talia went forward quickly. "What's wrong, Octavia? Are you hurt?"

She started to put a comforting hand on Octavia's shoulder but stiffened when she sensed the frissons of cold, dark energy seeping out the open door of the cabin.

"Oh, shit," she whispered.

Luke was already easing past her. He went to the door and disappeared inside.

"I hate this place," Octavia said. Rage seethed in the words, mingling with the tears. "I told Clive we should never have come here. But he wouldn't listen. It was all about the money, you see. The last big score, he said."

Luke reappeared in the doorway. His cold, hard eyes told Talia that whatever had gone down inside the cabin was bad. Nathan Gill was behind him. He, too, looked grim.

"Clive Venner is dead," he said, his voice flat and tense. "Looks like a heart attack or a stroke."

"Same as the assistant gardener," Marcella whispered. "What are the odds? Something terrible is going on here."

Octavia clenched her hands into fists. "There is a malevolent force on this island. It's going to murder all of us. We have to get off."

Talia put her fingertips on Octavia's arm. "Let's go to the lodge. I'll make some tea."

"Don't touch me." Octavia jerked back as if Talia's fingers were live electrical wires. "Get away from me. I don't trust any of you."

Talia went back down the steps.

Luke looked at Nathan. "You'll need help with the body. We can put it with Keever's."

Slick, Talia thought. Nathan's reaction might tell them if he was aware that the assistant gardener's body was no longer in the cabin.

But there was no chance to analyze Nathan's response, because Octavia spoke first.

"Leave Clive's body where it is," she said. "I am not going to spend the night in this cabin. I'll move into the lodge until the ferry gets here tomorrow."

"Assuming there is a ferry run tomorrow," Oliver muttered.

"All right," Nathan said to Octavia. "I'll help you pack a few things for tonight."

Octavia nodded once in brusque agreement and followed Nathan into the cabin.

"Good idea," Marcella announced. "I'm going to go back to my cabin, pack my things, and move into the lodge with Octavia. I don't want to be alone."

"I'm with you," Jasper said. "Safety in numbers and all that. The cabins are too isolated. I'll pick up my stuff and meet you in the lodge."

"I'll join you," Oliver Skinner said. He looked at Luke and Talia. "What about you two?"

"Talia and I are going to stick together in our cabin," Luke said. "We'll join you for dinner."

"Suit yourself," Oliver said. "But we don't know what the fuck is going on here, and Jasper is right. There's safety in numbers."

"You've got a point," Luke said. "We'll think about it."

He took Talia's arm and steered her back

through the labyrinth gardens, heading toward the cabin. She waited until they were out of earshot of the others before speaking.

"Let me guess," she said. "Another death by paranormal means?"

"That's what it felt like," Luke said. "But I can't be absolutely certain. It's not like I've had a lot of experience detecting murder by paranormal means, Talia."

"Sorry. I didn't mean to grill you." She touched the crystal at her throat. "I'm still fumbling along with my new talent, too. Hmm."

"What?"

"It will be interesting to see if Venner's body disappears, too."

"We are not hanging around to find out," Luke said. "Plans have changed. We're going into the conservatory now, not tonight. We can't risk wasting any more time. Two people are dead and our only lead is that hothouse."

"What if someone sees us trying to break in?" Talia said.

"It will be more interesting if someone tries to stop us," Luke said.

CHAPTER THIRTY-FOUR

"There's definitely no need for a jacket in here," Talia said. She surveyed the mass of vibrant green foliage that crammed the interior of the conservatory, awed and fascinated by the energy in the humid atmosphere. "It feels like we're in Hawaii."

The hothouse was laden with the earthy scents of vegetation that was thriving with uncanny vigor.

Luke looked around. "There's something going on with these plants. It's as if they're reacting to the storm. Listen."

He was right, Talia thought. There was a low-level rustling sound, and the leaves of many of the plants were gently shifting and undulating. The greenery in the outside gardens was agitated because it was being whipped and lashed by the wind and the rain. But here, inside the conservatory, the vegetation was protected by the glass walls and steel skeleton of the structure. The foliage should not be stirring, and yet it was.

The flashlight-shaped device had worked without a hitch. The pinging had become steady when she and Luke got close to the steel door. The black crystals had sparked a short time later and the heavy door had opened. They had stepped into an airlock-like chamber. When the outer door closed and relocked, the glass door inside had opened, allowing them into the plant-filled space.

"It's easy to talk about the power of nature, but when you're confronted with it like this there are no good adjectives," Talia said. "I wonder why these plants haven't smashed through the glass bricks and taken over the island."

"Good question." Luke looked down at the glowing crystal stones beneath their feet. "The root systems should have turned this flooring to rubble over the decades. Hard to believe this place has been running on old technology since the last half of the twentieth century. Hell, they were still working with slide rules in those days."

"They got to the moon in the last century using slide rules," Talia reminded him.

"Fair point. Anything new from Phoebe's necklace?"

Talia reached up to touch the crystal. Her

pulse skittered when she realized that the energy pulsing from it was stronger. "We're definitely closer to her, but I'm still getting the impression of a whirlpool."

"She must be in here somewhere."

"It's going to be hard to search this place. The plants look impenetrable. We would need machetes to hack through them."

"Maybe not," Luke said, cool certainty infusing his voice. "There's a path."

He walked across the stone floor and stopped at the edge of a wall of greenery. He reached out and pulled some of the leaves aside.

"Here we go," he said. "Whoever built this place used the same stones as those in the labyrinth gardens."

She went forward to join him and saw a path of faintly glowing stones set into the rich soil. Only three were clearly visible. The fourth peeked out from under a screen of violet orchids.

"Stay close," Luke said. "For all we know there may be several paths in here, just like there are in the gardens. If I lose you it could take a very long time to find you."

That hurt. Well, sure, she was being overly sensitive, but she had a right to a few emotions. A short time ago she had been in bed with the man, having the most amazing sex of her entire life and telling herself that she and Luke had some sort of special psychic bond, blah, blah, blah, and now he was complaining about the possibility of having to look for her if she got lost. It was too much.

"Right." She gave him an overly bright smile. "Wouldn't want you to be forced to waste time searching for me. Priorities."

He shot her a severe but baffled look. "I'm serious. This place is a miniature jungle."

"I noticed."

He hesitated for a beat. She got the feeling he was going to launch into a lecture on other potential or theoretical dangers that might be lurking in the conservatory.

"We should probably get moving," she said.

Evidently concluding this was not a good time for an argument, he turned around and moved forward along the path. She stayed close behind him. He was right. She really did not want to get lost in this place.

The stepping stones led straight into the thickest part of the foliage. She could feel the energy in Phoebe's pendant growing more intense. Excitement kicked up her pulse again. She decided to forget that she was irritated with Luke.

"This is the right direction," she said,

touching the crystal.

"You're sure she's still alive?"

Talia tightened her fingers around the stone and opened her senses. "Yes."

"Keever's device is pinging again," Luke said. "Maybe we're close to another door."

He shoved aside one last massive leaf and they moved into a clearing created by the stone paving tiles. In the center of the space was what looked like a bank vault door inlaid in the floor. A metal plate set with a grid of crystals was embedded in the steel.

"This isn't new," Luke said, crouching to touch the door. "It looks like it was constructed and installed at about the same time as the conservatory and the lodge."

The key device was pinging steadily now. The circle of black crystals sparked. The stones in the vault-like door blinked. Talia heard the muffled rumble of heavy gears. The vault door began to lift on massive hinges. A violet-and-green-tinged radiance glowed in the opening. Luke straightened, took the pistol out from under his jacket, and reached for Talia's arm. He tugged her back a few steps.

"If a big green tentacle comes out of there I may need my fainting couch," Talia warned.

"I'll join you," Luke said. He did not take

his attention off the opening. "According to my research, there was a time back in the middle of the last century when a lot of people built underground fallout shelters in their backyards in case of a nuclear war. I've never seen one, but maybe that's what this is."

"A fallout shelter inside a conservatory?" Talia shook her head. "Seems weird."

"This whole island is weird."

The vault door was several inches off the ground now. A flight of glowing blue steps appeared. The eerie violet and green radiance issued from the depths, carrying powerful currents of energy and the scents of rich, moist soil and vegetation.

The vault door clanged to a stop, now fully open.

"Not a bomb shelter," Luke said. He moved closer again and looked down the steps. "An underground conservatory, or maybe a grow house."

Talia joined him. She could see the fronds of some massive ferns near the bottom of the blue staircase. "Those definitely aren't marijuana plants."

"No, they're not."

Talia felt the pendant shiver. This time when she touched it there was no static. The vibe was clear.

"Phoebe is down there, Luke."

"Of course she is," Luke muttered. "Why would this case not get even more complicated? All right, I'll go first. Stay close. Keep the pepper spray handy. If I say run, don't ask questions, just do it."

"What makes you think I'd ask questions if you yell run?"

"I've come to the conclusion that you don't take orders well."

"I may have a few character flaws, but I've also got a strong sense of self-preservation. Don't worry, if you yell run, I'll run."

"Good to know." Luke considered briefly. "It's going to be hot down there. Might as well leave our jackets behind. I'll put the camera in my pack."

"Okay."

She gave him the camera and then peeled off her parka. She was careful to leave the garment on the stone tiles, a couple of feet from the nearest plants. Luke removed his jacket and then handed the key device to her.

"You're in charge of this gadget," he said.

"Okay."

Pistol in hand, Luke started down the steps. Talia took a deep breath and followed him into the glowing depths. The damp heat intensified rapidly as they descended. So did the strange light. The eerie glow emanated from the walls and the high ceiling, revealing a jungle of tightly packed foliage. The plants were bioluminescent, adding to the otherworldly atmosphere.

She tightened her grip on the device and told herself to breathe. She could do this. Panic was not an option.

Her glasses fogged up before she was halfway down the steps. Annoyed, she propped them on top of her head. The underworld scene blurred. She gripped the railing to make sure she did not trip.

Luke reached the floor of the vast underground chamber and studied the sea of glowing foliage.

"You know, I wouldn't be surprised to see a couple of dinosaurs walk past," he said.

"Hopefully not a T. rex." Talia shook her head, amazed. "We thought what was happening on the surface and in the conservatory was bizarre. This is jaw-dropping. It feels like something went very wrong down here."

Luke wiped sweat off his forehead. "There's a hell of a lot of energy in the atmosphere."

"The plants down here are even more agitated than those on the surface, but there's no wind or rain." Talia shuddered.

"Listen to them. It's almost as if they're whispering about us. Maybe wondering if we're food."

"You have a very vivid imagination. Forget the plants. There's a path. Same kind of stones that we saw in the conservatory and the aboveground gardens, but these look hotter."

"As in too hot to touch?"

"No, as in radiating stronger paranormal energy."

Talia slipped her glasses down over her eyes and took a quick look at the glowing path that sliced through the towering plants. "I get the feeling that the people who constructed this place lost control of their experiments."

"They were screwing around with forces they didn't understand," Luke said.

Talia looked at a cluster of radiant mushrooms growing in the shadows cast by massive leaves and then realized that her glasses were fogging up again. She positioned them back on her head.

"I wonder what happened to make the researchers shut down the project."

"Maybe the results turned out to be too dangerous to pursue," Luke suggested. "Or maybe the funding got cut off because experimenting with the paranormal became a third rail for any scientist or politician who was serious about a career. In the course of my own work I've come across several instances of projects involving psychic phenomena that were quietly closed down."

"Did any of those projects involve botanical research?"

"Yes, but most of those labs were small operations, usually attached to academic institutions. There was only one program that I'm aware of that would have had the resources to establish a facility like this, and officially it never existed. It's a legend among those who study the history of the paranormal."

"What was —" Talia began. She was interrupted by the quickening pulse of the crystal in Phoebe Hatch's necklace. She reached up to touch the stone. "The vibe from the crystal is very strong and clear now. Phoebe is down here somewhere, and she's close."

They moved cautiously forward. The plants on either side of the stepping stones stirred and swayed. Leaves clashed against each other. A frond came out of nowhere, brushing Talia's arm as if tasting her. She gasped and quickly pulled away. A particularly aggressive vine reached for Luke's neck. He yanked it off.

"Does the word *carnivorous* come to mind?" Talia asked.

"Yes, it does," Luke said. "Whatever you do, don't step off the path."

"Trust me, I'm not —" She stopped abruptly as the familiar dark frissons lanced her senses. "Oh, *shit.*"

Luke whipped around. "What?"

She turned to stare at the mass of greenery on one side of the path. "I think I just found Keever's body."

Luke lowered the pistol and reached out to push aside a curtain of wide leaves.

"You mean, what's left of the body," he said quietly.

Talia stared at the sole of a running shoe and the torn pant legs of a pair of trousers. The clothing looked as if it had been shredded by scissors, but the thorn-studded vines draped around what was left of Keever's legs told the real story. The rest of the body, or what was left of it, was concealed by a blanket of orange mushrooms.

Talia turned away, swallowing hard to suppress the nausea. Luke touched her shoulder.

"That answers one question," he said. "Whoever decided to get rid of Keever's body knew enough about this place to realize that the plants could make it disappear."

"Nathan Gill. He must have been the one who murdered Keever and later hid the body."

"I'm not sure he murdered Keever," Luke said. "I keep thinking about how he searched the body while trying to make us think he was checking for injuries. If he was the killer, why not do the search at the time?"

"Maybe he got interrupted and had to leave the scene."

"Maybe." Luke sounded doubtful.

"Do you think Clive Venner will end up down here, too?"

"I wouldn't be surprised."

Luke eased past some cascading foliage and stopped. Talia joined him. Together they looked at the doorway. It opened onto a large chamber illuminated with a familiar blue radiance.

There were no plants inside. A long workbench laden with lab apparatus stood in the center of the room. A table littered with a scattering of vintage scientific equipment had been pushed to one side. Faded charts and graphs hung on the walls. A collection of heavy-duty gardening tools was piled in a corner.

There was no one around, but a cot, sleeping bag, two suitcases, and some discarded energy bar wrappers occupied one corner. A white lab coat hung on a wall hook. A pair of muddy boots sat on the floor. A partially open door revealed the white porcelain tiles of a bathroom fitted with fixtures that were decades out of date.

"We now know where the Night Gardener hangs out," Talia said. "I wonder where she is?"

When there was no response from Luke, she turned to look at him. He was standing very still, the pistol in his hand. Something about his eyes made her wonder if he had gone into a trance.

"Luke?" she said gently. "What is it? What's wrong?"

He focused on her, his gaze suddenly rapier sharp. "I know this place. This is where they tried to turn me into a monster."

CHAPTER THIRTY-FIVE

The powerful emotions sweeping through Luke worried her. She reminded herself that she, too, would be in shock if the memories of her lost night suddenly returned, but they did not have time for him to process this new development right now.

She moved forward to stand directly in front of Luke. "I understand that you've had a jolt. This is the scene of the experiment that was designed to turn you into a psychic assassin. What you need to remember is that the experiment failed. Yes, you have a powerful psychic talent, but you are not an assassin. You did not become a rogue killer, either."

Luke watched her. "How do you know that?"

"Assassins do it for the money. Rogue killers do it for the thrill. You don't fit into either of those categories. Now it's time for you to do what you do so well."

His eyes tightened. "What is that?"

"Compartmentalize. We'll deal with the fallout from your recovered memories later. Is that clear?"

Luke almost smiled. Almost. "Thanks. I needed that."

"Anytime. Right now we have to find Phoebe Hatch. She is somewhere nearby."

"Yes, she is."

Talia realized he was now focused on a point behind her. She lowered her glasses again and turned to look at the closed doors of the two offices on the far side of the room. Each had a slim opening that must have contained glass at one time.

Luke was already moving. He went around her and crossed to the offices. She hurried after him. When she passed the stainless steel workbench her attention was snagged by the one item that looked out of place among the assortment of new scientific apparatus — a vintage leather-bound notebook that was open to a yellowed page covered in faded handwriting.

"She's here," Luke announced. "At least, I assume the woman in there is Phoebe Hatch. She's either asleep or else she's been drugged."

Talia saw that he was looking through the empty window of one of the offices. He wrapped one hand around the knob.

"The door's locked," he announced. He pounded on the metal panel. "She's not responding." He turned to take another look at the interior of the lab. "There must be something in here I can use to force it."

He crossed the room to examine the clutter of vintage gardening tools.

Talia moved to peer through the small window. She flattened one hand on the door panel and knew with unshakable certainty that the woman on the cot inside was Phoebe Hatch.

"Phoebe," she said. "Wake up."

There was no response from the woman on the cot.

"This should work," Luke said.

Talia glanced at him and saw that he was holding a sturdy garden trowel. She stepped out of the way and watched as he used the tool to pry open the door. The lock groaned and snapped with a sharp, violent crack. The door swung open on old, squeaking hinges.

"See if you can wake her," Luke said. "I'll keep watch. Pomona Finch must be somewhere nearby."

Talia slipped past him and leaned over the sleeping woman.

"Phoebe, it's me, Talia March from the

Lost Night Files podcast. Luke and I are here to get you out of this place."

Phoebe muttered something and her eyelashes fluttered, but she did not awaken. Talia put a hand on her shoulder and shook her gently.

"Phoebe. Please wake up."

Phoebe stirred. Her eyelashes shivered again. "Drugs. Can't stay awake. Help me."

"Hurry," Luke said. "If you can't get her on her feet I'll have to carry her."

"Please," Phoebe whispered. She moved her fingers in a shaky way. "Help me."

Talia looked at Luke. "She's aware of us and she's trying to surface, but the drug is pushing her under. Maybe you can use your talent to counteract it."

"What are you talking about? My talent is good for making people unconscious or worse. I don't know how to pull someone out of a sedated sleep state."

"Have you ever tried?"

Luke frowned. "No. It never occurred to me to try. There's never been an opportunity to run an experiment like that."

"Well, here's your big chance to prove your new talent is not the bad news you think it is. Pull Phoebe back to the surface or you're going to have to carry her out of here while you hold on to a gun and fight

272

off those plants. That's not going to be easy."

Luke hesitated and then he loped back across the room. He entered the office and crouched close to the cot. Talia felt energy lift in the already overheated atmosphere. Luke's talent suddenly electrified the small space. Powerful currents swirled.

"Where are you, Phoebe?" he asked.

The compelling energy in the words shuddered in the atmosphere.

"In a dream," Phoebe said. A shiver went through the words and her limp frame.

"It's time to wake up."

"Can't. Tried."

But she sounded a little stronger now, Talia thought. The energy in the room was still surging, but it felt steadier. More controlled. She realized that Luke was trying to locate the wavelengths he needed to manipulate in order to try to draw Phoebe out of the dream. There was probably a steep learning curve involved.

"You can wake up, Phoebe," Luke said. "Follow my voice. It will lead you out of the dream. Just follow my voice —"

Phoebe shuddered violently and sat straight up on the cot. She stared at Luke as if she was trying to decide if he was part of her dream.

"Who are you?" she gasped. "Don't hurt

me. Please don't hurt me."

Luke glanced at Talia, uncertain how to handle the new development. She stepped forward and put one hand on Phoebe's rigid shoulder. She held out the pendant in her other hand.

"It's all right, Phoebe," she said. "Luke is not going to hurt you. He and I are here to get you away from this place. I'm Talia March. Remember me? *The Lost Night Files.*"

Relief washed over Phoebe in a visible wave. She took the pendant with trembling fingers. "You found me."

"Thanks to that pendant," Talia said, easing Phoebe to her feet.

Luke went back to the doorway. "You can have that conversation later. Right now we need to get out of here. The light out there is changing. The violet energy is fading, turning more green. The plants are making a lot of noise. Doesn't sound good."

Phoebe looked toward the doorway. "This is their version of night. It's when they are most active. Lately they've been getting more aggressive during the green cycle."

"Who told you that?" Talia asked.

"I heard the Night Gardener say that to her assistant." Phoebe grimaced. "Google *mad scientist* and you'll find her picture."

"Where is she now?" Luke asked.

"Probably out in the gardens collecting specimens," Phoebe said. "She spends a lot of time with the plants."

"We may need weapons to fight off the plants on the way out," Luke said.

He tucked the pistol into his belt and crossed the room to the array of oversized gardening tools. He selected two wicked-looking pruning shears and a long gardening fork. After a moment's consideration he picked up a tool belt studded with various implements and slung it over one shoulder.

He went back to Talia and Phoebe and handed each of them a pruner.

"I'll go first," he said. "Phoebe in the middle. Talia, you're number three."

"Got it," she said.

How dare you interfere with my research?"
The screech of outrage came from the doorway of the laboratory. Talia and the others turned to see Pomona Finch on the threshold. She was wearing a white lab coat, white trousers, and white booties over her shoes. A white cap covered her hair. She gripped a canister with a trigger in a gloved hand. There were no markings on the canister, but Talia was sure it was not a fire extinguisher.

"You kidnapped Phoebe," Luke said.

"That happens to be illegal. We're taking her back to the surface."

Energy whispered in the atmosphere around him. Talia heard the low, mesmeric note in his voice and knew he was pulling on his talent.

"I didn't kidnap her," Pomona snapped. "Nathan brought her to me. She's on the list, you see. She is not an ideal candidate, but one must work with what's available. In a few more days I'll be ready to treat her with the new version of the drug."

"You're not going to be running any more experiments, Finch," Luke said. "We're leaving now."

He started forward, the lethal-looking gardening fork gripped rather casually in one hand. But Pomona did not appear intimidated. She aimed the nozzle of the canister at Luke.

"Stop or I'll spray you with the herbicide," Pomona said. "I'm not sure what it will do to a human. Haven't had an opportunity to run that experiment. But I know what it can do to the plants out there in the gardens. It is the only thing that can control them now."

"Well, shit," Luke said. "I don't think I've run into this particular problem before."

CHAPTER THIRTY-SIX

Luke Rand was a failed experiment. He should have gone insane. He should have been dead by now.

The only good news was that there was no indication he had any real talent, let alone one that could kill. As for Talia March, she was merely a low-level talent like the other two women involved with *The Lost Night Files.* Yet somehow Rand and March, working together, had not only managed to locate Night Island but had forced the shutdown of the Cold Fire project. There was only one logical conclusion — Rand's memories were returning. So much for the long-term amnesia effects of the sedative.

Fucked. Cold Fire 2.0 was fucked.

Nathan Gill shoved his way through the plant-choked conservatory, careful to stay on the radiant stone path. He wore heavy gloves, a leather jacket, and boots. To date none of the specimens inside the glass-and-steel walls were showing signs of turning carnivorous, but given what was happening down below, he didn't want to take any chances. Finch had warned him there was an elevated risk that some of the fungi might escape the lab. Once that happened, she said, it would be only a matter of time before the gardens on the surface became a serious threat.

The fucking fungi ruled the world and did it from underground.

A year ago his innate sensitivity to energy from the paranormal end of the spectrum had led him to the small antiquarian bookstore where he had discovered the logbook. The record of the decades-old experiments had made it possible for him to locate the entrance to the underground lab on Night Island.

Acquiring control of the island had been a simple process of altering the old tax and property records online, but it had taken months to set up the project. He'd had to find and hire the Venners. Then he'd had to track down the two disgraced pharmaceutical researchers who had been willing to take a contract to run the first round of Cold Fire experiments. Personnel management was tricky when you were forced to work with expendable employees, people who would not be missed.

Six months ago the project had finally gotten underway. Unfortunately, the first round of experiments had ended in disaster. The two test subjects had lapsed into comas and died. The researchers had tweaked the serum. There had been two more failures. Both subjects had gone mad and had to be terminated.

At last, three months ago, there had been a success. Unfortunately, there had also been another failure — Rand. But instead of sliding into a coma he had evidently awakened in a state of acute disorientation, grabbed a scalpel, slit the throats of the two researchers, and escaped the lab.

He should have gone insane within weeks, because he had never received regular boosters. He should have *died.*

Pomona Finch had been thrilled when she had been invited to take over the lab. She hadn't even blinked when she realized that the end product of her work would be psychically enhanced assassins. But then, Finch didn't much care for people in general. The only things that mattered to her were the plants.

A few weeks ago he had been unlucky enough to get caught in the lab when an unexpected storm system had struck the island. There had been no safe way to get back to the surface until morning. He had been forced to spend the night listening to Pomona Finch hum to herself while she conducted experiments and tests on various plant specimens.

When she finally announced that she was ready to run her first experiment on a human subject, he selected another name from the list. He had been making preparations to pick up the individual when another disaster struck: he had discovered that someone else was in possession of the very same list and was trying to market it online.

He had managed to track down Phoebe Hatch before the other buyers got to her through a combination of good luck and the psychic-grade digital talents of his half sister, Celina.

In theory, Celina had no reason to assist him in the Night Island project. A success would only serve to reinforce her status as a loser in the fucking succession game their father was forcing his three offspring to play. But Cutler Steen had not taken into account the complex forces at work in sibling rivalries. Celina's anger and resentment at dear old Dad had trumped her desire to see her half brother fail.

He now knew how Celina felt, Nathan

thought. Too many things had gone wrong with Cold Fire 2.0 because he had been forced to work with unreliable assets like Finch and Keever and the Venners.

It wasn't like he'd had much choice. There were not a lot of brilliant researchers who were eager to work in an underground lab dedicated to illegal paranormal experiments. And although there were plenty of con artists who could have run a scam like the Unplugged Experience, there weren't many who were willing to set up shop on a lonely island in the San Juans and agree to stay there for an extended period of time.

Nathan emerged from the thick foliage and stopped on the stone floor. He looked down at the big vault door. It stood open. The muddy footprints, the discarded poncho, and the jackets told him that everything he had feared was true. Rand and March had not only found the key on Keever's body, they had figured out how to activate it and it had led them straight to his secrets.

Cold Fire 2.0 was dead. Yes, he had one success — proof of concept — but Rand and March had made it impossible to continue the project on Night Island. It didn't matter if they lived or died. Either way they were a problem, because they would draw too much attention to the island. If they failed to return to the main-land, the damned podcast crew would come looking for them. If they made it back to Seattle, they would report the two deaths.

So, yes, time to cut his losses and clean up. Luckily he had Subject B, the one suc-cess of the Cold Fire 2.0 project.

He aimed the key at the steel door. The device pinged. The crystals flashed. The gate to the underworld closed and locked.

CHAPTER THIRTY-SEVEN

"I'm serious," Pomona said, her voice climbing. "The herbicide is lethal." She started to squeeze the trigger.

Talia held her breath but Luke was talking again, each word carrying currents of hypnotic energy.

"We believe you," he said. "You want to put the canister down. It's getting very heavy. You need to set it on the floor and get some sleep."

"No," Pomona whispered. The canister trembled in her grasp. She almost dropped it. "What are you doing to me?"

"I'm helping you get some sleep," Luke said. "You're exhausted."

Pomona shivered. "I'm cold. It's not cold in here. Why am I so cold?"

"Because your body is shutting down so that you can rest," Luke said.

Talia wasn't feeling the icy currents; nevertheless, she shivered when she heard them in Luke's voice. Phoebe took a step back and hugged herself.

"Something is wrong." Pomona watched Luke as if she was seeing a vision, but she did not go down. Instead, she stumbled backward. She was still clutching the canister but she was no longer aiming it. Her eyes widened. "I know who you are. Subject A. The failure. Nathan Gill told me you had gone insane and died."

Luke froze. Talia knew that Pomona's statement had fractured his concentration.

"What do you know about me?" he asked much too softly.

Pomona, no longer under the spell of his talent, raised the canister again, her finger tightening on the trigger.

"You're the test subject who disappeared after the first round of experiments," Pomona said. "Gill was sure you had not survived. He said you had gone insane and died within hours. Something about a boat fire. But then, he was convinced the enhancement drug hadn't worked on you, either."

"What made him so certain the drug didn't enhance my talent?" Luke asked.

"Because you used a scalpel to slit the throats of the two researchers who ran the initial trials, of course. Why use a blade and leave a mess if you had a lethal psychic talent? Regardless, you should be dead by now."

Out of the corner of her eye, Talia saw Phoebe flinch and turn to look at Luke as if he had metamorphosed into a monster. That was unfortunate, but there was no time to deal with the problem. She focused on Pomona.

"Why was Gill so certain that Luke had died?"

"I faked my own death," Luke said, his expression tight as he concentrated. "I remember some of it now. I stole the cruiser that was tied up at the dock. When I was near one of the other populated islands I set the boat on fire and sank it. I walked into town. I had some cash on me. I bought a ticket on a ferry and got off in Seattle."

"No," Pomona said, her tone that of someone lecturing a not very bright student. "The reason Gill was so sure you would be dead by now is because you never got the boosters."

"Boosters?" Luke said.

"According to the logbook, the original Cold Fire protocol was designed to require regular boosters," Pomona said, still in lecture mode. "They need to be administered every six to seven weeks. The idea was to make certain the subjects remained under control, you see." Pomona chuckled. "Can't have a bunch of psychic assassins take it into their heads to get rid of the boss and go off on their own, now, can we? They must understand that would be writing their own death warrants."

"Well, obviously the protocol is flawed," Talia said. "Luke is still very much alive, and quite sane."

"Yes, I can see that," Pomona said. Feverish excitement sparked in her eyes. "That is a fascinating outcome. I have a theory, but I need to do some more research."

"What's your theory?" Luke said, his voice dark and fierce.

"I was given a copy of your file to study," Pomona said. "You certainly fit the parapsych profile required for the project, but your innate talent was unusually strong, even before enhancement. You were born with the ability to handle a high degree of sensory overload. The Cold Fire serum strengthened your natural talent, but you were able to adjust to the change. This is fascinating. I'm going to need some blood samples and an MRI —"

"Forget it," Luke said. "Who was the other test subject who was in this lab at the same time I was here?"

Pomona frowned, distracted. "I have no idea. The file didn't contain that sort of personal information. All I can tell you is that Subject B was considered a success."

"If that's all you know, it's time to put the canister down," Luke said.

"Why should I do that?" Pomona shot back. "You're worth a lot to me alive, but I can learn almost as much from you if you're dead. A proper autopsy will yield a great deal of information."

"This ends here," Luke said. "You are not going to use the shit in that canister on me or anyone else."

The shuddering power of the currents in his voice slammed into Pomona. She reeled back, her mouth open on a silent shriek. She tried to squeeze the trigger of the canister, but she was shaking so hard she could not manage to aim the nozzle.

"You can't do this to me," she gasped. "You can't be allowed to interfere with my work. There's a Nobel Prize waiting for me."

"More likely a prison cell," Luke said. "Time to sleep, Pomona Finch."

Clinging to the canister with both hands, Pomona turned and staggered into the foliage. The greenery closed around her, as if attempting to swallow her whole. Talia realized that sometime during the last few minutes the agitated rustling of the plants had escalated to a thrashing sound.

A shrill, high-pitched scream sounded in the distance. Horror jolted through Talia. She stared at the doorway. So did the others. The terrible cry seemed to go on endlessly before it cut off with an abruptness that was as shocking as the scream.

"That was Pomona, wasn't it?" Phoebe whispered.

"Yes," Luke said, his jaw set in a grim line. "Evidently the herbicide was not enough to save her." He hitched the tool belt higher on his shoulder. "Let's get out of here."

Talia looked at Phoebe, who appeared stunned.

"Phoebe," she said quietly. "It's time to leave."

"What?" Phoebe pulled herself together with a visible effort. "Right."

She tightened her grip on the pruning shears and made to follow Luke.

But he stopped at the entrance of the lab.

"This is not good," he said quietly.

The light in the underworld gardens was an intense acid green now, and the energy level was rising. Some of the plants were whipping about as if tossed on invisible waves. There was a small cluster of iridescent mushrooms less than a foot away from the threshold of the door. Talia was certain they had not been there earlier. An odd tree with long, aboveground roots that looked a lot like legs hovered a short distance outside the entrance.

As she watched, a clawlike vine studded with needle-sharp thorns writhed through the opening. It stretched toward Luke as if sensing him.

He took pruners out of the tool belt, cut off the vine, and kicked the dismembered piece back through the doorway. The iridescent mushrooms got a little brighter.

"It's too late," Phoebe said, resigned. "It's full night down here now. We won't be able to get out until morning, not without the herbicide."

CHAPTER THIRTY-EIGHT

Talia surveyed the laboratory. "Why haven't the plants taken over this room?"

"It must be the blue radiation," Luke said. He was stationed at the doorway, pruners in hand. From time to time he executed invading foliage with ruthless precision. Somehow he had managed to achieve a deeper shade of grim. His eyes were cold and dark. "It looks like the same energy in the stones used in the garden paths and the conservatory."

"I heard Finch tell Keever she thought the plants were getting stronger," Phoebe said. "She had to use the spray a lot at night to keep the doorway clear."

"The plants are certainly aggressive," Talia said.

She and Phoebe were sitting on the edge of the cot that the Night Gardener had used, drinking bottles of water. They had found the water and a stash of energy bars in one of the cupboards. Phoebe and Luke had both eaten two each. Talia had resisted, but she was getting very hungry.

Luke was unusually quiet. She didn't have to be a mind reader to know what he was thinking. With the death of Pomona Finch he had lost what was no doubt his best hope of discovering more about what had happened to him during his lost night.

She knew he had paid attention when she gave him the stern little lecture informing him that he was not a real-world example of the Jekyll-and-Hyde syndrome, but she was afraid that, deep down, he wasn't entirely convinced. The Night Gardener's assumption that he was the one who had slit the throats of the two researchers had reignited his fears and questions.

Luke sliced off the tip of a creeper and glanced at Phoebe. "Are you sure that the plants will be calmer in a few hours?"

"I think so," Phoebe said. "I overheard Keever and Pomona arguing because she wanted him to modify his work schedule. She said he would have to start spending more time down here due to the changes in the behavior of the specimens. I could tell he did not want to do that."

"Can't blame him," Talia said.

Phoebe watched Luke with a wary expression. "You did something to Finch, didn't you? At the end, when she ran, she was terrified. Is what she said true? Did they really try to make you into an assassin with psychic powers?"

"They *tried*," Talia said before Luke could answer. "But you heard Finch. He's a failure."

"Are you sure?" Phoebe asked, clearly uneasy.

"Of course I'm sure," Talia said. "Luke isn't an assassin. Think about it. If he had the power to actually kill someone with psychic energy, he would have killed Pomona when she threatened to use that weed killer on us."

Phoebe got a thoughtful expression. "But the bottom line is that Finch is dead."

"Not because Luke killed her," Talia said.

Luke looked at her, and she read the truth in his eyes. *I could have killed her.*

She shook her head. "But you didn't."

Puzzled, Phoebe looked first at Luke and then at Talia. "What?"

"It's not important," Talia said.

Luke used the pruners to amputate a green tentacle studded with needlelike thorns. "It's going to be a long night."

"Longer than you know," Phoebe said. She glanced at the old-fashioned windup clock on the workbench. "I've lost track of time, but before Finch gave me the last dose of sedative she said that the gardens down here don't operate on a standard twenty-four-hour cycle. Nights are a lot longer than they are on the surface."

"Well, damn," Talia said. "I guess I'll have to eat one of those dumb energy bars."

She got to her feet and walked across the lab to open the cupboard Finch had used to store the water and snacks.

Luke's brows climbed. "What have you got against energy bars?"

"Everyone needs a motto," Talia said. "Mine is *Never waste calories on boring food.* Energy bars are at or near the top of the list of the world's most boring foods."

CHAPTER THIRTY-NINE

Clive was dead. So was Keever. And now the couple in cabin eight was missing. Nathan Gill had told everyone that he was going to check on Rand and March, but Octavia was certain they would be found dead — assuming they were found at all. Bodies were very easy to hide on Night Island.

She tightened her grip on the knife and sliced the plum tart into serving-sized pieces. Rand and March had been fools to return to the cabin. They should have joined the others in the lobby.

She set the knife down and began to pipe whipped cream onto each serving. Her hand shook, causing her to create a less-than-perfect swirl on the first slice.

Keever's death had alarmed her. Yes, it could have been an overdose. No one knew exactly what it was he smoked when he was alone in his cabin. Dried mushrooms of some kind. But he had died in the labyrinth gardens, not in his room. That did not look like an overdose to her.

The true danger had been brought home to her when she found Clive's body. She had come to loathe the man, had been planning a future without him. She did not mourn him. But she did not believe for one minute that his death was due to natural causes.

She did not know how Gill had murdered Clive and Eddy Keever but she did not doubt that he was responsible. And now he had gone after Rand and March. She was not sure why, but that didn't matter. He would come for her before the next ferry arrived. He could not afford to let her leave the island. She knew too much.

It was clear that Gill was cleaning up the operation he had been running down below in the tunnels. She was not sure what was going on in that old botanical research lab, but she no longer believed that it was a clandestine government project. She and Clive had fallen for Gill's con for the same reason marks always did — greed. It was embarrassing. Back at the start she had seen it as her last best chance to get enough money together to leave Clive and make her dream of a restaurant come true. For Clive it had promised to be the ultimate score.

She finally understood that Gill had never intended for her and Clive to leave Night Island. Her fight-or-flight instincts were screaming at her to run and hide, but there was no safe place on the island. If she fled into the woods she would get lost and disoriented. It was unlikely that anyone would even look for her body. After all, Nathan Gill owned the island. He had no reason to report a missing person.

She had to stay alive until tomorrow and try to get on the ferry with the guests. Assuming the ferry arrived. That depended on the weather. It also depended on Gill. He could decide to cancel the charter, but she was sure he wanted to get the guests off the island as soon as possible.

She glanced through the doorway into the dining room and the lobby beyond. Marcella Earle, Jasper Draper, and Oliver Skinner were sprawled on the furniture, methodically working their way through what remained of the liquor supply. She would stay close to them until the ferry arrived.

She set the piping bag aside. The peaks of whipped cream lacked her trademark sculptural elegance, but for once she did not care. She turned to open the door of the refrigerator.

"Looks delicious," Marcella said from the

doorway. Alcohol thickened the words.

Octavia started violently and turned around.

"Sorry," Marcella said. "Didn't mean to scare you. You really shouldn't be in here cooking for the rest of us. You lost your husband today."

Octavia flattened her hand on the counter to steady herself. "Cooking is therapeutic for me."

And he was never my husband, she added silently. *I was foolish enough to fall for him years ago but I was not dumb enough to marry him.* She had insisted on separate bank accounts from the very beginning.

"I understand." Marcella swallowed some of her drink. "You know, your talent is wasted here on this island. Ever considered opening your own restaurant?"

"Every chef thinks about that."

No need to mention that she had spent the last few months making plans for a future that did not include Clive.

"Well," Marcella continued, "if you ever do decide to launch your own restaurant in the Seattle area, you'll need to find a good location. Give me a call. I handle a lot of commercial real estate."

"I'll do that," Octavia said.

Marcella turned and wandered back

through the dining room and into the lobby.

Octavia hoisted the tray. A flash of lightning made her flinch so violently she almost dropped her burden. She looked out the window and saw Nathan Gill emerging from the gardens. He was on his way back from cabin eight. For a moment their eyes met, and she knew that either he had not found Rand and March or he had murdered them.

She was next on Gill's list. He would make certain she did not leave the island alive.

CHAPTER FORTY

"It was a trap and I fell for it," Phoebe said. "I was sure I had three legitimate buyers lined up to buy a copy of the list. I had been very careful. All three had figured out that they were on a list of people who had taken a certain psych test several years ago."

"Who was the first buyer?" Talia asked. "The one who kidnapped you?"

"It was supposed to be a woman named Nina Seldon. She was on the list. But the last thing I remember is the knock on the back door. The next thing I knew I was waking up in that little room over there."

"Sounds like a classic lost night situation," Talia said. "That's how it was for my friends and me. We walked into the lobby of an old hotel and woke up very early the next morning with no memory of what had happened to us."

"Same with me," Luke said. He used the pruners to slice off another encroaching creeper. Then he paused to look around the lab, his jaw hardening. "Mostly. By the way, Phoebe, someone murdered the assistant gardener."

"Yes, I know," Phoebe said. "I heard Finch and Nathan Gill arguing about it. Well, not about the murder, exactly. About the disposal of the body."

"What did they say?" Talia asked.

"I didn't catch all of it, but Finch was pissed, I can tell you that. She said that feeding human remains to the plants was affecting the entire ecosystem. She thought it was making the mushrooms and the plants more aggressive."

"About the list," Luke said. "Where is it?"

"The original was an old photocopy that someone posted online at a site I follow on the dark net," Phoebe said. "I grabbed a screenshot of it and put it on three memory cards for the three buyers. I have no idea what happened to any of those copies."

"We didn't find them in the house you were renting, so the kidnapper probably took them," Talia said. "All of your tech was gone, too."

"Don't worry," Phoebe said. "I hid a copy of the list on the dark net."

In spite of the rolling disaster that seemed to be her new normal, Talia got a ping of enthusiasm.

"You know how to navigate the dark net?" she said.

Phoebe shrugged. "I'm what you might call an online broker. I put deals together for people who prefer to remain anonymous. Which makes my current situation more than a little embarrassing. Usually I'm a ghost as far as my clients are concerned. Still can't believe I screwed up the one deal I tried to close for myself."

Luke looked at her. "The problem was that you moved out of the dark net to search for buyers on the surface web. You were more exposed there."

Phoebe grimaced. "I knew it was risky, but I figured that's where the legitimate buyers like *The Lost Night Files* operated."

"How many people on that list did you contact?" Talia asked.

"Five," Phoebe said. "Three of them blew me off. You two got back to me. So did Nina Seldon."

"You rented a house and set up the three buys," Talia said. "Why did you bother with the plant?"

Phoebe smiled somewhat ruefully. "I picked up the plant on a whim when I shopped for groceries. I've always liked to have flowers or a plant around. But after this place I may rethink that. What happened down here? Who built this lab?"

Luke bent down to whack a creeper. "Everything about this room — the metal furniture, the analog equipment, the old lab apparatus — looks like government issue from the mid-twentieth century." He cut off a writhing vine that was reaching for his ankle. "Your tax dollars at work."

Talia got to her feet. "That's an interesting thought." She went to the long workbench and picked up the leather-bound notebook she had noticed earlier. She opened it and studied the faded red stamp on the cover page. *"Top Secret. Restricted Access. Do Not Duplicate."* She looked up. "Ever heard of the Bluestone Project?"

"Bluestone?" Luke's eyes heated with interest. "Seriously?"

"That's what it says." Talia flipped through the handwritten pages. "It looks like lab notes relating to horticultural experiments." She glanced up. "What do you know about the Bluestone Project?"

"Not much. Remember that program I started to tell you about when we came down here?" Luke said. "The one that would have had the resources to create a facility like this?"

"You said it was a legend among those

302

who study the history of the paranormal."

"The Bluestone Project is it," Luke said. "Officially it never existed, but there have been rumors about it for years, and I've picked up a few solid leads. It was run by a little-known government entity, the Agency for the Investigation of Atypical Phenomena."

"Never heard of it," Talia said.

"What was the goal of the Bluestone Project?" Phoebe asked. "Weapons development?"

"I'm sure that was part of the mission," Luke said. "But assuming some of the stories about it are even half true, Bluestone was established to explore the potential for harnessing paranormal energy in a wide variety of fields. Looks like botanical research was one of the areas of investigation." He severed a vine that was trying to capture his wrist. "I'm going to take a wild guess here and speculate that something went wrong in this lab."

Talia turned the pages of the notebook until the faded handwriting abruptly ceased. "I think you're right. It looks like things were shut down in the middle of something called the Cold Fire program."

She took the logbook back to the cot and sat down to read.

■ ■ ■ ■

An hour later she looked up. "I admit I don't understand most of the scientific terms and references, but I can tell you what this lab was attempting to do."

"Increase the productivity of food crops?" Phoebe suggested.

"No," Talia said. "The plants and mushrooms out there in the garden were all considered potential sources of ingredients for drugs that could be used to activate the latent psychic abilities in the human brain."

"Figures," Luke said. He looked at Talia with haunted eyes. "I'll take another flying leap and guess that they weren't looking to enhance paranormal talents for the good of humanity, right?"

Talia cleared her throat, because she knew where he was going. "I'm sure the scientists working here in this lab anticipated that their findings would be useful in medical research."

Luke snorted and sliced off another snaky vine. "But?"

She sighed. "But you're right. The rationale for the funding was to explore drugs that could be used to enhance the abilities of intelligence agents."

"You mean spies?" Phoebe asked.

"And assassins," Luke said.

He cut off a vine dripping with blood-red orchids and fed it back to the gardens.

CHAPTER FORTY-ONE

The plants grew quieter and, as Phoebe had predicted, less aggressive as the acid-green night began to shift into the violet-infused twilight that passed for daytime in the underworld gardens.

Talia stood beside Luke in the doorway of the lab and watched as the illumination changed colors and intensity.

"The plants seem to have given up trying to get through the door," she said. "They aren't exactly dormant, but the change in lighting is putting them into a resting state, just like it says in the logbook."

"Time to move out." Luke glanced at the windup clock on the workbench. "It's almost one o'clock in the afternoon on the surface. If the ferry did make the usual run today, it will have come and gone by now."

Talia shot him another close look, trying to read him without revealing her concern. He had a right to be in a grim mood.

Evidently he was the latest in a recently revived off-the-books program designed to create assassins with paranormal talents. He was also faced with the fact that certain people had expected him to go insane and die. It was a lot to handle, but she gave him credit for staying focused. He was determined to finish the mission that had brought them to Night Island: rescuing Phoebe. There were advantages to being able to compartmentalize, she decided.

"I can't wait to get out of this awful place," Phoebe said.

"I'm with you." Talia tightened her grip on the pruners. "Let's go. Remember to step only on the paving stones. The mushrooms look even more dangerous than the plants. And watch out for the thorns. They are everywhere."

"Trust me, I'll be careful," Phoebe said.

Luke moved out onto the glowing path. "I wonder what the power source is down here," he said.

Talia pushed aside a wide leaf that seemed to be reaching for her. "Good question."

"There must be some machine generating the energy that controls the light cycles and feeds and irrigates the gardens," Luke continued. "If that's the case, it's been running since the middle of the last century.

Machines require fuel, and none of the conventional sources of power would have lasted this long."

He was back in professorial mode, Talia thought. All things considered, maybe that was for the best.

"I'll bet whoever built this facility figured out how to harness some form of paranormal energy," she said.

Luke eyed a small crop of innocent-looking pink mushrooms. "The fungi, maybe."

"It's an interesting problem, but thankfully it isn't our problem," Talia said. "We've got more immediate issues, such as what are we going to tell the authorities when we get back to the surface?"

"As little as possible," Luke said.

"Good plan," Phoebe muttered. "Pretty sure whatever is going on down here is way above the pay grade of the local cops. They won't believe us if we tell them what happened. Even if they agreed to investigate, I've got a feeling that whoever is behind this operation has the juice to keep them off the island."

"You're right," Talia said. "It's obvious we got tangled up with a secret government project. The alphabet agency running this very dark op will do whatever it takes to make sure it stays out of the news."

Luke glanced back over his shoulder. "Try not to fall too far down that rabbit hole. I've been wondering if this was a revived government operation run by the Agency for the Investigation of Atypical Phenomena, but the more I think about it, the more I doubt it."

"What makes you so sure?" Talia said. "Everything in that lab looked like government issue."

"*Vintage* government issue," Luke corrected. "Back in the day, Bluestone was as top secret as the Manhattan Project. But it was shut down decades ago, and believe me, the cover-up was thorough. That happens with old programs that might be awkward to explain to the public."

"Like paranormal horticultural experiments," Talia said, using the pruners to cut off a branch studded with small suckers.

"Exactly," Luke said. "It looks like someone discovered the old Bluestone facility here on Night Island, got his hands on the formula for the enhancement drug, and found a way to open up the old lab and the gardens."

"Nathan Gill," Talia said.

"Or whoever is providing the funding for this project," Luke said.

"It's absolutely terrifying to know that Finch was working for someone who wants to turn people into psychic assassins," Phoebe said. "What a creepy idea. Talk about creating Frankenstein monsters."

Luke did not respond to that, but Talia could feel the tension in his energy field. She knew what he was thinking. *Not Frankenstein monsters. Jekyll and Hyde killers.*

"So what makes you think this isn't Bluestone Project 2.0?" she asked quickly, hoping to distract him.

"The whole setup is too small," Luke said. "The security is minimal. The Unplugged Experience is inadequate as a cover. None of the people involved, including the Venners, are trained, professional agents. Pomona Finch was obviously unstable. She may have been a genius, but it's clear she required constant supervision. Management problems must have been overwhelming. Gill has been forced to control things both underground and aboveground for months. He appears to be working alone. He doesn't seem to have been able to delegate any of the responsibilities. It's also clear he's working with a limited budget. Say what you will about the government, it isn't in its DNA to do things on the cheap."

"I've got to admit those are insightful

observations," Talia said.

"Glad you're impressed," Luke said. "I worked hard on them."

Luke humor, Talia thought. She opted to ignore it.

"How do you know all that stuff about how secret government ops work?" Phoebe asked.

"Before I became a history professor I was in the intelligence business for a while," Luke said. "I learned a few things."

"So if we don't report this situation to the local authorities, who do we report it to?" Talia asked.

"I've also learned a few things as a history professor," Luke said. "I've spent a lot of time doing research in the parapsychology library at Adelina Beach College. I think I know who to contact."

That should have been good news, Talia thought. So why did it sound like the very last thing Luke wanted to do was contact the individual he thought might be able to deal with the situation?

CHAPTER FORTY-TWO

Some twenty minutes later Talia followed Luke and Phoebe through the last of the underground jungle and stopped at the foot of the glowing steps that led up into the conservatory. The vault door was closed. A whisper of panic iced her senses.

"Luke," she said.

He put his hand on her shoulder. "Use the key."

She realized the device was pinging. "Right."

She aimed the key at the door and breathed a sigh of relief when she heard the rumble of gears.

The door began to lift on the big hinges. The gray light of a cloudy day streamed into the stairwell.

"I was a little concerned, too," Luke said quietly as he moved past her into the conservatory.

Talia noticed that he still had his pistol in

one hand.

"Glad I wasn't the only one," she muttered.

Phoebe stepped out of the opening and glanced first at Luke and then at Talia. "What are you two talking about?"

"We were just commenting on the fact that the door unlocked without a hitch," Talia said. "Frankly, we weren't sure what to expect."

"Oh." Phoebe managed a weak smile. "Thanks for not letting me know you were worried that we might be locked inside those gardens forever."

"You're welcome," Talia said. "All part of the *Lost Night Files* service."

Phoebe surveyed the glass-and-steel chamber. "What is this place?"

"It's a conservatory," Luke said. "You would have been unconscious when Nathan Gill brought you through here to take you down below."

"These plants look a lot like the ones down below, but they aren't as aggressive," Talia said. "Maybe this place was used to create hybrids and cultivars that had the characteristics the researchers wanted. The successful specimens would have been introduced into the hot paranormal climate underground."

"Another creepy thought," Phoebe said. "Maybe not as bad as psychic assassins, but definitely creepy."

Talia could not see Luke's face, but she noted the renewed tension in his shoulders. Best to change the subject.

She looked up at the murky daylight filtering through the glass block ceiling. "If the clock down in the lab was accurate, it must be, what? One thirty in the afternoon?"

"Yes," Luke said.

Talia groaned and leaned down to retrieve the jackets and Luke's rain poncho. "You were right — if there was a ferry run today, we missed it."

"The weather appears to have settled down," Luke said, taking his jacket from her. He started along the path that led to the entrance. "So it's likely the ferry was able to dock, in which case the other guests will be gone. But with luck the landline will be working again. We'll be able to call the mainland and get an emergency pickup."

"What about Nathan Gill?" Talia said.

"If he shows up, I'll deal with him, but I think he'll be gone, too."

"Why?" Phoebe said.

"When Talia and I disappeared into the conservatory yesterday, he had to know that his operation was falling apart. He won't

314

stick around to explain things to the authorities."

"Unless he assumes we're dead," Talia said.

"That won't reassure him," Luke said. "He has no way of knowing how many people will come looking for us. Any way you look at the situation, there are now too many bodies to explain. Too many missing people."

"We're finally getting answers," Talia said. She tightened her grip on the logbook. "I can't wait to get hold of the rest of the podcast team. They'll want to see this island for themselves."

"If the person I'm going to contact, the one I think is responsible for what's left of the old Bluestone Project, takes charge, there won't be any more unauthorized visitors allowed on the island," Luke said. "That rule will probably go double for podcasters."

"We can't give up on the investigation," Talia said, outraged.

"We aren't giving up on it," Luke said. "But we've got to be smart about how we handle this new development."

Talia cleared her throat. *"We?"*

Luke's mouth tightened. "Looks like I'm on the podcast team."

"I appointed you a *temporary* member," Talia reminded him.

"Like it or not, I'm permanent now. You need me, and I need you and the rest of your team."

"Can't wait to tell them that we have a new, self-invited member who thinks we should keep our mouths shut," Talia said, swiping aside a wide leaf.

"Don't worry, you'll get used to me," Luke said.

He stopped to open the front entrance of the conservatory. They moved into the air-lock and then through the steel door. They worked their way through the labyrinth gardens.

"This really is one very strange place," Phoebe observed with a shudder. She eyed a nearby fern. "Are these plants glowing, too?"

"Everything seems to be getting hotter up here," Luke said.

He moved out of the labyrinth gardens and stopped at the edge of the driveway. Talia and Phoebe halted beside him. The van was no longer parked at the entrance of the lodge.

Luke walked to the top of the drive and looked down at the dock. "The van is down there. That answers one question. The noon

316

ferry made a run."

"The next question is, did they all leave?" Talia said, looking around.

"The guests definitely will be gone," Luke said.

"And Chef Octavia," Talia said.

"Maybe." Luke did not sound hopeful.

"Why would she stay behind?" Talia asked. "She was determined to get off this island."

"She lived here for the past several months," Luke said. "Gill may have decided that, like Keever and her husband, she knew too much."

Talia shivered.

"Who's Octavia?" Phoebe asked.

"The chef here at the lodge," Talia said. "She and her husband, Clive, ran the Unplugged Experience operation that Nathan Gill used as a cover. Clive was found dead shortly before we went down below to look for you. We think he was murdered."

Phoebe's eyes widened. "By Nathan Gill?"

"Yes," Talia said.

"Maybe," Luke said.

Talia glanced at him, but he did not offer any explanation for the hesitancy to declare Gill the prime suspect.

Phoebe looked around uneasily. "Are you sure Gill left?"

"Yes," Luke said. "The cabin cruiser is

gone. By the time we get back to the mainland, he will have disappeared."

He sounded certain, but Talia noticed he still had the pistol in his hand.

He went up the front steps and opened the door of the lobby. "Looks like they couldn't wait to get away."

Talia moved to stand behind him at the entrance. The interior was littered with carelessly discarded blankets, a few half-empty liquor bottles, plates holding the remains of sandwiches, and a partially completed jigsaw puzzle. There was no luggage. The fire was slowly dying on the big hearth.

Phoebe peered into the room. "How many people were here?"

"When we went looking for you, there were three other people besides Luke and myself who had booked the Unplugged Experience," Talia said. "In addition, there was Nathan Gill and Chef Octavia. So five in all."

"I'll see if the phone is working," Luke said.

He went down the hallway and disappeared into the office. It seemed to Talia that he was inside an inordinate length of time. When he returned he had a file in his hand. His eyes were hard.

"Please don't tell me the landline is still

out," Talia said.

"The landline is not just temporarily out of commission," Luke said. "The cord has been cut."

Phoebe gasped.

"Gill sabotaged it, didn't he?" Talia said. "He wanted to make sure we couldn't call for help if we made it back to the surface."

Phoebe groaned. "So we're stuck here until the ferry makes its regular run tomorrow?"

"I don't think we can count on the ferry," Luke said.

Phoebe looked at him, alarmed. "What do you mean?"

"Excellent question," Talia said. "Explain yourself, Rand."

He held up the file he had brought with him out of the office. "This is a contract with the charter service that handles the private ferry. The agreement states that the service can be canceled at any time. If Gill went to the trouble of making sure the phone wouldn't work, there's a high probably that he terminated the regular ferry service. We should assume that the Unplugged Experience has been unplugged."

Phoebe looked at Luke, her eyes stark with a new fear. "Does this mean there's no way off this island?"

"No," Luke said. "We will get off, but it may take a couple of days."

Phoebe cleared her throat. "How, exactly, are we going to get off?"

"My friends know we are here on Night Island," Talia said quickly. "If we don't contact them in the next couple of days they will charter a boat and come looking for us."

"I doubt we'll have to wait for them," Luke said. "We're not sitting on a deserted island in the middle of the Pacific. We're in the San Juans. There are boats coming and going within visual range every day. All we have to do is get the attention of one of them."

"I knew that," Talia muttered.

"Of course you did," Luke said. "You've just been a little stressed lately. Sometimes it's hard to focus on the obvious when you're under pressure."

He did not actually pat her on the top of her head, but he did not need to. The pat was there in his voice and the quick flash of amusement was in his eyes. Luke humor.

Talia narrowed her eyes. "Careful. You're on thin ice, pal."

"I'll remember that," he said.

Phoebe frowned. "How are we going to signal a passing boat?"

"With a fire," Luke said. "No one ever ignores fire."

Talia looked at the fireplace. "There isn't a lot of wood left, and those plants out in the gardens don't look like they will burn well."

"The cabins are old," Luke said. "They'll go up like matchsticks. There are ten of them, so we've got ten chances to hail a passing vessel. But before we start signaling for rescue I want to take a look around the cabins that Gill and the Venners used. We need as much information as we can get."

"Good idea," Talia said. "Gill had to work quickly when he decided to shut down his project. He may have left some evidence behind."

"You two stay here," Luke said. He took the gun out of his jacket and handed it to Talia. "I won't be gone long, but if you get nervous, just fire a shot."

"Okay." She took the weapon, surprised at how heavy it felt in her hands. "While you're gone I'll see what's left in the way of good food."

Luke startled her with a quick grin. "Have I ever told you that I like your priorities?"

Chapter Forty-Three

Luke stood in the doorway and opened his senses to the atmosphere inside Nathan Gill's cabin. His intuition whispered that there was nothing useful to be found there, but old training habits kicked in, reminding him he had to take a look.

It didn't take long to confirm his initial assumption. Gill might as well have been a ghost. He had been prepared to leave in a hurry and he had left nothing of himself behind. The closets and drawers were empty. The bathroom had been cleaned out. The bed was neatly made.

Luke went outside and took the path through the gardens that led to the Venner cabin. When he opened the unlocked door two things became clear. The first was that Clive Venner's body was gone. It was unlikely that it had been taken back to the mainland for burial. Gill had probably dumped it. There were so many options —

the labyrinth gardens; the conservatory; the deep, cold water of the Sound.

The second thing that was obvious was that Octavia had not made it off the island. Her clothes were still in the closet. A suitcase was open on the bed, but there was only a handful of items inside.

Luke went out onto the front steps, closed the door, and started toward cabin eight, the one he and Talia had used. On his way through the gardens he tried to decide if he should ask Talia to find the Venners' bodies. He knew she would do it if he told her it was important, but it would be hard on her and she had been through a lot lately. He remembered what she had said about the owner of the forensics investigation agency she consulted for in Seattle. *Sometimes I catch him looking at me as if I'm a member of the Addams family.*

"I don't think you're Wednesday Addams," Luke said under his breath. And, really, what was the point of locating the dead couple? The Venners had been pawns for Gill. Alive they probably could have provided some useful information — that was why they had been killed — but there was little to be learned from their bodies.

No, Luke decided, he would not put Talia

through the ordeal of finding two more dead people.

He realized he was suddenly desperate to make sure she did not classify him in the same category as the Seattle forensics investigator. He assured himself he wasn't using her. She had a vested interest in the outcome of the investigation here on Night Island.

Yes, they had started out as allies — yes, they had been using each other back at the start — but things were different now. The sex had crystallized his new reality. His life had changed in ways he was only beginning to comprehend — because of Talia.

He opened the front door of cabin eight and moved inside. His attention went straight to the still-tumbled bed. Memories of yesterday morning hit him in a wave of heat. He forced himself to focus. Talia said he was good at compartmentalizing. Time to do some of that.

The cabin had been searched. Gill had evidently taken a look around, but he hadn't spent much time on the business, probably because he hadn't expected to find anything useful. He had been right. The important things were safely stowed in the day pack.

Chapter Forty-Four

"How long have you and Luke known each other?" Phoebe asked.

"It's all been a blur, to tell you the truth," Talia said. She opened the industrial-sized refrigerator. "Let's see, we met at your house in the early morning, then came here to Night Island the next day. Spent one night here, and the following day we went down below to find you. We spent last night in the lab, and now here we are. That makes about three and a half days, give or take a few hours."

"Seriously?" Phoebe sounded shocked. "You just met him three and a half days ago?"

"That's right," Talia said. Her spirits leaped skyward when she saw the untouched potato-and-leek pie on the center shelf. She picked it up and turned around. "Why?"

Phoebe was sitting on a stool on the far side of the long worktable, a mug of tea in front of her. After Luke had left she had followed Talia into the kitchen. It was clear she did not want to be left alone. Talia understood. She didn't want to be alone on Night Island, either. Luke's pistol was on the table within easy reach.

"I don't know," Phoebe said. She hesitated and then shrugged. "I guess I sort of assumed that you two had been together for a while. I figured you were a couple."

Startled, Talia set the pie on the table. "What in the world gave you that idea?"

"I dunno. Something about the energy between you two. Like you're more than friends."

"Luke and I have been through a rather stressful experience together," Talia said. She turned away to give herself a moment to compose a logical explanation for a relationship that defied logic. The connection she felt with Luke was growing stronger by the hour. It was not simply physical attraction. It was as if something deep inside her recognized Luke on a primal level. *You. You're the one.* Yes, they were more than friends.

Her gaze fell on a knife lying on the counter. There were crumbs on it. That wasn't right. Octavia never would have left one of her high-quality knives lying around.

"That sort of thing tends to create a bond between two people. It doesn't necessarily imply a romantic relationship."

Although it could, she added silently. But probably not in her case, because she had a poor track record in the relationship department, and so did Luke. *Commitment issues,* she reminded herself. Nevertheless, when she envisioned a future with Luke in it she didn't get the usual this-is-okay-for-now-but-won't-last warning from her intuition.

"So you're, what?" Phoebe pressed. "Partners?"

"In a way," Talia said. "We worked together to find you."

"Weird," Phoebe said. "I could have sworn you two were a couple."

"We posed as a couple when we arrived on the island, but it was just a cover story," Talia said.

"So you are sharing a cabin?"

"Just one night," Talia said. "Separate beds."

One hot morning in the same bed did not count, she decided. It wasn't like they had been sleeping in the bed.

She could not stop staring at the knife. It should not have been left on the counter. It was wrong. Out of place. But what did it matter? Octavia was dead. Murdered by

Nathan Gill. *Let it go. Picking up the knife will only confirm that she's dead. You don't need that.*

But she could not stop herself. She had to know. She braced herself and reached out for the knife. Her fingers closed around the handle just as Luke spoke from the doorway.

"Thanks for clarifying our relationship," he said.

"Oh, shit," she yelped.

"Is it that bad?" Luke said. "I realize it's been a little rocky at times, but on the whole I thought we were getting along okay."

She ignored him because the shock of energy from the handle of the knife was rattling her senses. For a moment the kitchen was too bright and too loud. The room was starting to spin around her. *Sensory overload,* she reminded herself. She could handle it.

She caught her breath and managed to stave off the anxiety attack with sheer willpower. She turned around and saw Luke standing in the doorway. He was carrying his duffel and her overnight bag. The pack was slung over his shoulder. He was watching her from the Luke zone.

"Luke," she gasped.

"Something about seeing you with a knife in your hand will always remind me of our first couple of dates," he said. "The one you aimed at me the morning we had biscuits together definitely got my attention. But I think it was the vegetable cleaver you used that night that sealed the deal."

Luke humor.

Talia glared at him. "That is not funny."

"I've got news that is not funny, either." Luke dropped his duffel and her overnight bag on the floor and let the shoulder pack slide off onto a nearby counter. He picked up the pistol and tucked it under his jacket. "Clive Venner's body is missing, and all the evidence indicates that Octavia did not make it off the island. Looks like she was in the middle of packing, but she never finished."

Phoebe's eyes widened. "So the cook really is dead?"

"She's a chef," Talia corrected automatically. "And she's not dead — not yet, at any rate. She's still here on the island. She's terrified. We have to find her."

CHAPTER FORTY-FIVE

"Any idea where we should start looking for Octavia?" Luke asked.

He stood with Talia and Phoebe on the front porch of the lodge, surveying the labyrinth gardens. From time to time he glanced at Talia, trying to get a read on her mood. He wanted to ask her pointblank what she had been thinking when she told Phoebe that a bond generated by shared stress did not imply a romantic relationship, but now was not the time. There never seemed to be a good time to talk about his relationship with Talia.

"I think she slipped out the kitchen door and went into the labyrinth," Talia said. "She was terrified. She wanted to hide. After spending six months on the island she knew her way around the gardens, and maybe the conservatory, as well."

"It would have been just a matter of time before Gill found her," Luke said. He gave that a few seconds' thought. "But maybe he didn't have time. His first priority would have been to get the guests off the island and cut his losses. He may have decided to leave Octavia stranded here."

"All I can tell you is that she isn't dead," Talia said.

She gripped the knife, went down the porch steps, and started across the driveway. Luke and Phoebe followed.

The sky was still a murky gray, but there was no rain and the wind was calm. Talia, knife in hand, moved steadily through the gardens and stopped in front of the conservatory.

He watched her closely. There was a sheen of bright energy in her eyes. He could feel the heat in her aura.

"Did she go inside?" he asked. "If so it means she had a gadget like Keever's, a device that can unlock the door. I wonder how many of those are floating around?"

"She's not inside," Talia said. She was tense with concentration now. She led the way around the conservatory and stopped at the cabin that had been assigned to Pomona Finch. "She's in there."

Luke walked up to the door and knocked. "Octavia, it's Luke Rand. I've got Talia with me and a friend. It's okay to come out. Gill is gone. So are the others."

There was a short, stark silence from within the cabin. Luke saw a curtain twitch. A moment later the door opened. Octavia stood in the shadows, her eyes stark with fear. She had a large carving knife in one white-knuckled fist. She stared at Luke.

"I thought you were dead," she said.

"I've been getting that a lot lately," Luke said. Gently he took the knife from her hand. She did not resist. "Let's go back to the lodge and figure out how we're going to get off this damned island."

"There is no way off Night Island," Octavia said. "Not now. It's too late."

"Too late?" Talia asked.

"Can't you feel the forces that have been unleashed here?" Octavia gestured with one hand to indicate their surroundings, the gardens, the glass-walled hothouse, the lodge, and the cabins. "Something is wrong. The plants are too bright at night. The storms are coming more frequently. It's too warm for this time of year. There's a bad feeling in the atmosphere."

"All the more reason for not hanging around," Luke said. He glanced up at the rapidly descending tsunami of night. The plants in the garden and the conservatory were already starting to glow. The change in the tides would make it impossible to bring a boat in close to the dock. "We're stuck here tonight, but we'll get off tomorrow."

"How?" Octavia asked, twisting her hands in her apron.

"Luke has a plan," Talia said. "He always does."

And as any battlefield commander will tell you, the plan always goes sideways as soon as the war starts, Luke thought. But there was no point mentioning that old adage. Got to stay positive.

CHAPTER FORTY-SIX

"I hoped that if Gill assumed I'd tried to escape by going into the conservatory he wouldn't bother to look for me," Octavia said. "Even if I survived he knew he controlled the private ferry, and that is the only way off the island. I'm not surprised that he sabotaged the landline."

"We'll get off the island," Luke said around a mouthful of potato-and-leek pie.

"How?" Octavia asked.

"Tell her," Talia said.

The four of them were gathered around one of the dining room tables, drinking an excellent red from the well-stocked wine collection and eating the savory pie. Night had fully shrouded the island, bringing with it a heightened buzz in the atmosphere. Outside in the gardens the plants glowed.

Earlier Luke had built a fire in the lobby. It provided some reassuring energy and warmth, but Octavia was right, Talia thought. The ominous feeling that settled on the island after dark had grown more intense just in the short time she and Luke had been there.

"We'll use fire to get the attention of a passing boat," Luke said.

Octavia stiffened. "Of course. I totally forgot."

"What did you forget?" Luke asked.

"About the emergency flares," Octavia said. "The kind that are carried on boats. Gill had some on board his cabin cruiser."

"The cruiser is gone," Talia pointed out gently.

Octavia snorted. "But the flare guns are still here. I went down to the dock and stole a couple of them a month ago while Gill was in the tunnels. He never missed them."

"Why did you take the flare guns?" Phoebe asked.

"I was getting more and more nervous about Gill," Octavia said. "There was no way to get a real gun, because we weren't allowed to leave the island. I thought that the flares might serve as weapons if my worst fears came true."

"Where are they?" Luke asked.

"I hid them in one of the kitchen cupboards," Octavia said. "Gill never went into the kitchen. But yesterday when I panicked and decided to run I forgot about the flare guns. I grabbed a knife instead."

Talia nodded approvingly. "The instinctive action of a smart chef."

"That settles it," Luke said. "The flares will grab someone's attention. Getting off the island is not going to be the hard part. Making sure we all get our story straight is what we need to work on."

"What is the big picture of your plan?" Talia asked.

"The primary objective is to dump the problem of Night Island into the lap of the government contractor that is responsible for it," Luke said.

"What about the four of us?" Octavia asked.

"We are going to keep a very low profile," Luke said.

Phoebe set her fork aside. "I know people on the dark net. For a price I can get new identities for each of us."

Talia looked at her, intrigued. "Really? You can do that?"

"I told you, I'm a broker," Phoebe said. "In spite of appearances, I'm pretty damn good at it. I put deals together. You'd be amazed how many people want to buy new identities."

"That is impressive," Talia said. "It sounds

slick, but it won't work for me, because I am not going to vanish. I've got friends. Also family. Okay, maybe we're not the closest family in the history of the world, but my relatives would definitely notice if I disappeared. Also, I'm part of the *Lost Night Files* podcast team. We are going to stick together until we find the people responsible for stealing a night of our lives and running experiments on us."

Phoebe's expression tightened. "I'm with you. I'm not going back into hiding. I want to find those creeps as much as you do."

Talia smiled. "Want to join the team? We could use the help of someone who knows her way around the dark net."

Phoebe looked startled by the offer. But in the next moment she got a thoughtful expression. "That sounds . . . interesting."

Octavia cleared her throat. "Personally, I like the idea of getting a new identity. I want nothing more than to leave my old life behind and start fresh."

"No problem," Phoebe said. "But it will take cash."

Octavia nodded. "I've got some money hidden away in a bank account that I never told Clive about. I've been saving up to open a place of my own, but buying a new identity is more important. Once I have that

I can get a job in a good restaurant."

"Okay," Phoebe said. "I'll order the package as soon as I can get online. My preferred vendor can deliver within forty-eight hours."

Talia was truly awed. "That is amazing."

Phoebe blushed. "Thanks."

"We really need someone with your skills on our team," Talia said. It dawned on her that Luke had not said anything about ordering up a new life. Dread clenched her insides. She looked at him. "Are you going to disappear?"

"No," he said. His eyes heated. "I tried that. Didn't work. I'm a member of the *Lost Night Files* crew now. That means I'm going to live by the code."

Talia smiled. "We're in this together until we get answers."

CHAPTER FORTY-SEVEN

"It was just too perfect," Octavia said as she smashed garlic and salt into a paste using a mortar and pestle. "Clive and I fell for it, hook, line, and sinker. We had been running the Unplugged Experience project for nearly four years in various locations. Before that we operated a string of similar projects. We, of all people, should have recognized a con."

"You said that Gill told you it was a secret government project," Talia pointed out. "You had no reason to doubt him."

She was sitting at the long kitchen worktable watching Octavia make parsley and basil pesto the old-fashioned way — no food processor involved. It was after ten in the morning and they were all hoping to be off the island before lunch but Octavia had insisted on starting preparations for the noon meal, just in case. Talia knew she needed to keep herself occupied.

The four of them had spent the night camped out in the lobby. From time to time Talia had heard Luke get up from his bed on the floor to throw another log on the fire. They had all awakened early but there was nothing to be done until the tides changed. An hour ago Luke had found a pair of binoculars in the office. He had collected the two emergency flare guns and walked down to the dock to watch for passing vessels.

None of them had slept well. Phoebe was taking a nap on one of the sofas in the main room of the lodge.

"The big red flag was the amount of money Gill promised to pay us for the job," Octavia said. She tossed a handful of roughly chopped basil into the stone mortar and went back to work grinding the greens into the garlic and salt paste. "Clive saw the project as the score he had been waiting for his whole career. I saw the cash as my ticket to a new life."

"You may not have the cash, but you will have a new identity, and you've got your culinary skills," Talia said. "You'll be able to find a position in a good restaurant and make a name for yourself that way."

"Maybe," Octavia said. She tossed more chopped herbs into the mortar. "But I've been running the con with Clive for so long, I might not be able to handle a real job."

"There's something you need to remember," Talia said. "The Unplugged Experience may have been a con, but there is nothing fake about your talent. The wonderful food you served to your guests was the real deal."

Octavia paused in the task of smooshing the herbs. Pride and determination sparked in her eyes.

"You're right," she said. "You can't fake good food."

"That's better," Talia said. "You're a chef. You need to act like the diva you were born to be."

Octavia smiled faintly. "I'll keep that in mind."

CHAPTER FORTY-EIGHT

Talia walked out of the kitchen, through the dining room, and into the lobby. The icy tingle of energy came out of nowhere and zapped across her senses with enough energy to make her flinch. Her pulse leaped as if she had just avoided a fall down a staircase. She stopped, caught her breath, and instinctively turned on her heel, searching for the source of the threat.

There was nothing to be seen. Phoebe was still asleep on the sofa, a blanket draped over her. The sound of pots clattering in the kitchen indicated that Octavia was going about the task of preparing the noon meal everyone hoped they would not have to stick around long enough to eat.

Maybe they could pack a picnic lunch to take with them when they were rescued, Talia thought. The very idea of leaving the beautiful pesto behind, uneaten, was depressing. Octavia intended to serve it on hot pasta, but maybe a cold pasta-and-pesto salad would work as a getaway dish.

She took a step forward and halted again when another icy thrill shivered through her. *I'm overreacting. My nerves are still on the fritz because of all the dead bodies lately and that really bad night down in the lab.*

The logic sounded solid, but her intuition wasn't buying it. She realized she was staring at her overnight bag. It was sitting in the corner next to Luke's duffel. Octavia's suitcase was nearby. The clothes and other things they had rounded up for Phoebe were in a fabric sack. They were all ready to leave on a moment's notice.

She walked slowly across the lobby. The closer she got to her bag, the stronger the vibe. The only thing inside that did not belong to her was the old Bluestone logbook. For some reason it suddenly seemed very important. But why now?

Phoebe stirred and pushed herself upright on the sofa. "What's going on? Are you okay?"

"Yes, I'm fine," Talia said.

Phoebe shoved the blanket aside and stood, stretching her arms overhead. "Is Luke back?"

"Not yet," Talia said. She did not take her attention off the bag.

"Do you really think he'll be able to attract the attention of a passing boat?"

"In my experience, if Luke says he's going to do something, you can safely assume he will do it."

"That's good to know." Phoebe groaned. "I still feel like I'm moving through molasses. I'm going down the hall to the restroom to wash up and then I'll get some tea from Octavia. See you in a few."

"I think I saw a slice of leftover salted-chocolate-and-caramel tart in the kitchen," Talia said. "Chocolate is an excellent source of energy."

"Good idea."

Phoebe disappeared down the hall.

Talia crouched, unzipped her bag, reached inside, and touched the logbook with cautious fingers . . .

. . . and yelped when she got a small shock.

"Shit," she whispered.

Setting her teeth against the hot-and-cold sparks that were crackling across her senses, she picked up the logbook and got to her feet. She took a few deep breaths and forced herself to focus. The sharp, unstable energy left behind by Pomona Finch was much stronger and more intense than it had been earlier. It was not the hollow echo of death.

The Night Gardener was alive, and she

was nearby.

Logbook in hand, Talia started toward the front door.

"Octavia," she called. "I'm going down to the dock. I've got to talk to Luke."

Octavia appeared in the arched opening that connected the dining room to the lobby. Fear had transformed her face into a stiff mask. She was not alone. Pomona Finch was directly behind her.

The Night Gardener wore the protective trousers, jacket, gloves, and boots that she'd had on when she fled into the underground gardens. But the clothes were ripped in several places and there were bloodstains on the fabric. Her face looked as if it had been slashed in a couple of places. She had lost her cap. Wormlike vines were twisted in the limp strands of her hair.

Her eyes were wild with rage and, perhaps, insanity. The canister of potent herbicide was in her hands. The nozzle was aimed at Octavia.

"You have destroyed my life's work," Pomona rasped. "You are all going to pay."

CHAPTER FORTY-NINE

"Congratulations on surviving the plants," Talia said. She stopped in front of the fireplace, the logbook clutched in one hand behind her back. "I'm impressed."

"You have no idea what you've done," Pomona said. She pushed Octavia forward into the lobby and followed, finger on the trigger of the canister. "You stupid woman — the work I was doing in that lab would have changed the world."

"Is that right?" Talia said. "Could have fooled me. It sure looked like you were trying to create assassins. I've got news for you. The world doesn't need any more killers."

"Completing that project for the Institute was the price I had to pay for the opportunity to work in that incredible facility," Pomona said. "I was so close to making countless new discoveries and now everything is in ruins. *Because of you and that failed Subject A, Luke Rand.*"

"I assume you used that high-octane weed killer to get through the gardens," Talia said. "But how did you make it out of the underworld?"

"I have one of the keys," Pomona said.

"How many keys are there?"

Pomona snorted. "Who knows? Nathan Gill said he found a couple in one of the old lab desks. There was another one in the conservatory and one in the lodge office. There are probably more. No one has been able to explore the entire lab facility. In some places the vegetation is impenetrable."

"I see," Talia said. "Well, if it makes you feel any better, your research has suffered a setback, but nothing more. Setbacks happen all the time in science, right?"

"What are you talking about?"

Talia brought her hand out from behind her back, revealing the logbook. "I have the notes from the original researcher. They are the foundation for your own recent work, aren't they?"

Pomona stared at the logbook, distracted. "Give it to me."

"I will if you put down the sprayer," Talia said.

Phoebe appeared at the entrance of the hallway. Pomona, focused on Talia, did not see her.

"Now, why would I do that?" Pomona said. "Toss the logbook to me or I swear I'll use this on you. From this distance I can't miss."

"You might kill me, but what happens when the herbicide splashes on the logbook?" Talia said. "I imagine whatever is in that canister will eat right through the leather cover and the pages."

Pomona hesitated. Panic flashed in her eyes. *"Give it to me."*

Talia opened the logbook and prepared to tear out the first page. "I'm going to toss these notes into the fire one sheet at a time until you put down that sprayer."

Pomona screamed, *"No."*

Phoebe moved. She grabbed a ceramic vase off an end table and ran toward Pomona.

"Bitch," Phoebe yelled. She raised the vase, preparing to slam it against Pomona's head.

Startled, Pomona whipped around. She managed to scramble partially out of the way of the descending vase. It struck her shoulder, sending her off-balance. Talia dropped the notebook and launched herself at Pomona.

Pomona struggled to find her footing and raise the canister at the same time. Talia caught her arm, forcing her to aim the canister toward the fireplace.

Pomona screamed and pulled the trigger again and again. She fired three bursts of the herbicide into the flames. There was no fourth jet of chemicals. The canister was empty. Talia realized Pomona must have used most of it to survive her battle with the plants.

Pomona dropped the canister and fell to her knees, sobbing. Talia released her and stepped back. She realized the lobby looked a little blurry.

"My glasses," she said.

"Here." Octavia handed them to her.

Luke came through the front door, pistol in hand. He took in the scene and lowered the gun.

"I think I saw this movie," he said.

Talia sucked in air. Her heart was pounding. She was riding an adrenaline rush. "The one where the monster everyone thinks is dead keeps coming back to life?"

"Yeah, that one." His eyes burned. "You scared the living daylights out of me." He looked around. "Everyone okay?"

"Yes." Octavia took a deep breath. "I never did like that woman. She did not appreciate good food."

"I wasn't very fond of her, either," Phoebe said. She gave Talia a shaky smile. "You saved us. No telling what that weed killer would have done if it had struck one of us."

Luke looked at the fire. "We'll never know how that stuff affects humans, but it's acting like gasoline on the fire."

It dawned on Talia that the flames on the big hearth were no longer crackling in a comforting way. They were roaring. She turned to see what was happening. So did the others.

The fire rapidly became a small inferno. Flames leaped out and upward, scorching the mantel. Smoke began to fill the room. Sparks flew, igniting small fires on the rug.

"I've got a kitchen fire extinguisher under the sink," Octavia said.

"Forget it," Luke said. "There's too much energy in the atmosphere, and this place is a tinderbox. Everyone, grab your stuff. We're getting out of here."

Talia seized her overnight bag. "What about Finch?"

Pomona leaped to her feet and staggered down the hallway, evidently heading toward the back door of the lodge.

"Let her go," Luke said. He slipped the gun back inside his jacket and grabbed his duffel. "We've got a boat to catch."

No one argued. They headed toward the door. Talia paused briefly before going out onto the porch. She glanced longingly back toward the arched doorway that led to the dining room and the kitchen.

"The pesto," she said.

Luke wrapped one hand around her upper arm and hauled her through the doorway.

"Move," he ordered. "The lodge is going to blow."

"I was thinking a chilled pasta-and-pesto salad," she said.

No one paid any attention.

"You said we've got a boat to catch?" Phoebe called over her shoulder. "Were you able to signal one?"

"Yes," Luke said. "That's why I came back to the lodge when I did."

They made their way down the rutted lane to the dock. Talia saw an expensive-looking yacht sailing toward Night Island.

"Wow, first class," she said. "I like your style, Rand."

There was a low rumble from the burning lodge at the top of the drive. She turned around. So did the others. They watched as the building exploded in a fireball. A hellish storm of debris rained down on the plants closest to the structure. A moment later the gardens burst into flames.

"I like your style, too, March," Luke said,

studying the conflagration with deep interest. "Never a dull moment around you, is there?"

She glared. "That fire is not my fault."

"You were the one who forced Finch to aim the weed killer at the fireplace," Luke pointed out. "I'm not criticizing, by the way. That was a very smart move, under the circumstances."

"Why would the herbicide cause the fire to explode?" Phoebe said, unable to look away from the burning gardens.

"Who knows what chemicals were in that canister," Luke said.

Octavia shook her head, stunned. "I don't understand. I never thought those plants would burn so easily."

"I think it's the energy in the atmosphere on the island," Talia said. "Octavia, you told us things have been escalating, getting more intense."

"So?" Phoebe said.

"There is something in the logbook about fire being one of the elemental forces that can burn from the normal end of the spectrum all the way into the paranormal. As Luke said, the weed killer acted like gasoline on the fire."

"Okay, that's scary," Phoebe said.

"I always knew there was some malignant

force on this island," Octavia said.

"I don't know that it's fair to say it's malignant," Talia said. "Energy is energy. It doesn't have a moral compass. What matters is how it's used."

Octavia shook her head. "I'm telling you, it's bad energy."

"I agree with you," Phoebe said. She shuddered. "Bad things happened on that island."

"Listen up, people," Luke said. "We don't have time for a discussion of metaphysics. Our ride is almost here. Here is rule number one. There will be no mention of a mad scientist, paranormal energy, hidden underground labs, carnivorous plants, or anything else that will make all of us sound like we need a psych evaluation. Is that clear?"

"Clear," Talia said.

Octavia grimaced. "Absolutely clear."

"I've had enough of being locked up," Phoebe said. "I don't want to do time in a psychiatric hospital."

"It's settled, then," Luke said. "Phoebe, Talia, and I were all guests at the lodge. Octavia was the cook."

"Chef," Talia said.

Octavia squared her shoulders and raised her chin.

"Chef," Luke corrected. "Management

and the other guests left on the ferry yesterday. We were expecting the ferry to return today. It didn't. Probably a communications mix-up. We decided to flag down a passing vessel. Then came the fire. Got it?"

"Got it," Talia said.

Octavia and Phoebe nodded.

Phoebe shook her head. "It's hard to believe they were trying to create psychic assassins."

"Nathan Gill and Pomona Finch are obviously delusional," Talia said crisply. "*Dangerous,* I admit, but delusional. Nathan Gill stumbled into the ruins of an abandoned government project that dates from the last century and decided to try his hand at creating killers with enhanced psychic talents. He ignored the glaring evidence that his grand plan was doomed from the start."

Octavia frowned. "What evidence?"

Talia waved a hand to take in the whole of Night Island. "The Bluestone Project was shut down. There's only one reason why a top secret research and development project gets terminated. That's because it was unsuccessful."

Octavia's expression cleared. "You're right. The government never would have abandoned a program like that if it had appeared even the least bit promising."

Luke gave Talia an admiring look that did not quite conceal the amusement in his eyes. "You're good. Very, very good."

"Thank you," she said. "I'm a podcaster. I know how to tell a story. But I would remind you again that I'm a professional. Don't try this at home."

CHAPTER FIFTY

The yacht was named *I've Got Mine.* It was sleek and luxurious. Talia was right, Luke thought, he had done a nice job arranging transport off the island. The owners were a retired couple named Bev and Ben Thompson and they were delighted to play the role of rescuers.

"Don't worry, there's room for all of you," Ben said as he ushered them on board. He looked up at the smoking ruins of the lodge and the labyrinth gardens. "Anyone hurt in that fire?"

"No," Luke said.

"How did it start?" Ben asked.

"Fireplace," Luke said. "Evidently management hadn't cleaned the chimney in quite a while. Once it got going, that old building went up like a pile of kindling."

"Are you four the only people on the island?"

"Management and the other guests left on

the noon ferry yesterday," Luke said. "We expected to get picked up today, but obviously there was a problem."

"For as long as I can remember Night Island was off-limits," Ben said. "Private property. But about a year ago it was sold. Next thing we knew that meditation operation opened up, but it never seemed to do much business."

"I think it's safe to say the Unplugged Experience is closed for good," Luke said.

Talia, Phoebe, and Octavia accepted Bev Thompson's invitation to have coffee in the vessel's elegantly appointed main cabin. Luke stayed outside and lounged on the rail while he waited for his heavily encrypted phone to wake up. When he was finally able to get a couple of bars he dialed the number in Las Vegas.

His call was answered on the first ring.

"Who are you and how did you get this number?" The voice was male, gravelly, and infused with intensity.

"I want to speak to Victor Arganbright," Luke said.

"You're talking to him. Now, who the hell are you?"

"A blogger. I write *The Anomalies Report*."

"Never heard of it."

"Yeah, well, I'm still building my brand," Luke said. "The point is, in my work I pick up a lot of rumors. Does the word *Bluestone* mean anything to you?"

There was a short, stunned pause on the other end of the line. While he waited, Luke watched five members of an orca pod knife through the cold waters. The sleek apex predators looked like they were frolicking in the waves, but he knew that was an illusion. They were hunting.

"I'm listening," Arganbright said. "But if this is a crank call . . ."

"According to my research, you're the CEO of the government contractor that is responsible for securing the old Bluestone labs," Luke said.

There was another startled pause before Victor spoke again. This time he sounded more cautious. He was paying attention.

"I'm the head of the Foundation," he said. "Tell me about this rumor you say you picked up on your blog."

"The story is that about a year ago someone using the name Nathan Gill found one of the Bluestone labs on Night Island in the San Juans. He managed to get it open. For the past six months it's been used for some off-the-books experiments designed to create assassins with psychic talents."

There was another long silence.

"That's a pretty wild story," Victor said.

"It is, isn't it? Are you going to hang up?"

"No."

Luke tightened his grip on the phone. For better or worse, Arganbright was hooked.

"The project on Night Island operated under the cover of a retreat," Luke continued. "The Unplugged Experience."

"Keep talking," Victor Arganbright said.

Luke kept talking.

CHAPTER FIFTY-ONE

The Foundation, Las Vegas, Nevada . . .

Lucas Pine watched his husband end the call. Victor looked annoyed, impatient, and tense. It was his default mode. Lucas, uncharacteristically, was feeling much the same way. He had heard the entire conversation because Victor had put the phone on speaker. Any mention of Bluestone got their attention. The possibility that another one of the lost labs had been discovered was a major event.

"Ever heard of *The Anomalies Report*?" Victor asked.

"Nope." Lucas glanced down at his phone. "But I pulled up the blog while you were talking to Mr. Anonymous. Looks like just another small-time online site that claims to report on incidents of paranormal phenomena. For the most part it focuses on sensational claims and junk science. It's clearly aimed at the tinfoil helmet crowd. But I found a couple of interesting articles on the history of parapsychology that look well-researched."

Victor grunted. "So our anonymous tipster is trying to build a brand as a paranormal investigator."

"Lot of those out there. These days everyone thinks they can play detective using the online search engines. But the Bluestone tip sounds solid."

"Yes, it does." Victor got to his feet behind his desk. His eyes heated with anticipation. "Which is why we're going to take it seriously. Contact our people on the ground in Seattle. I want a team on the island claiming it as government property immediately. Then call the airport and get the jet readied. You and I are going to fly to Seattle today."

"Right." Lucas headed toward the door.

"Don't forget to warn the Seattle people that there may be a deranged scientist running around the island armed with possibly lethal herbicide. Oh, and they'll need camping gear, because evidently there was a major fire that destroyed much of whatever infrastructure was there."

Lucas wrapped his hand around the door handle and looked back over his shoulder. "We're in a strange business, Victor."

Victor contemplated the vast collection of

paintings that lined the walls of his office. The pictures dated from various eras. The quality of the artwork ranged from the mediocre to the transcendent. Some were framed. Some were not. They all had one theme in common: each pictured the artist's vision of the Oracle of Delphi.

"Maybe we're in a strange business because we are not exactly normal ourselves," Victor said quietly.

"The older I get the broader my definition of *normal* becomes," Lucas said.

He went next door to his office, got on the phone, and started making the calls that would put the Foundation in charge of Night Island.

CHAPTER FIFTY-TWO

Talia watched Luke out of the corner of her eye while she sipped coffee and chatted with Bev Thompson and the others inside the yacht's main cabin. She had not been able to hear the phone conversation going on outside but it was clear Luke had been intensely focused on the call. Now he was leaning on the rail, watching the orca ballet.

"I can't believe the Unplugged Experience management people left the four of you behind." Bev shook her head. "Talk about unprofessional. I mean, I see a potential lawsuit here."

Octavia and Phoebe looked at Talia, silently signaling her to take the lead.

She smiled. "I'm sure it was not intentional. Nathan Gill no doubt planned to return to pick us up. But the ferry that services the island is just a small, private business. There were probably mechanical problems and the run was unavoidably delayed. No one could notify us because the one landline phone was out and there was no cell service."

Octavia rolled her eyes. Phoebe looked angry. But Luke had emphasized the importance of sticking to their story, and they were doing just that. There would be no mention of mysterious deaths, underground gardens, or illegal experiments. He was right. She knew that no good would come of trying to convince their rescuers or the local authorities of the truth. For starters, no one would believe them, and it would be downhill from there.

Talia took another look at Luke. She could tell by the grim set of his face that he was still focused on strategy and logistics. Compartmentalizing. He was certainly not giving any thought to their relationship. Why would he? Yes, he wanted to be part of the *Lost Night Files* team, but that did not mean he wanted a serious relationship with her.

She knew now that a serious relationship with him was the only kind she was interested in having.

She got to her feet. "If you'll excuse me, I'm going to have a word with Luke."

"Why don't you take him a mug of coffee?" Bev suggested.

Talia smiled. "Great idea."

She picked up the coffeepot and filled a mug half full as a precaution against spilling the contents. The water was smooth, but why take chances? She went out onto the covered deck.

Luke sensed her approach and turned to watch her come toward him. She thought his eyes warmed at the sight of her, but she told herself not to make any assumptions. She was sure there was a bond between them, and she was certain he was aware of it. But she did not know how he interpreted the connection. Would Luke recognize love if he slammed into it the way she had during the past few days? If he did acknowledge it, would he lose his nerve and surrender to his commitment issues?

She stopped beside him and handed him the mug.

"Bev thought you could use some coffee," she said.

"Bev must be psychic." Luke took the mug. "Thanks."

Talia gripped the rail with one hand and used her other hand to hold her wind-whipped hair out of her eyes. "Were you able to contact the head of that Las Vegas outfit?"

"The Foundation. Yes, I got straight through to Victor Arganbright. He keeps a low profile, but he's not trying to hide."

"Unlike, say, you for the past three months?"

"Unlike me."

"I could tell you were reluctant to get him involved," Talia said. "I assume that's because he's got government connections and neither of us wants to become the target of a federal investigation. Is he going to be a problem?"

"I don't think so, at least not right away," Luke said. "I used my credentials as the anonymous blogger who writes *The Anomalies Report.*"

It took a second for that news to register. When it did, she wasn't sure whether to laugh or groan.

"Of course you write *The Anomalies Report,*" she said finally. "I'm psychic. Why did I not see that coming?"

"No psychic gets it right every time."

"Moving right along, did Arganbright recognize your blog?"

"No." Luke's mouth twisted a little in a wry smile. "Which is embarrassing, of course, but, under the circumstances, good news."

"I understand, believe me."

"I think I managed to leave the impression that I'm just a small-time blogger who hangs out on the fringes of the online paranormal community."

"In other words, you didn't mention that, in your other life, you are a mild-mannered professor of history or that in a former life you worked in the intelligence business."

"Nope. I told him that I picked up a weird rumor about an old government project called Bluestone and figured he would want to know about it given his connections to a certain government agency."

She smiled. "Did you use your talent to convince him you were telling him the truth?"

"Unfortunately, my ability doesn't work on the phone; only in person. But I didn't need any extra juice to get his attention. I could tell the word *Bluestone* did it. Arganbright struck me as a very single-minded guy, and at the moment he is focused one hundred percent on securing Night Island."

"What about those keys that he'll need to open the conservatory and the underground lab?"

"I mentioned that according to the rumors a unique device was required to access the old lab, but I didn't say we left two of them in plain sight on the dock. I also warned him that there might be a mad scientist running around."

"All in all, it's a wonder he believed you."

"It's obvious he's obsessed with all things Bluestone. Even if he doesn't believe me he'll feel compelled to check out my story."

"You do realize that sooner or later he's going to start wondering about your sources for those rumors," she warned.

"There's nothing I can do about that. I'll just have to take my chances and hope my security and privacy protocols hold."

"So once we get the new ID for Octavia, the *Lost Night Files* team can go back to hunting for the people who kidnapped us."

"Yes."

She rested her forearms on the railing, clasped her hands, and watched the orcas for a moment before she turned her head to look at Luke.

"Can I ask why you were so concerned with maintaining your anonymity when you contacted the Foundation?" she asked. "I know you said you don't want to draw the attention of the feds, and I agree that's not a good idea, but I get the impression that you had other reasons for not wanting to make that call to Arganbright."

Luke drank some coffee and lowered the mug. "If even half the rumors about the Foundation are true, it isn't only in the business of securing the old Bluestone labs."

Talia went cold. "What else does it do?"

"It maintains a quasi-police force that hunts down people with dangerous paranormal talents. People like me."

"Well, shit."

"My sentiments exactly."

CHAPTER FIFTY-THREE

Shortly before six o'clock that evening Luke took the glass of wine that Talia had just poured, opened the glass-paned door, and moved out onto the apartment balcony. He stood quietly for a moment, taking in the evening. It felt good. Normal. There was none of the eerie, disquieting energy that had accompanied night on the island. The buzz in the atmosphere here in Seattle was the familiar vibe of a busy city.

He turned and looked at the small group on the other side of the glass door. Phoebe and Octavia were on the sofa drinking wine and nibbling on the cheese and crackers Talia had prepared. Earlier she had contacted the concierge of the apartment tower to reserve one of the guest suites that management provided as an amenity. Phoebe and Octavia would spend the night there.

That opened up the question of where he was going to sleep, but he was not ready to raise the subject. Talia had not brought it up, either. He had no idea how to read her silence on the topic. Maybe she assumed things would go back to pre–Night Island status and offer him her podcast studio bedroom. Or suggest a hotel.

He was sure she was not thinking about the sleeping arrangements, because she was perched on a dining counter stool, her laptop open to display the delivery menus of nearby restaurants. Dinner first, relationship second. The woman had priorities. For some reason that made him smile.

A lot of things about Talia March made him smile, he realized.

The others were making plans to get on with their lives. Phoebe had commissioned the new identity packet for Octavia and paid extra for rush service. The new documents were going to be delivered tomorrow. As for Phoebe, she had made her decision. She was going to join the *Lost Night Files* team. She was making plans to rent an apartment in the same tower as Talia. Her logic for moving into the building was that proximity would facilitate their working relationship. That made sense, but he was equally sure that Phoebe liked the idea of having someone she trusted close by. She liked the idea of being part of the podcast crew. He didn't blame her.

He was done with hiding. Done with fighting the battle on his own. He was ready to go on offense with Talia and the *Lost Night Files* team.

His immediate concern, however, was not his future in podcasting — it was his relationship with Talia. He felt as if he was treading water, waiting to see if she would throw him a lifeline or at least a hint that she envisioned a future for the two of them.

This wasn't his fault, he decided. He wasn't having commitment issues. When it came to Talia, he no longer had problems with the idea of a forever relationship. The treading-water sensation was her fault. He could not be sure if she even classified their association as a relationship. If she did, it was possible that her definition of one did not align with his.

The good news was that he was still afloat.

On the other side of the glass door, Talia apparently made the big decision. She got up, said a few words to Phoebe and Octavia, and then walked across the small living room and opened the door. She stepped out onto the balcony and closed the door.

"Everything okay?" she asked.

"Yes." He took a fortifying swallow of the wine and lowered the glass. "Dinner decision made?"

"Yep, and I have to tell you, it wasn't easy. I went through every interesting menu with Phoebe and Octavia and made my recommendations based on my experience with the various restaurants, but in the end, Phoebe said she wanted pizza."

"So we're having pizza?"

"Phoebe got kidnapped and held in that horrible lab. I figure she's entitled to eat whatever she wants for dinner tonight. Octavia agreed. Besides, who doesn't like pizza?"

"Fine by me." He drank some wine and tried to focus on a non-relationship issue. "There's something we need to talk about."

Talia went very still. Her eyes sparked with energy. Expectant tension shivered in the atmosphere. It was as if she was waiting for him to announce the winning number of the lottery.

Time to compartmentalize.

"It's about my Jekyll-and-Hyde problem," he said.

The spark did not exactly go out of her eyes — nothing that dramatic — but the aura of excited expectation energizing the atmosphere around her definitely faded. It was replaced with knowing concern. Sympathy was the last thing he wanted. He wondered what she had been hoping to hear. That he planned to check into a hotel this evening?

"I understand, believe me," she said, very earnest now. "I certainly haven't told my parents that I now excel at finding dead bodies. They would insist that I go back into therapy. Roger Gossard, the forensics psychologist I consult for, is the only person outside the *Lost Night Files* team who knows. I think Roger has convinced himself I've just got really good intuition. Let's face it — I doubt that most people really want to know what I can do, and those who would be interested are probably weird."

"Pretty sure that applies to my talent, too." He swallowed a little more wine. "Are you going to tell the podcast crew about my new skill set?"

"No. It's your secret. It's up to you to decide how much you want to reveal. You are a man with an extraordinary ability, one that could potentially be lethal, but you are not an assassin."

"What's the difference?"

She surprised him with a smile. "One is a talent; the other is a career path, a choice. You chose to become a history professor, not a killer. Now let's go back inside and enjoy the wine and cheese with Octavia and

Phoebe. The pizza will be arriving soon."

He smiled a little. "Priorities."

"Yep."

He followed her back inside, wondering what he had screwed up. It was obvious he had missed some important cue. He excelled at that when it came to Talia.

CHAPTER FIFTY-FOUR

Talia curled one leg under the other and helped herself to a slice of pizza. A few minutes ago she had opened another bottle of wine and refilled everyone's glass. The food and booze were having the desired effect, she decided — taking the edge off, at least temporarily. She and the others had spent a lot of time in fight-or-flight mode on Night Island. They needed to breathe. They needed to debrief.

"What do you think will happen to those plants in the conservatory and the underworld gardens?" Phoebe asked around a mouthful of pizza.

"I doubt if the fire made it into the conservatory," Luke said, "or down into the old lab. My guess is that the plants will continue to grow and mutate as long as the power source that keeps the facility running is undamaged."

Talia munched some pizza while she

thought about that. "Maybe the fire will affect the machines that run the conservatory and the lab."

Octavia shuddered. "I'm telling you, that whole island is contaminated with bad energy."

"Night Island is now the Foundation's problem," Luke said. "We're done with it."

"I still can't believe the government shut down such an expensive project," Talia said. "And then forgot about it."

"I told you, there was a very thorough cover-up," Luke said. "But as is always the case with cover-ups, eventually there are leaks." He swallowed the last of his pizza and looked at Octavia. "Of all of us, you spent the most time on Night Island. Would you mind if I ask you a few more questions? Talia, Phoebe, and I and the rest of the podcast crew are going to try to find Nathan Gill and whoever else is responsible for what happened to us. We can use all the data we can get."

"No problem," Octavia said. She drank some wine. "Just promise me you'll keep my name out of it."

"You have my word on that," Luke said.

Phoebe smiled. "As of tomorrow you'll have a new name anyway, Octavia."

"Yes," Octavia said. She nodded, satisfied.

"That's right."

Luke took his phone out of his pocket and prepared to take notes.

"That reminds me," Talia said. "We need to get the roll of film that we found in Keever's camera developed."

"We'll take care of that first thing tomorrow," Luke promised.

Some time later Talia escorted Octavia and Phoebe down the elevator to the guest suite on the fourth floor. When she returned to her apartment she found Luke waiting, duffel bag in one hand, pack slung over his shoulder. Her spirits plunged so fast and so far that she felt a little light-headed.

"Where are you going?" she asked, trying for casual and cool. Just curious.

"You tell me," Luke said.

She knew him well enough now to understand that he was serious. He needed an answer. So did she.

"All right, let's try this again," she said "Where do you want to go?"

"I don't want to go anywhere," he said.

Her spirits pulled out of the dive and reversed course.

"Well, don't," she said.

He watched her, his eyes burning. "Don't. That's what you said when I told you thought I could stop someone's heart with my talent. Just don't."

"You have a tendency to overthink things, Luke. Probably your academic side."

"Maybe. To be clear, if I stay here, I don't want to sleep in your spare bedroom."

She smiled, went toward him, and slipped her arms around his neck. "Well, don't."

He dropped the duffel on the floor and let the pack slide off his shoulder. His mouth came down on hers in a kiss that was charged with his unique heat and energy. The zing was intoxicating. Intimate. Joyful.

He might not stay forever, but he was here tonight, and he wanted her as much as she wanted him. That was enough. For now.

CHAPTER FIFTY-FIVE

While he had waited for Talia to decide his fate he had vowed that if he got the chance to make love to her again he would not rush things the way he had the first time. He would take it slow, show her that he could be a thoughtful lover. He wanted to seduce her in the truest sense of the word. He wanted to make certain that she never forgot him — because he would never forget her.

By the time he joined her in the shadowed bed he was already forced to pull hard on his self-control. The urge to lose himself in her warmth and scent threatened to overwhelm him. The feel of her sleek, soft body was intoxicating. He opened all of his senses, savoring the vital, sensual energy of her aura.

"Luke," she whispered, her voice husky with desire.

She twisted against him, twining one leg

around his. Her response thrilled and delighted him but it was also a challenge. When she wrapped his erection in one small fist it was all he could do not to climax.

Determined to maintain control, he reached down between her thighs. She was hot and wet and shivering with tension. He probed gently, searching out the sensitive places.

"Yes," she gasped. "Yes."

He was not satisfied until he made her shiver and tighten, until he felt her nails sinking into his back. Until she was commanding him to finish what he had started.

Only then did he settle between her upraised knees and propel himself slowly, deliberately into her tight, tense heat.

Finally, inevitably, the fever broke. Talia went over the edge with a muffled shriek, her hands clenched in his hair. He drove himself home one last time and followed her into the soft darkness.

Chapter Fifty-Six

He'd had the nightmare many times during the past three months, but until now it had always come in the shape of vague scenes and scraps of conversation. Tonight the dream unfolded in a startlingly coherent way, offering more context . . .

The voices of the two men bring him awake . . .

". . . Subject A is not responding. We will have to terminate."

"Wait. He may pull out of it. We can't afford another failure. He's worth a fucking fortune."

"Only if he's a success. If he does survive there will be a high probability of insanity. The client is paying for a psychically enhanced assassin, not a monster with a lethal talent."

"We can't be sure the subject will be insane if he survives. If he is we can terminate later."

"He's a failure. I'll take care of this."

"What the fuck? Stop —"

The screams start then.

He sits up on the gurney and discovers that he is in a small room lit by a blue radiance that emanates from the floor, ceiling, and walls. He is wearing his trousers but his shirt is gone. There is a needle in the crook of his arm. It is attached to a line that is connected to a bag of fluid hanging from an IV pole. He yanks the needle out and gets to his feet.

The room floats around him. It takes him several seconds to find his balance. When he does, he searches for an object that can be used as a weapon. The screams have stopped, but that is not reassuring.

He sees a tray of medical equipment near the gurney and selects a scalpel. He lurches across the small space, opens the door, and looks into a large laboratory lit with the same blue light.

There are two men in white lab coats sprawled on the floor. Their throats have been slashed. There is a horrifying amount of blood. Bloody footprints lead to the door on the far side of the lab. A mass of luminous plants can be seen through the opening . . .

"Luke, wake up. You're dreaming."

Talia's calm, quiet voice brought him to the surface on a surge of energy. She did not sound alarmed, just concerned. He opened his eyes and saw her shadowed face looking down at him. His talisman. A sense of wonder whispered through him. He reached up and touched her cheek.

She caught his hand in her own and squeezed it gently. "A nightmare?"

"Yes, sorry," he said. He levered himself up to a sitting position, swung his legs over the edge of the bed, and tried to push the dream fragments out of his head. "I was back in that damned lab."

Talia sat up beside him. "Was there anything different about the dream this time?"

"Yeah." He rubbed the back of his neck. "More details. How did you know?"

"I didn't. But things have changed since your last nightmare. It's not surprising that the experience of returning to Night Island has brought back some more memories and influenced your dreamscape."

"Yes," he said.

He summoned up the scenes from the latest version of the nightmare. A sense of certainty hit him like a splash of ice water. "I know where I got the scalpel. It was on a tray in the room where I woke up. I heard two men talking about having to terminate Subject A. Then I heard the screams. I figured I might need a weapon."

"You grabbed the scalpel." Talia watched him intently. "A perfectly reasonable thing to do under the circumstances. Go on."

"I opened the door and looked into the lab. I saw the two bodies on the floor and the blood. So much blood. Someone had walked through the blood."

"Barefoot?"

"Good question." He concentrated. "No. Shoe or boot prints, I think, but they were badly smeared."

"You saw the killer's footprints."

"Yes. They led to the door of the lab and disappeared into the gardens. I knew I had to get out of the lab, so I followed the footprints to the door. I saw the path through the gardens and followed it."

"So there you have it," Talia said. "You were not the one who murdered those two men in the lab. Pomona Finch told us the other test subject was considered a success. Subject B is the killer."

"But we're back to the same question I brought up in the beginning. If Subject B has a lethal psychic talent, why not use it to commit the murders in the lab?"

"For the same reason you suggested when we talked about this on Night Island. Subject B had probably just awakened and was still in a foggy state. You said you didn't know what you could do with your enhanced talent until after you escaped the lab. Subject B would have been in a similar situation."

Luke thought about it and shook his head. "Something doesn't add up. If B was a success and not being threatened, why murder the two researchers?"

"The hallucinations were probably a factor. Subject B wasn't thinking clearly."

"I've seen a lot of crime scenes. Trust me, if Subject B had been hallucinating there would have been more chaos. Multiple stab wounds. Instead, there was only one on each victim. The killer worked fast and knew how to slice open a throat. Neither target had a chance to fight back or run."

"What are you saying?" Talia asked.

He got to his feet and reached for his pants. "I think Subject B had a lot of experience with killing before becoming a psychically enhanced assassin."

"You're going to try to identify Subject B."

"That's the plan."

"Okay," she said. "But I can tell you right now that we'll never persuade the police to arrest a criminal who uses paranormal energy to commit murder. *The Lost Night Files* tried that on one of our first cold cases. It didn't go well."

"So I will set up a scenario that will force the assassin to resort to a lethal weapon."

"I was afraid you were going to say that,"

Talia said, resigned. "But first we have to identify the killer. At least we have the advantage of a relatively short list of suspects. We know the killer was on Night Island, because two people died by paranormal means there. Nathan Gill?"

"I think he's in the body-dumping business, but I don't see him as the assassin. He was trying to create one, not become one. Finch told us the serum is very risky. If Gill wants to acquire a lethal talent he'll wait until he knows the drug is safe."

"We know Clive Venner wasn't the killer, because he was a victim," Talia said. "I hope you're not thinking Chef Octavia is a murderer."

"I considered it," Luke said. "But she feared Gill. She would have gotten rid of him if she had the ability to do so. Instead, she went into hiding."

"Right," Talia said, relieved.

"It's one of the guests." Luke headed for the bedroom door. "Has to be. Let's take a look at that bookings file we picked up in Octavia's office."

Talia scrambled out of bed and grabbed her robe. "I knew the file was important but I didn't know why. Even if we get a name, how do we draw the killer out into the open?"

"That's the easy part. The killer will be obsessed with me now, watching and waiting for an opportunity to get rid of me."

"Because you're potential competition?"

He moved out into the hall and paused in the doorway, one hand on the frame. "No, because the mission was to assassinate me. As long as I'm alive I'm proof that the killer is a failure."

"I see what you mean. Psychology 101. You said drawing the assassin out into the open is the easy part. What's the hard part?"

"I need to figure out how to force a killer with paranormal talent to resort to using a regular weapon. And we'll want to get it all on film, of course."

"That won't be a problem. These days, there are cameras everywhere." Talia paused. "Except on Night Island."

CHAPTER FIFTY-SEVEN

Rand should have been dead by now.

The following night the assassin stood in the shadows of the parking garage and watched the door of the elevator lobby. Subject A was a fucking *failure.* Yet in spite of a severe reaction to the enhancement drug he had somehow managed to escape the lab, fake his own death, and disappear for three months. He had survived the first attempt to terminate him a few nights ago here in Seattle. He had even managed to find Night Island, rescue the Hatch woman, and escape a second time.

Rand had been lucky, but tonight his luck would run out.

The elevator doors opened. Rand walked out, a duffel bag in one hand. There was a day pack slung over his shoulder. He was dressed for leaving town, planning to disappear again.

Too late, Rand.

The assassin waited until the target was about fifteen feet away, close enough to be sure of a sharp focus, before moving out of the shadows. Time to make the kill.

CHAPTER FIFTY-EIGHT

Luke stopped. "Jasper Draper. Right on schedule. Figured you'd show up tonight."

Jasper's mouth fell open. He recovered quickly. "What the fuck are you talking about?"

"You've been monitoring Talia's phone because you couldn't get into mine. I knew you were watching so I had Talia send a few messages about my plans to leave town tonight."

"Shut your fucking mouth."

"I've been waiting for your review of the Unplugged Experience to appear online. But there never was a travel blog, was there? You had to come up with a cover story in a hurry and that was the best you could do. It's that kind of sloppy thinking that made it easy to figure out you were Subject B."

"That's right." Jasper showed a lot of teeth in a cold grin. "I'm the success. You're the failure."

"The weak cover story wasn't the only thing that put you at the top of my list. If you had been a legitimate guest at the lodge there would have been a record of your reservation in Octavia's files. There wasn't, because you never made one and Nathan Gill didn't bother to create a fake one. He was in a hurry, too, because he had just found out that Talia and I had booked the Unplugged Experience. He wanted you on the island because he figured it would be easier for you to take care of me there."

Jasper relaxed a little. "Gill damned near pissed himself when you hit the online app and made a reservation. I'm impressed. Takes a lot to make him nervous. It wasn't the first time you surprised him. He was in a panic when he found out that you had escaped the lab that night and stolen his boat. He was sure you were fucking insane, you see. There was no way to know if your talent had been enhanced. No way to know if the amnesia drug would suppress your memories. Just too many unknowns. But he was certain you wouldn't survive long."

"Because there was no way for me to get the boosters."

"That's right. He wanted to believe you had died in that boat fire you rigged up but he looked for you real hard for a month or so anyway, just in case. Then he decided you had to be dead. Imagine his surprise when you turned up as one of the people who wanted to buy the list from the Hatch woman."

"Were you the one who kidnapped Phoebe Hatch, or was that Gill?"

"I grabbed her and handed her over to Gill. Then I went back to watch Hatch's house. I knew there were two other buyers. I had seen a photo of you but I didn't recognize you in the dark."

"And besides, I was supposed to be dead. Were you planning to kill the other two buyers?"

"No. Gill just wanted to identify the competition. He's not a fan of leaving dead bodies around unless he can dump them on Night Island. Says they draw too much attention."

"You followed Talia and me when we left Hatch's house, didn't you?"

"I finally got good shots of you and Talia March when you went into that restaurant. I sent the one of you to Gill. He got it just before he left for the island with the Hatch woman. He freaked. He told me to take care of you."

"But your drive-by didn't go well."

Jasper reddened with fury. His eyes got

hot. "Couldn't get a solid fix. You were too far away."

"Whatever. You failed, so Gill went with plan B. He told you to finish the job on the island. You tried, didn't you? I'll give you credit for that. You attempted to set up an ambush at the cabin that had been assigned to me the first night, but you screwed that up, too."

"I didn't fuck up." Jasper's voice rose. "There was a witness. I couldn't risk having him tell someone that he had seen one of the guests breaking into your cabin."

"You panicked and took him out, but that just complicated things, didn't it?"

"I didn't panic."

"Your problem is that you lack impulse control, Draper. Were you that way before they injected you with the formula or is that a side effect that developed after you were enhanced?"

"Shut your fucking mouth."

A lightning strike of icy energy slammed into Luke. He had thought he was braced for it but the paranormal shock wave caused him to stagger back a few steps. He dropped the duffel. The pack slid off his shoulder and landed with a thud on the concrete floor. He managed, barely, to stay on his feet.

"You were the one who murdered those two researchers in the lab," he rasped.

Jasper made a visible effort to pull himself together. This time his toothy grin was jittery. "I wanted to make sure they didn't create any more enhanced operatives like me."

"I thought that might be the reason. You don't want any competition, do you? As long as you are the only psychic assassin around, you're extremely valuable. You used the scalpel instead of your talent because you wanted to make Gill think that I was the one who had murdered his two, no doubt very expensive and hard to replace, lab people."

"You were supposed to be a failure so I couldn't use my talent to do the job. Had to make it look like the work of a non-enhanced killer."

"The hits on the two researchers looked like the work of a pro."

"It's not like I haven't had some experience," Jasper said. "I was trained in the military. When I got out I went to work for a private security firm."

"I don't see you as a night guard trudging around a warehouse checking to make sure doors are locked, so I'm assuming that when you say you worked for a private security firm you mean you were a merce-nary."

"Let's compromise on the term *consul-tant,*" Jasper said. "It was my experience and my skill set as well as my psychic vibe that convinced Gill to recruit me for the Night Island project."

"You were recruited?"

"Gill found me because I'm on the same list you're on. He tracked me down and made me the offer of a lifetime. There was no need to dose me with the amnesia drug before I got enhanced."

"You jumped at the opportunity."

"To get that upgrade?" Jasper snorted. "Oh, yeah. You, on the other hand, were a problem right from the start. Gill said he almost changed his mind about grabbing you."

"Why?"

"He was worried that you didn't have the *temperament* for the work. But those old test results indicated that you had the potential to become a useful asset for his team."

"What team?"

"We all have dreams, right?" Jasper chuck-led. "Gill is trying to assemble an elite squad of assassins for hire, assets that can terminate their targets without leaving a trace. He calls the operation Cold Fire 2.0. But he's running into problems."

"What kind of problems?"

"He's done enough experiments to know that the enhancement drug doesn't work on everyone. Most people can't handle it. The more he tweaks the parapsych profile to select the best candidates, the more he narrows his options. There are only so many people on that list, and most of them don't have the vibe he thinks he needs."

"Do you think Gill realizes that it's only a matter of time before he enhances the wrong assassin, a killer who decides he doesn't want to work for Gill's outfit and decides to terminate him?"

A dark excitement flashed in Jasper's hot eyes. "Between you and me, Gill has already made that mistake. He just doesn't know it yet."

"Got it. You're the mistake. You've got plans."

"Fucking right. Gill needs me but I don't need him."

"So why haven't you gotten rid of him and gone solo?"

The excitement in Jasper's eyes dimmed, replaced with frustration. "The maintenance booster is still being perfected. Gill is the only one with access to it. For now I have to play the part of the loyal employee. But it's just a matter of time."

"Pomona Finch said something about the boosters. You have to get one every six or seven weeks, don't you? Doesn't that worry you?"

Jasper raised one shoulder in a twitchy shrug. "Why should it? Like I said, Gill needs me. He's going to take very, very good care of his asset. I'm the only success he's got. He tells me I'm proof of concept."

"You do realize that by now he will be having second thoughts about your usefulness."

"Bullshit. He knows what I can do."

"What you do is screw up a lot," Luke said. "That's not a useful trait in an asset."

"I told you to shut up."

Another blast of high intensity cold slammed across Luke's senses, but this time he was ready with the counterpoint wavelengths. He infused them into his voice.

"By now I'm sure Gill has figured out that you're unstable," he said. "You may have some talent, but you're not reliable. That makes you a failure, Draper."

"Stop talking," Jasper snarled. "You're going to be a dead man in a minute, but I can make that death fast or slow. Your choice."

"When you screw up this job Gill will

decide you aren't worth the trouble and the risk. He'll cut his losses. He's probably already trying to decide where to dump your body. He won't be able to go back to Night Island."

"He can't kill me," Jasper said, his voice rising. "I'm too powerful."

"You're dangerous at close range but you're as vulnerable to a bullet as the next man. Or maybe Gill will engineer an accident. Of course, there's always poison. There are so many ways to kill someone, aren't there? Psychic energy isn't necessarily the most efficient way to do it."

Jasper shuddered and clutched at his chest. Confusion and disbelief sparked in his eyes. "What . . . what are you doing?"

"Do you really want a lesson in metaphysics right now?"

"Can't breathe." Jasper's teeth were chattering now. *What are you doing to me?*

"Helping you to get some very deep sleep," Luke said. He injected a little more power into the words.

Jasper stared at him, shocked. "You haven't had access to the boosters. You should be *dead.*"

"Evidently there's a lot to learn about the effects of the serum," Luke said, putting a little more energy into the words.

Jasper yelped and doubled over, as if in gut-wrenching pain. When he straightened he had a military-grade knife in his hand.

"Old habits and all that," he grunted.

He lunged forward, sending out yet another chaotic burst of heavy energy, laying down paranormal cover fire until he was close enough to use the blade.

Luke pulled hard on his talent, locked onto the wavelengths that emanated directly from Jasper's psychic core, and sent one last blast of ice. He knew he had struck home because the shock of the recoil nearly shattered his own senses. The act of psychic destruction came at a price.

Jasper stumbled, lurched forward a couple more steps, and then went down hard on his knees. Stunned, he released the knife to clutch at his chest again. He stared up at Luke.

"You're the failure," he said, his voice hoarse.

"I know," Luke said, "and I'm okay with that."

"Fucking failure," Jasper whispered.

He shuddered, closed his eyes, and collapsed.

CHAPTER FIFTY-NINE

Talia threw herself against the heavy glass door of the elevator lobby and rushed out into the parking garage. Her heart was pounding with a mix of relief and dread. She released her grip on Luke's pistol, which was tucked out of sight inside her open shoulder bag. He had given her the weapon in the event that things went badly and told her to use it without hesitation if necessary. She had her phone in her other hand. Luke's phone had been on throughout the confrontation, allowing her to listen in.

"Did it work?" she asked. She stopped a few feet away from the unconscious man. "Were you able to permanently neutralize his talent?"

"I think so," Luke said. He took out his phone.

"You *think* so? Aren't you sure?"

Luke punched in 911 and then glanced at Jasper Draper. "It's not like I've had a lot of experience destroying someone's psychic senses. But I don't think he will be able to commit any more murders with his talent. Something . . . flatlined. I can't explain it, but I'm pretty sure of it because the recoil almost flatlined me."

Panic arced through her. "Are you okay?"

"I don't know. I'm not even sure what the definition of *okay* is right now. I'll worry about it later. Right now we're dealing with a professional killer who just tried to murder me with a knife." Luke glanced up at the surveillance cameras. "And it's all on video. The police should be able to work with that."

The story was a minor one as far as the Seattle media was concerned. It appeared briefly online and vanished almost immediately, crushed under a pile of more spectacular crime reports.

Suspect Collapses During Attempted Armed Assault in Parking Garage

A man tentatively identified as Jasper Draper is believed to have suffered a seizure while allegedly using a knife to attack an individual in a parking garage. Police took Draper into custody and transported him to a hospital for treatment. At last report Draper was listed in serious condition.

In addition to a statement from the victim and a witness, police collected a knife at the scene and will be reviewing security camera video to obtain more evidence . . .

CHAPTER SIXTY

Jasper Draper stared hard at the ceiling, trying not to look at the ghosts of the people he had killed during the course of his career. The specters of his victims surrounded the hospital bed, each trying to get his attention. Somehow he knew that to acknowledge any of them would be disastrous.

He had awakened a couple of hours ago to the realization that something was wrong. The first thing he had discovered was that he was in restraints, bound to the hospital bed. When the door opened to admit a nurse he caught a glimpse of the police officer stationed outside the room.

It had taken him a while to figure out that his powerful psychic talent had vanished. He had run a couple of feeble experiments on a medical assistant who had come into the room to check his vitals. Nothing. The target had been oblivious to the invisible assault.

Cloudy memories of the encounter in the parking garage were slowly trickling back. The hit had failed, he was sure of that much. He was also certain that it wasn't his fault. The intel he had been given was bad. Rand had not only survived the initial dose of the serum, his talent had been enhanced to a lethal level. The kicker was that he did not require the boosters to maintain his enhanced abilities.

The hospital door opened again. A figure dressed in scrubs entered the room, closed the door, and came to stand over the bed.

For a few seconds Jasper worried that he was hallucinating. And then a throat-tightening wave of relief coursed through him.

"Gill," he whispered. "About time you showed up. You've got to get me out of here. I need a booster."

"Don't worry," Nathan Gill said. "I'll handle everything." He took a syringe out of his pocket and plunged it into Draper's shoulder. "There you go. In a few minutes you'll be fine."

"Fuck. That is good news." Jasper flopped back onto the pillow. "The intel on Rand was wrong. He's got some heavy-duty talent."

"No, the serum nearly killed him. He

survived but there's no indication that his senses were enhanced."

"You don't understand."

"For a while I thought you were my proof of concept, and to some extent that's true. But you were unstable before you were given the serum and unfortunately the enhancement protocol has accelerated your deterioration."

"*No.* I'm proof that the formula works."

"Initially it enhanced your talent, but it has become obvious that you don't have the strength and control to handle the upgrade. You collapsed at a very inopportune time in the garage, didn't you?"

"I didn't collapse. I'm telling you, Rand used his talent on me."

"We both know that if he had any serious talent he would have used it to kill you. After all, he was fighting for his life. The fact that you're still alive tells me that he didn't have anything to do with your collapse."

"As soon as the booster takes effect I'll deal with Rand."

"I'm afraid you won't be leaving here alive," Gill said. "That wasn't another dose of the serum that I gave you. It was something else. You're going to have a heart attack in about thirty seconds."

"You can't do this. You need me. I'm the only asset you've got."

"You're of no use to me now."

Jasper pulled hard on his senses, marshaling every ounce of strength he could summon, but there was no response. A great weakness was rolling over him, suffocating him. There was a crushing weight on his chest. The ghosts of his kills were gathering closer around the bed.

He was vaguely aware of the sound of the door closing.

And then there was nothing.

CHAPTER SIXTY-ONE

The podcast team got together on a video call the next morning. Pallas and Ambrose wearing sunglasses, beamed in from Phoenix resort where they were drinking coffee on a sunny patio. Amelia was also wearing dark glasses. She was on the balcony of her San Diego apartment. There were a couple of palm trees in the background.

Talia and Luke were at the dining counter of her apartment, mugs of coffee in front of them. They were not wearing sunglasses. It was nearly eight o'clock, so, technically, the sun was up in Seattle — barely — but there was no visible evidence of that, because was raining.

"Jasper Draper died during the night," Talia said. "They're calling it a heart attack associated with his seizure, but Luke and suspect that Nathan Gill got to him."

"It makes sense that Gill would want t

get rid of him," Amelia said. "Draper knew too much and he was a ruthless, unstable assassin endowed with a lethal psychic talent."

"Right," Talia said. "What could possibly go wrong?"

She ignored Luke's enigmatic glance. She put up with his weird humor. He could learn to tolerate hers.

"So much for the value of being a successful proof of concept," Ambrose said.

"Evidently," Talia said.

She was aware that Luke was sitting quietly beside her. Too quietly. She didn't have to be a mind reader to know that he was braced for the possibility that her friends would figure out what he could do with his talent and realize that he was the real Night Island project proof of concept.

She rushed to change the subject. "I have two bits of good news. *The Lost Night Files* has hired the perfect virtual assistant, Phoebe Hatch. She's actually only semi-virtual. She will be renting a place right here in my apartment building. She knows her way around the dark net and she has already started working."

"That's great," Pallas said, "but we can't afford a virtual assistant."

"Phoebe says she will start off as a volunteer," Talia said. "Apparently her other online project is quite profitable, so she can forgo a salary for now."

"What's the other good news?" Amelia asked.

"Luke is joining us as our official historian," Talia said. "He, too, is a volunteer."

Beside her, Luke grimaced and drank some coffee. She slanted him a quick, searching look. She had stopped asking him if he was okay, because the repeated question obviously irritated him. As far as she could tell, he *was* okay, but he seemed to have retreated back into that other zone, the one he had inhabited when she had first met him.

"Always happy to have more help," Pallas said. "But what, exactly, will he be doing?"

"Turns out Luke has uncovered a lot of the history of the research into paranormal phenomena, including the top secret work done by various government agencies in the last century. He was the one who knew who to contact when we realized Night Island was a problem that the local authorities would not be able to handle."

Ambrose nodded. "That outfit called the Foundation. Good work."

"Right," Talia continued. "Also, believe it or not, he collects a lot of interesting bits and pieces of information from his blog."

Pallas looked interested. "What blog is that?"

For the first time Luke spoke up. "*The Anomalies Report.* Maybe you've heard of it?"

There was a short silence.

Amelia mumbled something about having read it a couple of times.

"Yes," Pallas said, her voice painstakingly neutral. "I believe we are all familiar with it."

Ambrose chuckled.

Luke smiled the serenely confident smile of a cruising shark. "Think of it as the online equivalent of the *Lost Night Files* podcast. You know, a site that collects and analyzes rumors and chatter about the paranormal."

"Okay," Amelia said slowly.

Pallas and Ambrose got thoughtful expressions.

"I got the tip that led me to the Foundation off the blog," Luke concluded.

"We need all the leads we can get," Talia said, rushing to fill another moment of silence.

"Very true," Pallas said. She was starting to look intrigued. "Your knowledge of the history of paranormal research certainly came in handy during this case."

"It's hard to believe that a secret govern-ment lab has been sitting there on a private island in the San Juans all these decades," Amelia said. "I wonder how Nathan Gill found it."

"Good question," Luke said. "It's obvious that Gill and the people he's working with have also been doing a deep dive into the history of paranormal research. What's more, it's safe to say they're well-financed."

"There's never been a shortage of ec-centric billionaires willing to throw cash a bizarre projects," Ambrose pointed out.

"Too bad one of them doesn't offer to toss some money our way," Talia said. "We could use the funding."

"Be careful what you wish for," Luke said "That kind of easy money always come with strings attached."

"He's right," Ambrose said.

"Well, that does it for my good news," Ta-lia said. She jumped up off the dining stool and went around the counter to pick up the coffeepot. "Now Luke has some for you."

"A fresh lead?" Pallas asked, looking hope-ful.

"Maybe." Luke opened an envelope and took out the contents. "We got the film in Keever's camera developed by a firm that does specialty work here in Seattle. We were able to supervise the process to make sure there were no copies made, and we got the negatives back."

Amelia was suddenly riveted. "You have photos?"

"We do," Luke said. "Keever used black-and-white film, and most of the shots were done underground in the lab. He had to deal with the weird light down there, which meant extended exposure times. The result is that the images are grainy, not sharp and clear. Most of the photos are pictures of mushrooms, but there are some of the interior of the lab where Pomona Finch did her work."

He held the photos up to the laptop camera.

Ambrose leaned closer to his screen to get a better look. "Definitely mid-twentieth-century tech."

"Nothing digital works down there or anywhere else on the island," Talia explained. "Probably something to do with the paranormal environment."

"The most interesting shots are the ones taken on the surface," Luke said. "They are also black-and-white, but unlike the others, they are sharp and clear."

He held up one of the prints.

"Two men standing on a dock," Pallas said. "Why are they important?"

"That's the dock at Night Island," Luke explained. "The individual on the left is Nathan Gill. We don't know who the older man is but we think he's important. In the background you can see two cabin cruisers. The first is the one Gill used. We are assuming the other man arrived in the second boat."

Ambrose studied the photo. "You're sure the unknown man wasn't a guest who had booked the Unplugged Experience?"

"Chef Octavia was adamant that the guests always arrived on the chartered ferry," Talia said. "She did not know who the man was, but she said he was definitely not a guest. He did not stay very long."

"According to Octavia, the unknown man made two visits to the island while she was there," Luke added. "Each time Gill met him at the dock and took him straight through the gardens and into the conservatory. Presumably they went down into the lab. When the two emerged from the conservatory, the visitor went back to the dock and left. He never came into the lodge."

"How did Gill explain the visits to Octavia and Clive Venner?" Pallas asked.

Talia answered as she replaced the coffeepot on the burner. "He told them that the stranger was a research scientist from the Institute and that he came occasionally to get progress reports."

"The Wynford Institute for the Study of Medicinal Botany is a fake operation," Luke added. "It exists only on the internet. It was a cover for Gill's project."

Talia went back around the counter and perched on the dining stool. "The unknown man has to be important."

"We've got the hull identification numbers of the two boats tied up at the dock," Luke added. "They're both rentals, but I'm going to try to track down the people at the marina who dealt with Gill and the unknown individual. There has to be a paper trail. Both men had to sign rental agreements and buy fuel. Someone may remember something."

"Anything else of interest in the prints you made from that roll of film?" Amelia asked.

"We don't think so, but we can't be sure," Talia said. "As you can see, the underground photos are not good quality. We think the photos of the two men and their boats are the critical shots, mostly because they are the exceptions to the mushroom shots."

"Send the negatives to me," Amelia said. There was a fierce urgency in the words. "I

415

need to develop them myself and take a close look. I've got some software that will enable me to enhance the images."

"Will do," Talia said. "When it comes to photography, you're the expert."

"I feel like we're making some real progress at last," Pallas said. "We've got the list, thanks to our new semi-virtual assistant, and we've got photos of two people we know are involved in this thing."

"I can't wait to get my hands on those negatives to see if I can find something else that might help us," Amelia said.

"I'll overnight them to you today," Luke promised.

Pallas shook her head. "I'm still trying to wrap my brain around the idea that Nathan Gill and his little team of whack jobs were trying to create psychic assassins."

"Not just trying," Ambrose said. "Sounds like they succeeded in creating one — Jasper Draper."

"He was a killer before he was enhanced," Talia said, determined to stomp on any conversation that involved the word *assassin.* "The drug apparently gave him some temporary ability to commit murder with his paranormal senses, but it's obvious he couldn't handle the sensory overload."

Pallas shuddered. "Thank goodness you

failed to respond to the drug, Luke."

"And even luckier that the stuff didn't kill you," Amelia added.

"My lucky day," Luke said.

CHAPTER SIXTY-TWO

The Night Island Project was a failure, and now his father would demand answers.

Benedict Steen walked off the air-conditioned private jet into the humid tropical warmth of the other island, the one he was supposed to think of as home. What bullshit. The island was a fortress.

He had shed the Nathan Gill persona as soon as he had seen Draper and the others off on the last ferry. He had explained that he would wait on the island for a while in case Talia March and Luke Rand managed to find their way back to the lodge. But as soon as the ferry was out of sight he had jumped into the cabin cruiser and another identity and headed for the mainland.

There had been only one loose end — Jasper Draper. He had become increasingly unstable, and that made him uncontrollable and unpredictable. He hadn't been proof of concept, after all. Just another failure. He hadn't even managed to take out an un-armed Rand.

It probably would have been a good idea to get rid of March and Rand, but the body count was already unacceptably high. The problem with killing them was that too many people would notice — including the *Lost Night Files* podcast crew. They were already getting too close for comfort. Luckily they were small-time players in the podcast universe. The last thing he wanted to do was give them a story that might go viral.

Benedict climbed into the waiting SUV and sat back for the ride up the hillside to the sprawling villa that overlooked the sparkling waters of the South Pacific. Time for the confrontation with the old man. It was not going to be pleasant.

Cutler Steen had never been what anyone would call the understanding and forgiving type. He had a low tolerance for failure. His temperament suited a man who controlled a global empire founded on the arms trade and a private security business that catered to dictators, warlords, and the extremely wealthy.

The flight to the island had given Benedict ample time to compose his version of events. True, his sister Celina's project had imploded a short time ago, but Cutler had been less concerned with the disaster in Carnelian. That project had been significant but it had been more in the nature of a drug trial.

The Night Island Project, however, had held out the prospect of an astonishing result — the creation of a squad of psychically enhanced assassins who could be controlled with the boosters. Cutler had been so obsessed with his vision of becoming the ultimate player in the private security world that he had broken his own rules. He had left his tropical fortress to make no one but two trips to Night Island to assess progress.

The armored SUV came to a stop at the entrance of the villa. A member of the Steen security team was waiting.

"Your father is waiting for you in the great room, sir," he said.

"Thanks," Benedict said. "Are my sisters here?"

"Yes, sir. Ms. Celina and Ms. Adriana are out on the veranda. Cocktails will be served soon."

"In that case, might as well get the business with Dad over and done. I need a drink," Benedict said.

He walked through the high-ceilinged

halls to the vast, tiled great room that opened onto the veranda. He thought he was prepared for the confrontation; nevertheless, his gut twisted when Cutler turned to face him.

"Welcome home," Cutler said. "I hope you had a smooth flight."

Benedict chilled. Dealing with his father was always a high-wire act. Cutler was the ultimate Janus-faced man. You had to be careful not to assume that what you saw on the surface reflected Cutler's real state of mind. Growing up, Benedict and his half sisters had learned that the truth was in Cutler's eyes.

In the past it had been hard to read his eyes. Doing so had required attention, analysis, and caution. But lately it had become easier. Benedict still wasn't sure why that worried him.

Today Cutler's eyes glittered with cold disapproval and contempt. *No surprise,* Benedict thought. But it seemed to him that there was something else going on just beneath the surface.

"Good to be home," Benedict said. He could lie as easily as Cutler. Like father, like son. "Unfortunately, as you know, the Night Island Project had to be terminated."

"Because of Rand and March," Cutler

said, his voice tightening. "Hard to believe you let a fucking failure of a test subject and that amateur podcast investigator take down such an incredibly promising enhancement project."

"For what it's worth, the project was doomed from the start."

"What are you talking about? You had that logbook. You had that amazing lab. You had the scientists. You had everything you needed to succeed and you failed."

"The project was doomed because the formula is flawed. It killed the first two subjects. It nearly killed Rand. I'm convinced it drove Jasper Draper mad."

"Bullshit," Cutler shot back. "He was no doubt unstable before he was enhanced."

"Maybe, but the serum pushed him over the edge."

"Why didn't it kill Rand or make him insane?" Cutler demanded.

"No way to know for certain, but the logical answer is that the formula simply didn't affect him. Maybe his system was immune to it. Or maybe he had the wrong parapsych profile. It's not like we can measure innate ability and accurately assess how someone will respond to the new version of the drug. All we had to go on was the fact that his name was on that list and that he had a military and intelligence background."

Cutler began to pace the floor. Benedict watched with interest. This was new. Cutler had never had a habit of pacing.

"Now that ridiculous podcast crew has the list," Cutler said.

"There's very little they can do with it," Benedict pointed out. "They might track down some of the people on it, but so what? It's just a list of names that was compiled several years ago. We don't even know who conducted those old psych studies. There's no way that list can lead *The Lost Night Files* to us."

Cutler reached the far side of the room, turned, and started back. He stopped a couple of yards away from Benedict.

"Let's hope you are right," Cutler said. "And let's also hope that Adriana's project will have a more successful outcome than yours and Celina's did."

Benedict considered his options and decided he had nothing to lose. "Back at the start, Adriana, Celina, and I assumed that you were playing a succession game with us, using the three enhancement projects as a test. The winner would be anointed as the next in line to take control of the business."

Cutler slammed a fist on the table. "It's

not a *game.* Don't you understand? We are talking about power of a kind that has never before been available. If we control the enhancement drug, we control anything and everything we touch. But the operative word is *control.*"

"You're talking about the boosters."

"It's one thing to be able to switch on an individual's psychic senses, and, yes, people will pay any price for true paranormal talent. But we must have a means of making sure the subject is stable. We also need a way to shut down an asset with enhanced senses if it becomes necessary."

"I get it. But the bottom line here is that the new version of the serum that was used in the original Night Island experiments doesn't work any better than the original. Boosters won't solve the problem."

"We will see what Adriana can accomplish with the version I provided to her," Cutler said. "Your sisters and I will meet you on the veranda for cocktails in fifteen minutes."

He had regained most of his composure, but there was still an edgy tension sparking in his eyes.

"Yes, sir," Benedict said. "Fifteen minutes."

He walked out of the great room trying to find the right word to describe what he had glimpsed in Cutler's eyes. It came to him a few minutes later when he was standing in front of a mirror fastening the buttons of a short-sleeved sports shirt.

Fear.

That was what he had seen in the old man's eyes. Cutler was afraid.

But what would it take to scare Cutler Steen? He was a ruthless man driven by a craving for power. He had fathered three offspring by three different mothers as an experiment designed to discover whether or not innate paranormal talents could be passed down through the bloodline. He had never told Benedict and his half sisters the truth about their origins, but they had done some quiet ancestry research on their own.

Among other things, they had learned that all three of their mothers had exhibited indications of psychic ability. Each had died shortly after giving birth. Benedict, Adriana, and Celina had been raised by nannies, private tutors, and high-end boarding schools. They had been brought up in the family business.

Cutler Steen had given his offspring everything they needed to take their place in a world that was fueled by wealth, power, and secrets. In return he had demanded constant proof of achievement and absolute loyalty. *Family is everything* was the motto of the Steen clan. The corollary, *Trust no one outside the family,* had also been drilled into the Steen heirs.

Cutler had always ruled his empire with an unshakable certainty in his own off-the-charts intuition, a talent that had been so unerring Benedict knew it qualified as psychic. But now he was showing signs of fear, maybe even panic. It was as if he was running out of time.

Benedict studied his reflection in the mirror. What did it take to make Cutler Steen panic? He had made enemies in the course of his climb to the top of a dangerous business, but enemies were nothing new for him. Something else was going on.

Benedict smiled. A new range of options and possibilities had just opened up. He turned away from the mirror and went to meet his sisters and his father for cocktails on the veranda.

Cutler was right, family was everything — including the source of the greatest danger.

CHAPTER SIXTY-THREE

"Time to ponder the most important question of the day," Talia said. "What's for dinner?"

Luke was sitting at the dining counter, working on Talia's laptop. He looked up, amusement glinting in his eyes. "This morning you said that 'What's for breakfast?' was the most important question of the day. Around noon I recall you saying something similar about lunch."

"I believe in treating each meal with respect." Talia opened the refrigerator door. "How does pasta with brown butter and parmesan and a nice watercress salad sound?"

"Sounds great," Luke said. "But I have to tell you, just about anything would sound good."

"That was easy." She reached for the watercress. "You'll eat anything I feed you. I like that about you."

"Is there anything else you like about me?"

He wasn't teasing. He was serious — Luke serious. She took a breath, closed the refrigerator, and set the watercress on the counter, giving herself a moment to consider her response. When she turned around she saw that he was watching her from the Luke zone. That meant her answer mattered. A lot.

"Yes," she said. She crossed the small kitchen, leaned forward, and folded her arms on the counter. She smiled a polite, deliberately enigmatic smile. "Your turn. Is there anything you like about me?"

"I like being here with you. I need to know how long you want me to stay."

"You are really lousy at this kind of conversation, aren't you?"

"Yes."

"Okay, let's try this. How long do you want to stay?"

"As long as you'll let me," Luke said. ". fell in love with you that first morning when we ran into each other at Phoebe's house."

She almost stopped breathing. Almost. A fierce joy flooded her senses.

"Luke," she whispered.

"I don't want to leave, Talia. Ever."

She smiled. "Well, don't."

His eyes tightened. "That's what you said

428

when I told you I was sure I could stop someone's heart with my talent. It's what you said when we got back from Night Island and I told you I didn't want to stay in a hotel."

"So?"

"So this is a very different situation." Luke got up and moved around the counter to stand a couple of feet away from her. "I think something more is called for."

"You're overthinking this, as usual. Some things really are simple and straightforward." She slipped her arms around his neck. "I love you. I've been afraid you wouldn't realize that we have something very special together."

Luke put his hands on her shoulders. "Aren't you worried about our commitment issues?"

"In hindsight, I think it's clear that we never had commitment issues," she said. "We were just waiting for the right person to come along."

His eyes burned. "About time you figured that out. I knew it from the start."

She opened her mouth to give him a short lecture on the importance of communication, but she had to refocus, because he was pulling her close and tight and his mouth was on hers.

Priorities.

CHAPTER SIXTY-FOUR

The Lost Night Files *Podcast*
Episode 7: "Island of the Vanished"
Podcast transcript:

TALIA: His name was Edward Keever. He was a lonely, reclusive botanist, a failed academic with a special interest in mushrooms. He was lured to a private island in the Pacific Northwest with the promise of a position in a top secret government research lab. He died under mysterious circumstances. And then his body vanished.

AMELIA: Once the setting of dangerous botanical experiments, Night Island conceals many mysteries. Several months ago some of the secrets buried there were uncovered by a ruthless man named Nathan Gill.

PALLAS: Thanks to a *Lost Night Files* investigation, Gill's criminal activities on the island have been halted. The long-lost lab is once again under the control of the government agency tasked with maintaining its security. But questions linger.

TALIA: This is the story of a case that involves kidnapping, murder, and illicit paranormal research designed to produce assassins endowed with lethal psychic talents. Welcome to *The Lost Night Files.* We're in this together until we get answers.

ABOUT THE AUTHOR

Jayne Ann Krentz is the author of more than fifty *New York Times* bestsellers. She has written contemporary romantic suspense novels under that name and futuristic and historical romance novels under the pseudonyms Jayne Castle and Amanda Quick, respectively.

The employees of Thorndike Press hope you have enjoyed this Large Print book. All our Thorndike Large Print titles are designed for easy reading, and all our books are made to last. Other Thorndike Press Large Print books are available at your library, through selected bookstores, or directly from us.

For information about titles, please call:
(800) 223-1244

or visit our website at:
gale.com/thorndike

$39.99

LONGWOOD PUBLIC LIBRARY
800 Middle Country Road
Middle Island, NY 11953
(631) 924-6400
longwoodlibrary.org

LIBRARY HOURS

Monday-Friday	9:30 a.m. - 9:00 p.m.
Saturday	9:30 a.m. - 5:00 p.m.
Sunday (Sept-June)	1:00 p.m. - 5:00 p.m.